**"I should go." Brayden jerked a thumb over his shoulder in the direction of his dog, Echo, who was snuffling along the edge of the lawn.**

Even though he said the words, he made no movement.

That awareness of each other was growing and building, causing the air around them to crackle. Instinct told her he wouldn't make the first move. The damage he'd suffered—whatever it was— wouldn't allow him to risk rejection. And Esmée wasn't ready to act on these feelings...no matter how compelling they might be.

Placing a hand on his shoulder, she rose on the tips of her toes and brushed her lips against his cheek. It was intended to be a chaste kiss. Instead, when her mouth made contact with his skin, it instantly became the most decadent thing she had ever done. A jolt of desire shot through her, and she had to force herself to step away instead of gripping the front of his T-shirt and pulling him closer.

"Good night, Brayden." It was hard to breathe, let alone speak.

He stared down at her for a moment or two, the look in his eyes stealing the remainder of her breath. "Good night."

**Jane Godman** was a 2019 Romantic Novelists' Award and National Readers' Choice Award winner and double Daphne du Maurier Award finalist. She wrote thrillers for Harlequin Romantic Suspense and also wrote paranormal romance.

### Books by Jane Godman

### Harlequin Romantic Suspense

#### Sons of Stillwater

*Covert Kisses*
*The Soldier's Seduction*
*Secret Baby, Second Chance*
*Family in the Crosshairs*

#### The Coltons of Mustang Valley

*Colton Manhunt*

#### Colton 911

*Colton 911: Family Under Fire*

#### The Coltons of Roaring Springs

*Colton's Secret Bodyguard*

#### The Coltons of Red Ridge

*Colton and the Single Mom*

Visit the Author Profile page
at Harlequin.com for more titles.

# ON THE TRAIL OF A KILLER

## JANE GODMAN

Previously published as *Colton and the Single Mom*

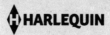

Special thanks and acknowledgment are given to Jane Godman for her contribution to The Coltons of Red Ridge miniseries.

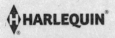

ISBN-13: 978-1-335-47375-2

On the Trail of a Killer

First published as Colton and the Single Mom in 2018.
This edition published in 2022.

Recycling programs
for this product may
not exist in your area.

Harlequin Enterprises ULC
22 Adelaide St. West, 41st Floor
Toronto, Ontario M5H 4E3, Canada
www.Harlequin.com

Printed in U.S.A.

# ON THE TRAIL OF A KILLER

# Chapter 1

"It's official." Chief Finn Colton faced his K-9 officers in the morning briefing. "The Groom Killer has claimed a fourth victim."

Brayden Colton remained silent throughout the buzz of conversation that followed. Four dead men... and this time it felt personal. Again. The first victim had been the half brother of a cop. This time, the murdered guy was an ex-cop. Although he shared the shock and grief that gripped his colleagues, Brayden had even more reason to feel anger and frustration.

He was aware of the chief watching him closely and guessed Finn was concerned about how he would react to this latest bombshell. Brayden was aware of his role. He knew how he was supposed to play this. He should keep an open mind, stay professional. Although the evidence against his kid sister was stacking up hard and fast, inside this building he was a police officer first and Demi's brother second. Right now, he should be doing everything he could to convince his cousin, the chief, that he was impartial.

Reaching out a hand, he placed it on the head of Echo, his K-9 partner. As always, the dog's calm, quiet presence soothed him. Brayden made sure his gaze was steady on Finn's face as the chief continued with the briefing. Crime-scene photographs appeared on a large screen behind him. "Like the other victims, Jack Parkowski was shot through the heart. A black cummerbund was stuffed in his mouth. He was forty-eight years old, born and raised in Red Ridge, but hadn't lived here for over twenty years. Came back six months ago in preparation for his marriage to Sarah Mull. She was the one who found his body."

"How is she?" It was a voice from the back of the room. Sarah Mull had to be about the most popular person in Red Ridge. She had been Brayden's first-grade teacher.

"Not good. She's being treated in the hospital for shock. As far as the Groom Killer case goes, there is nothing new to report. Since we have another murder, let's recap on why finding Demi Colton is our priority. When the first victim, Bo Gage, was found, he had written *Demi C* in his own blood. Then, a gold heart necklace with the initials *DC* was found under a pickup wheel near Bo's body. We also have a witness who saw Demi close to the scene just before the murder. When we add in the fact that she went on the run as soon as we got a warrant for her arrest, it's hardly surprising that every finger in town is pointing her way. Last month, a witness also claimed to see her shoot the third victim— a witness who ended up dead soon after. However, the FBI reported a sighting of Demi across the state at the time of that murder." Finn's gaze moved purposefully around the room, lingering for a second on Brayden. "So, just because we are focusing our resources on the search for Demi, I don't want anyone to stop looking at other angles."

"There are rumors that Demi is pregnant," Officer Juliette Walsh said. "If that's true, we have to hope she'll seek medical help at some point. Is there an alert out to the medical centers in the region?"

Finn nodded. "Demi's photograph has been circulated throughout the county."

"Demi Colton is half feral. Why would she care about the welfare of her baby?" The sneering voice came from behind him and Brayden kept his head down, riding the wave of anger that swept over him. This was the way it had been from the minute Demi took flight. This constant fight between his job and his loyalty to his sister. It was getting harder each day.

"We suspect that Demi is pregnant with Bo

Gage's child and is several months along. All we know for sure is that Bo ended their relationship and became engaged to another woman. Unfortunately, that speaks to Demi's motive." Finn's voice was firm.

"Yeah. But then again, Bo might not be the father. Anything is possible with Demi—"

Brayden was on his feet before he had time to think, swinging around to face the unknown speaker. "What are you trying to say about my sister?"

Among the faces looking back at him, one stood out. Lucas Gage, Bo's brother, was a bounty hunter who had been deputized to the police department. Since Demi was in the same profession, they were fierce rivals and Lucas had been convinced from day one that Demi was the killer. Although Brayden couldn't be sure Lucas was the person who had spoken, the other man stared back at him, provocation in his eyes. It was a challenge Brayden was more than happy to take.

*To hell with impartial. To hell with all of it.*

"My sister is not a killer."

"Let's calm this down." Finn's cool, authoritative voice cut across Brayden's overheated senses. "Personal comments have no place in this investigation." His gaze swept the room. "They have no place in this department. I hope that's clear to everyone?"

There was a general murmur of agreement as Brayden returned to his seat. His fingers sought the reassuring softness of Echo's fur and the dog gave the inside of his wrist a quick lick.

When the briefing ended, Finn spoke quietly to Brayden. "My office."

With Echo keeping close to his heels, Brayden followed the chief to his room. "I know." He spoke as Finn was closing the door. "I was out of order. I shouldn't let it get to me."

"This has got to be hard on you, Bray." The change in Finn's manner told Brayden this was his cousin speaking, not his boss. "You're one of the best officers I have, and I need all the friends I can get. The Groom Killer case is the biggest thing to hit Red Ridge since I took over as chief. If I start taking officers off the investigation because of family loyalties, we'll struggle to keep up with what this murderer throws at us next. Not to mention our regular caseload."

Brayden knew exactly what he meant. "While this is going on, the Larson twins are stepping up their criminal activities."

"Our attention is split two ways." Finn's expression was grim. "We have a killer with a grudge against engaged couples, and the Larsons, who are intent on growing their crime empire. Our resources are stretched to the limit. In addition to that, you are the lead search-and-rescue officer on the team. I've never doubted your loyalty and you know the problems I face."

Finn didn't need to elaborate. The mayor, their uncle Fenwick, was breathing down their necks to get an arrest in the Groom Killer case. The Colton-Gage feud that had torn Red Ridge apart for a century was alive and well right here in the police department. The tensions were never far from the surface. The Gage officers on the team would grasp any opportunity to stir up old hostilities.

"You have a temper, Bray. You've said publicly you believe in Demi's innocence. Don't give anyone a chance to push you on this."

It was good advice. Brayden couldn't help Demi by getting himself thrown off the force. And Finn was right about the search-and-rescue side of his job. The pressure increased as summer approached. The Coyote Mountains attracted large numbers of tourists. There were always the inevitable cases of inexperienced hikers wandering off the trails, falling or staying out after dark. Brayden and Echo were often all that stood between them and disaster.

"You want me to focus on the Larsons?"

"If you can. Obviously, if anything comes your way to do with the Groom Killer case, you'll need to follow it up. And, Bray?" Brayden paused with his hand on the door handle. "Esmée da Costa tells me she's having trouble contacting you."

*That would be because I've been ignoring her calls.* Apparently, Esmée da Costa, the documentary maker who wanted to make a film about the Groom

Killer, couldn't take a hint. So, instead of respecting Brayden's privacy, she had gone to his *boss*. His antagonism toward the woman he'd never met spiked higher. He was the Colton cop from the wrong side of the tracks. His sister was on the run, wanted for a series of grisly murders Brayden knew she wasn't capable of committing. He was half out of his mind with worry for Demi, as he tried to focus on his job and deal with the taunts of the Gages and the arrogant skepticism of his better-off Colton relatives, and he was also aware that the eyes of the town were upon him wherever he went. Why the hell would he want to put his feelings on the record for a true-crime documentary film? If Brayden ever did come face-to-face with Ms. da Costa, he would give her his opinion of how she made her living. He doubted she'd enjoy hearing it.

Brayden smiled for the first time that morning. "You know me. I'm not much of a talker."

As she pulled into Hester Mull's drive, Esmée da Costa gripped the steering wheel so tight it hurt. Determined not to cry in front of Rhys, she battled back the tears. Her son had seen too much high drama in his two years. While Esmée knew it wasn't possible, or healthy, to cocoon him from every negative emotion, she did her best to keep his world on an even track.

Even so, hiding her sorrow was tough. She supposed it was because, until now, she hadn't really believed Jack Parkowski was dead. It had been impossible for her to accept that the big, strong man who had been such a powerful force for good in her life wouldn't be there forever.

Seeing Sarah, Jack's fiancée, her face pale and her smile strained as she lay in that hospital bed, was what had made it real. Esmée had held one of Sarah's icy hands in her own while Hester, Sarah's sister-in-law, held the other. As they talked, Rhys had played one of his noiseless games with the wooden animals he took everywhere. That was when the truth had come crashing down on Esmée, gaining speed until it reached the full force of an avalanche. She would never again see the man who had been there for her and Rhys when they had most needed a friend.

"The dog show is one of the most popular events in Red Ridge." Hester's voice brought Esmée back to reality. She had stowed a large picnic basket in the trunk of the rental car and was getting into the passenger seat.

"And you're sure *all* the K-9 officers will be there?" Esmée asked. She wasn't interested in all of them, but Hester didn't need to know that.

In the course of her research about the Groom Killer case, Esmée had learned that there was one man who was prepared to speak out in support of Demi Colton, the chief suspect in the murders. Despite his job as a member of the K-9 police team,

Brayden Colton was brave enough to declare his belief in his half sister's innocence.

As she delved deeper, Esmée would need to talk to all three of Demi's half siblings, but Brayden was the one who fascinated her. He must be going through hell right now. His sister was accused of murder, with most of the town happy to vocalize her guilt, yet Brayden had to turn up for work each day and investigate the crimes. He had to hear the details and listen to the theories about Demi's guilt. How did that make him feel? How did he balance the two different sides of his life? Colton and cop. Which did he put first?

Brayden's was the voice Esmée wanted to hear, his was the story she wanted to use as her starting point. If she could only get in touch with him.

"Oh, yes. Chief Finn Colton insists on it. Part of the trust that funds the unit provides for the K-9 team to do outreach work in the community."

Esmée and Hester had only just met and the circumstances hadn't exactly been pleasant. Sarah Mull had been happily married to Hester's older brother until he died in a car crash a few years ago. Now, Hester was helping her sister-in-law recover from another shock death, that of her fiancé, Jack.

Esmée, having met Hester a few times at the hospital when she visited Sarah, had instinctively liked the other woman. Hester was warm, kind and she had offered to show Esmée and Rhys around Red Ridge.

Before Hester had retired, she'd been a police officer herself, so Esmée was confident she knew what she was talking about. "The police dogs take part in demonstration events, and the officers are there to answer any questions members of the public have about the unit."

Hester turned to wave a hand at Rhys, who was in his safety seat.

"Rhys will enjoy today," Esmée said. "He loves all animals, but he really likes dogs."

"Such a pity he can't talk." Hester lowered her voice to a whisper as she fastened her seat belt. "Isn't there anything the doctors can do to cure him?"

"Rhys *can* talk." Esmée dealt with this all the time. People meant well, but they didn't understand. "There's nothing wrong with him," she explained to Hester. "He had a very bad experience when he was just twelve months old. Before that, he made the usual babbling noises all babies of his age make. Then he went quiet. Not speaking is his way of dealing with the trauma. It's called selective mutism."

"Oh." Hester cast a sidelong glance at Esmée, obviously wondering what to say next.

"It's okay." Esmée placed her hand briefly on the older woman's knee. "You didn't know and I don't mind talking about it."

It was true…in a way. Of course she minded that Rhys didn't talk. But she had always been open about it, even if the reason for his emotional distress filled her with guilt. The toxic downturn in her relationship with Gwyn Owen, Rhys's father, had been gradual. Even so, the deterioration into violence had taken Esmée by surprise. It was only Jack's intervention that had saved her from serious injury. Her old friend had come to her rescue, removing her from the scene of a vicious attack and helping her deal with the aftermath. But the damage had been done. Rhys had witnessed his mother cowering with her hands over her head as his father punched and kicked her.

"Why don't we go see some dogs?" Change the subject. Yeah, that always worked. For a while.

Rhys clapped his hands together before holding up both hands with his fingers curved as he imitated a begging dog. Esmée's heart expanded with pride and love and she clapped her own hands in response. It was important to praise any efforts he made to communicate, even if they weren't verbal. She wanted to use the dog show to meet Brayden Colton and set up an interview, but the most important thing was for Rhys to have a good time.

Her sweet, silent boy spoke to her in his own way. And one day he would use words. She had to stay positive that it would happen. Every time she looked into his dark eyes, thankfully like her own rather than his father's, an icy shard of guilt pierced her heart. She should have gotten away sooner, should have known it was never going to have a happy ending…

Hester laughed delightedly. "He's so clever."

Esmée already liked Hester, but her admiration for Rhys sealed the deal.

She chatted to Rhys as she drove, describing the late-afternoon scene. Hester picked up on what she was doing and joined in. Esmée didn't need the psychologist and the speech therapist who saw Rhys regularly to tell her that he needed lots of talk to stimulate him. She was his mom—her instincts told her what to do. At the same time, talking to Rhys, singing songs to him and telling him stories were all reminders of her own childhood. Esmée was a talker. It was who she was, and it made Rhys's silence so much harder to bear.

The dog show was held at the K-9 training center. Located at the far end of Main Street, the center was a large one-story brick building that edged onto the woods. They got out of the car and headed toward a large backyard with a five-foot-high wooden fence all the way around. The gates were open and the event had spilled out onto the surrounding grass with stalls lining the route all the way to the trees.

Hester explained that the major part of the K-9 unit funding came from a trust left by Mayor Fenwick Colton's late first wife. "That's him." Even though the man she indicated was too far away to hear, Hester murmured the words out of the corner of her mouth.

Esmée had heard a few things about Fenwick Colton, none of them good. According to the Gages she'd spoken to, the short, skinny man with the blond hairpiece thought he owned Red Ridge. He was a wealthy businessman in his midfifties, with three divorces behind him. Apparently having finally decided marriage wasn't for him, he now preferred to have a new young girlfriend on his arm, and changed them every few months.

"His daughter, Layla Colton, was supposed to marry Hamlin Harrington, the owner of Harrington Inc., at the end of the year." Hester's voice took on a gossipy ring that triggered Esmée's human-interest radar. "There's a rumor that Fenwick's business, Colton Energy, is in trouble. Hamlin has signed the documents that will save Colton Energy once he marries Layla. But since the Groom Killer murders, Hamlin has gotten nervous and called off the engagement. Now the clock is ticking and Fenwick faces losing everything. He needs millions by December 31st or it's all over. The problem is, if Fenwick loses Colton Energy, the funding for the K-9 unit will be pulled."

Esmée looked around her at the training center and the people who had gathered to celebrate the work it did. "That would be awful."

Hester spread her picnic blanket on the ground. "Fenwick is putting pressure on Chief Finn Colton to get a quick arrest. There is no such thing as family loyalty for our mayor. He can't stand his lowlife cousin, Rusty, who owns a bar, or any of his kids. As far as Fenwick is concerned, he doesn't care whether

Demi is guilty or innocent. He just wants her arrested and locked up so folks won't be scared of getting married and he can get his money-making plans back on track with his daughter's wedding."

"Nice man."

Hester snorted. "You think?"

Although Fenwick wasn't the Colton that Esmée was interested in right now, the story added color to her research. There clearly wasn't much family feeling between the three Colton patriarchs, Fenwick, Judson and Rusty. No wonder Demi had gone on the run. Guilty or innocent, there didn't seem to be much sympathy for her in Red Ridge. On the subject of the dysfunctional Colton clan...

She looked over at the enclosure in the center of the grass, where the officers were gathering with their dogs. "Which one is Brayden Colton?"

"I don't see him." Hester shielded her eyes with her hand as she looked toward the enclosure. Some of the officers were standing in a group nearby. "But it will be easy to pick him out when he does get here. He's the search-and-rescue officer on the team, so he wears an orange vest over his uniform. His K-9 partner, Echo, is a golden retriever. Echo also wears an orange vest."

It was a useful piece of information, and Esmée kept checking on the K-9 team as she and Hester took Rhys around the stalls and activities.

Her feelings about Red Ridge were mixed. Jack was the reason she had come to this town. He had worked closely with her mother, assisting Portia da Costa on several of her best-selling true-crime books. After Portia died and Jack left the force, he had helped Esmée with her own research. He had even joined her in Wales, where she'd spent almost two years filming her award-winning documentary, *What Remains*. When Jack alerted her to the Groom Killer case, Esmée had immediately been intrigued. But arriving in town to find her friend had become one of the victims had tilted her whole world off course. It also made her motivation for staying a whole lot stronger.

Even without Jack's death and the background of the Groom Killer story, there was enough of an undercurrent here in Red Ridge to stimulate her interest. Esmée's stories were about the individuals, families and communities that had been torn apart by acts of violence and lawlessness. It was hard to explain to anyone else, but she could also tell when a *place* was suffering. And, even though she'd only arrived recently, she knew Red Ridge was hurting more than any other town she'd known.

When Jack had called her with the news he and Sarah were getting married, Esmée had just finished delivering an online course to murder-mystery writers. She was in the unusual position of being between jobs.

"There's a story here, if you're interested," Jack had said. "How about a town where folks are scared to get married in case the groom is murdered? Couples are making a big deal of publicly calling off their weddings. Flower stores, cake shops, caterers and wedding-dress designers are seeing their incomes plummet. No one is going on dates or out for romantic meals. Hell, most people are even scared to hold hands with their partner." Jack always did have a knack for catching her attention and hooking her into a story, making her see the human-interest angle.

Esmée had reached for a notepad and pen. "Red Ridge, South Dakota. The town where romance died?"

She recalled that conversation as she looked around her now. Although there were couples at the show, she noticed a definite lack of any displays of affection. It created a strange, false atmosphere.

Hester entertained her by explaining that there were competitions for the saddest eyes, waggiest tail, floppiest ears and scruffiest dog. "There was a campaign to have a crossbreed disqualified after he won all four categories last year."

Esmée burst out laughing. "Now that's a dog I need to see." She noticed that a tall, dark-haired officer in an orange search-and-rescue vest had entered the K-9 enclosure. "Hester, would you watch Rhys for a few minutes? There's someone I need to talk to."

# Chapter 2

"You know how hard you've been working to stay out of Esmée da Costa's way?" Finn asked.

Brayden regarded him warily. "Yes."

"Looks like she found you anyway."

Brayden followed the direction of his chief's nod. Until now, he wasn't aware he'd had any expectation about how Esmée would look. He certainly hadn't expected to see a petite, pretty woman with long auburn hair and huge dark eyes. She was holding the hand of a little boy, who wore a red sweatshirt, and she was laughing at something Hester Mull was saying. Having looked her way, Brayden was having a hard time dragging his gaze away again.

After a moment or two, he realized Finn was waiting for some kind of response. He shrugged and turned away. "I need to get Echo ready for the manhunt."

Each of the K-9s in the unit had a different specialty and the dog show was an opportunity to show the public what they did. Echo was trained as a scent-specific search dog, also known as a trail dog. If he was given something belonging to a missing person, Echo would discriminate that scent from the others around it and use it to hunt for the person it matched. Each year, during the dog show, Brayden would select members of the public and ask them to hide before using Echo to find them in a canine game of hide-and-seek. It was one of the most popular features of the day.

"Officer Colton?" The voice was low-pitched and musical and the aroma that invaded his nostrils was subtle and floral.

He swung around quickly, encountering a smile that, in any other circumstances, would have done him a whole powerful lot of good. Up close, Esmée was even more beautiful than from a distance, with dainty features and golden skin tones. The top of her head was level with his shirt pocket and she tilted her head back to look at him.

She was eye-catching in her short, brightly patterned skirt, over which she wore a lace blouse and a faded denim jacket. Black lace-up ankle boots drew Brayden's attention to her slender legs.

"I'm Esmée da Costa. We seem to keep missing each other."

"No, Ms. da Costa. I've been avoiding you."

Her smile widened. It was possibly the most enchanting smile he'd ever seen and he was working hard to *not* be enchanted. "I knew that. I was being diplomatic."

She was stunning and just gazing at her was a reminder to his body that it had been a long time since he had been this close to a woman. Maybe it was time to do something about that. Not with *this* woman, obviously...

"This must be Echo." As she stroked the dog's head, Brayden's well-trained K-9 partner forgot his manners and licked her bare knee. Esmée laughed. Smiling and laughing seemed to come naturally to her. If she hadn't been making a documentary that had the potential to ruin his sister, he'd have been tempted to join in. "Oh, hey...is that a Red Ridge greeting? The knee licking?"

"Looks like it is now." He really couldn't blame Echo for his lapse. She had the nicest knees.

"I know you're busy." She waved a hand to indicate the compound, where the K-9s were waiting patiently for their partners. "And I need to get back to my little boy, but I'd love to fix up a time to speak to you."

"That isn't going to happen." He was about to launch into his rehearsed speech about her chosen profession, when the sound of a woman's voice raised in shrill alarm drew his attention back to the training area.

"Esmée! Oh, dear Lord." He narrowed his eyes, catching sight of Hester Mull standing at the edge of the K-9 compound with her hand over her mouth. "I just turned away for a second…"

With lightning speed, Esmée had already broken into a run. Catching a glimpse of a small figure in a red sweatshirt among the dogs, Brayden was just behind her. He overtook her before she could run into the compound.

He caught hold of her arm, pulling her back until she was behind him. "Leave this to me."

"Rhys…" The word was choked from her as she gazed at her son. Weaving his way among the dogs, the boy appeared smaller than ever. There were gasps and exclamations from some of the onlookers.

"Somebody do something. Those dogs will tear him apart." The unknown woman's voice grated on Brayden's nerves.

Catching sight of Danica Gage, a K-9 trainer, he gestured for her to keep the onlookers away and ask them to be quiet. As Brayden stepped into the compound, Rhys approached Echo. Wrapping his arms around the dog's neck, the boy pressed his face into thick, golden fur. When Brayden reached them, Echo gave him a look that seemed to say, "Don't worry, I've got this."

Echo stayed perfectly still as Brayden carefully

loosened Rhys's hands from around his neck. As soon as he had freed the boy from the dog, Esmée was there. Dropping to her knees at her son's side, she scooped him into her arms.

"Dog," Rhys said, pointing to Echo.

"What did you say?" Esmée stared at him, her face growing pale.

"Dog." Rhys seemed slightly impatient at being asked to say the word again.

Esmée's hand shook as she raised it to cover her lips. Tears filled her eyes, spilling over as she gazed at him.

"I know it looked bad, but he wasn't in any real danger." Since she was clearly in shock, Brayden attempted to reassure her. "These dogs are well trained. None of them would hurt a child, and Echo is just a big cuddly toy."

She shook her head, the tears flowing faster now. "You don't understand. Rhys doesn't talk. That was his first word."

Brayden squatted next to Rhys, who stood within the circle of Esmée's arms. She was still having a hard time believing what she'd just heard.

"This is Echo." As Brayden pronounced each word slowly and deliberately, Esmée held her breath.

"Ko." Rhys tried out the word carefully.

"Close enough." Brayden held out his hand, inviting the little boy to come closer. "It's okay." He raised his eyes to Esmée's face and she knew the re-assurance was for her sake more than Rhys's. "Echo is great with kids."

*So are you.* Her son could be a little shy around strangers, but she watched him take Brayden's out-stretched hand. She got to her feet as they approached the dog.

"Esmée, I'm so sorry. I don't know how he got away from me." Hester came to stand beside her.

She shook her head. "He said a few words, Hes-ter." Tears blurred her vision again momentarily. "The dog got him talking."

"Oh, my." Hester slid an arm around Esmée's waist and she leaned her head gratefully against the older woman's shoulder as they observed Rhys interact-ing with Echo.

Brayden was talking patiently to the little boy. "Echo can shake hands, but you have to tell him what you want him to do. You have to say 'paw.'"

As soon as he said the word, Echo raised his paw and Brayden took it, shaking it to demonstrate what he meant. Rhys started to laugh. It was a sound Esmée hadn't heard since that awful night in Wales when Gwyn had attacked her. Although he often smiled, when Rhys had retreated into his silent world, he had stopped laughing.

Now, watching Brayden shake hands with Echo, her little boy's musical chuckle rang out. It was the sweetest sound she had ever heard.

"Now you say it." Brayden positioned Rhys in front of Echo. "Say 'paw.'"

Instead, Rhys gave the dog another hug. "Ko." His voice was muffled by Echo's fur.

"Can I get a picture?" Esmée's hand shook as she took her cell phone out of her pocket.

"Sure. Echo is a narcissist, he loves posing for photographs," Brayden said.

As if to demonstrate, as soon as Esmée aimed her phone to take the picture, Echo shifted position so his search-and-rescue vest was on display. He looked up at her, big eyes shining, his mouth wide as if he was smiling. She had never had much contact with dogs. Her mother's job had kept them moving around too much for them to own one when Esmée was growing up. Now, looking at Echo's kind, intelligent face, she thought there was probably a lot to be said for the benefit of a canine companion.

"Let's try the paw thing once more."

Esmée realized what Brayden was doing. He was using his dog as therapy, getting Rhys to talk to Echo. Her throat tightened with gratitude toward this man she didn't know. No one had grasped what Rhys needed so quickly, or done something about it with such efficiency.

Slowly, patiently, Brayden got Rhys to say the word *paw* to Echo. Rhys squealed with delight when Echo lifted his paw on command. He shook it, then insisted on doing it over and over.

"That dog is going to have a sore leg." Even though she was laughing, Hester had tears in her eyes as she hugged Esmée.

"Now it's Mommy's turn to shake hands," Brayden said. "Tell her to come over here."

Esmée held her breath as Rhys looked over his shoulder, his eyes shining. "Mommy, say 'paw.'" He pointed. "Ko."

Although she had stayed positive, telling herself he *would* talk, there had been times when she had wondered if she would ever hear him call her "Mommy." All she knew was she'd have given everything she owned to hear that word on his lips. As she sank to her knees next to Brayden, wrapping an arm around Rhys's waist, she wanted to relish the moment, to imprint it on her memory forever.

Rhys wasn't going to give her time to get emotional. "Say 'paw.'" Having found his voice, he seemed determined to use it.

Laughing, Esmée went through the routine of shaking hands with Echo, who, she decided, must be the most patient dog in the world.

Brayden straightened and stood over them. "Sorry to break this up, but Echo and I have to go put on a show for the crowd."

"Of course." Esmée lifted Rhys into her arms. "We have to say goodbye now."

"Bye, Ko." He waved a hand over her shoulder at the dog.

Esmée wondered if Brayden had any idea what he'd just done. For an instant, they gazed at each other. His eyes were unusual. More green than blue and fringed by thick, dark lashes, their expression was intense. When she first saw him, her first thought had been that he was unapproachable. Devastatingly handsome, but, oh, so severe.

Now she was being forced to rethink her first impression. Because she was sure he *had* deliberately taken time out of his busy schedule to spend with Rhys when he had figured out that her little boy needed a push to keep him talking. Maybe he didn't know he had just changed her life, but Brayden Colton had done a good thing for a stranger. That had to make him a special kind of person. She hadn't formed any idea about his sister, but Brayden thought Demi was innocent. More than ever, Esmée wanted to hear his opinion.

"Thank you." It seemed an inadequate thing to say, but it was all she had. The emotion was still close to the surface. Even those two words had her throat tightening painfully all over again.

"All part of the service." Somehow, she sensed Brayden understood the raw emotion that was churning through her. He placed a hand briefly on Rhys's shoulder. "He's a great kid."

"He is." She rested her cheek against Rhys's curls. "He's the best."

He reached into his top pocket, pulling out his shades. "Oh, and that interview you wanted?"

"Yes?" Her heart beat a little faster. She wasn't sure whether it was at the prospect of the interview, or the chance to spend more time with him. Possibly it was both.

He slid the shades on, hiding his eyes. Hiding *himself.* "Still not happening."

It was a good thing Echo knew what he was doing because Brayden had been afflicted by a curious inability to concentrate. It was a unique experience for someone who was usually focused, and it was annoying him intensely.

He was well aware of the reason for his distraction. Throughout the K-9 demonstration, during which the police dogs showed off their different skills, his eyes seemed to have developed a will of their own. No matter how hard he tried to keep his gaze on what was happening around him, his eyes insisted on wandering to the picnic rug where Esmée was sitting with Rhys and Hester.

Although they were some distance away, Rhys was a splash of bright color in his red sweatshirt, and Esmée's skirt was equally eye-catching. Brayden choked back a laugh. She could be camouflaged to blend in with her surroundings. He'd still find her.

The truth was, Esmée da Costa had shaken him and he wasn't sure how to feel about it. The fact that she was five foot three inches of delicious femininity hadn't escaped his notice, but it was not the only reason she had grabbed his attention.

Even though she looked like every man's hottest fantasy, he'd been ready with a few well-chosen words of angry dismissal when she'd mentioned an interview. Then the drama with her little boy had unfolded. What he'd seen then had been remarkable. When Rhys said his first words, Brayden had been able to feel the emotion coming off Esmée in waves. In her eyes, he had seen hope mingling with a love so intense it was fierce.

He had spent time with Rhys for the kid's own sake. Something about the little boy had reminded Brayden of himself. When Esmée said her son hadn't spoken until today, it was clear Rhys had problems that went deep. Brayden didn't know what they were. As a child, his own intense shyness had been crippling. After knowing Rhys for only a matter of minutes, he wouldn't presume to say he knew how the boy felt. All he could say was he remembered what it was like to wish he could retreat behind an imaginary wall in a grown-up world. He'd seen a way to reach out, and Rhys's smile had been the only reward he'd wanted.

When he saw Esmée's reaction to Rhys's first words, he had experienced a strong desire to go further and help her as well as her kid. The feeling was so strong he had put aside his personal animosity toward her purpose for coming to Red Ridge. Had even possibly forgotten all about the story she was covering and just enjoyed that brief encounter with her and her son. As incredible as it seemed, for the first time since Bo Gage had been found shot dead with a cummerbund stuffed in his mouth, Brayden had stopped thinking about the investigation.

As his gaze strayed in Esmée's direction again, he decided it was worth a reminder that the presence of a child indicated there was a father around somewhere. Not that he had any intention of letting a pair of big dark eyes and those pretty legs with their lickable knees divert him from who she was. A few wrong words from Esmée could hurt Demi, and Brayden wasn't going to add to his sister's problems.

With that thought in his mind, he glanced at his cell phone. He had gotten into the habit of willing Demi to get in touch, even though he knew she wouldn't. Brayden didn't have much of a relationship with any of his half siblings; they'd all been raised by different mothers. They were all close in age, and had lived nearby when they were growing up—he and his older sister, Quinn, had even been in the same class at school—but their mothers had instilled a sense of distrust in them that had lasted into adulthood. Brayden, Quinn and Shane didn't dislike each other. They just had nothing in common and no reason to get to know each other.

Demi was different. They weren't exactly friends,

but their shared love of the outdoors had brought them together when they were growing up and a bond had developed between them because of events that had come their way. It was the reason Brayden was certain his sister wasn't a killer. It was also how he knew she wouldn't contact him. Strong-willed, stubborn and feisty, Demi was also fiercely loyal. She wouldn't put Brayden in a position where he had to choose between her and his job.

He just wished she would get in touch with *someone* to let them know she was okay. Those rumors were swirling around town that Demi was pregnant with Bo Gage's baby. Her critics were claiming it as further proof of her guilt. Bo dumped her and was marrying someone else while she was carrying his child, so she killed him? Brayden shook his head. Demi had a temper, but she was more likely to confront Bo and land a punch on him that would break his nose. And the idea that Demi had then continued killing other bridegrooms? Jack Parkowski was the fourth victim. *Fourth.* Brayden just didn't buy into the idea that his sister was out somewhere close by, stalking and killing engaged men.

Even so, the evidence against Demi wasn't good. A search of her house had revealed photos and love letters to Demi from Bo, with big *X*s across them and the word *Liar* scrawled in marker across one letter. No matter how bad things seemed, if she would just give herself up, Brayden was sure they could clear her name.

The K-9 demonstration was over and Brayden looked in Esmée's direction once more. She was chasing Rhys in a circle around their picnic rug, letting him stay just ahead of her. Almost as if she sensed him watching, she looked up and stared back at Brayden across the distance between them. Hurriedly, he turned away to help Danica dismantle the agility equipment.

A heavy hand landed on his shoulder and alcohol fumes greeted him as he turned his head. Brayden resisted the temptation to groan.

"Saw you talking to that pretty little reporter a while ago, son." His father, Rusty, only ever called Brayden "son" when he wanted to borrow money from him.

"She's not a reporter."

"Whatever she is, that would be one mighty fine way to spend an afternoon." Rusty winked and elbowed Brayden in the ribs. "Maybe I'll invite her over to the Pour House. Tell her my side of the story while we, uh…relax."

Brayden had given up on wishing Rusty would treat women with respect. Usually, he called his father out on the worst of his comments without much hope that he would be listened to. For the first time ever, real anger blazed through him at his father's attitude. The thought of Rusty leering at Esmée infuriated

him almost as much as the idea that he would con-
template discussing Demi's situation with a stranger.
A stranger who was here to make a *documentary*. To
expose every aspect of their lives to the world.

"Stay away from her." The words came out harder
than he'd intended.

"Whatever you say." Rusty held up his hands in a
gesture of peace. "Look, I have a problem—"

"How much?" Brayden didn't want to hear the latest inventive reason why Rusty needed cash.

"Fifty should do it."

Brayden handed him the money and Rusty stuffed
it into the back pocket of his jeans. He stooped to pat
Echo before wandering away, whistling tunelessly.
Despite telling himself he wouldn't, Brayden turned
once more to look at Esmée.

She'd gone. He already had plenty of reasons of
his own to stay away from her. The fact that he was
more disappointed than relieved that she was no longer around added about a dozen more.

# Chapter 3

Two days had passed since the dog show and Esmée congratulated herself that she hadn't contacted Brayden during that time. The temptation had been almost overwhelming, but she had resisted for a number of reasons.

The first was that he had made it clear he didn't wish to speak to her. The man had to be dealing with a world of pain right now. She had caught some of that in his expression before he lowered his shades. She had also heard it in his voice. The last thing he needed was for her to disrespect his wishes and trample roughly over his feelings. Esmée hadn't given up on her desire to talk to him, but she worked within a strong code of ethics. She wasn't going to try to coerce him into it.

Her hope was that, once he saw other people opening up to her and became aware that she was treating his sister's story with sensitivity, he would change his mind. If he didn't? She would take her research in another direction. She'd done it before. A documentary of this kind took a long time to make and there would be many twists and turns along the way. Right now, it felt like Brayden was her starting point, but that could change.

An approach to the subscription TV company that had bought the documentary about the murders in the Welsh farming community of Glanrafon had proved promising. They were keen to work with her again and loved the Red Ridge idea. Viewing figures for *What Remains* had been phenomenal and it had won several prestigious awards. Esmée's terms were simple—a good price and total artistic control over her work.

Her second reason for keeping her distance from Brayden was more personal. Rhys was talking. She wanted to hold her breath every time he spoke in case he stopped again. The remarkable thing was that he was good at it. All that listening to Esmée must have paid off. He was speaking in simple sentences, his vocabulary was good and he could pronounce most words well.

Esmée had called both his speech therapist and

psychologist to discuss this new development. The speech therapist had been encouraging.

"You know what to do as well as I do. Give him a context to talk. Keep modeling what to do. Ask him questions. This is the turning point—it will all move forward from here."

The psychologist, while also optimistic, had added a word of caution. "You say this started with a dog? Make sure Rhys doesn't develop a reliance on the animal."

"He's been talking just fine without Echo," Esmée had explained as she watched Rhys eating the cookie he had asked for. Not signed. Not gestured. *Asked.*

"Just something to be aware of."

While Esmée had no doubt that Echo had been the trigger for Rhys to start talking, she didn't believe that his continuing recovery depended on the dog. Even so, he had several times asked the same question.

"See Ko?"

"Echo is busy. He has to work." Although Rhys had accepted the explanation, his disappointment had been obvious. Once or twice, he had asked to see the picture of Echo on Esmée's cell phone. And, after watching Brayden and Echo demonstrate their search-and-rescue skills at the dog show, Rhys had developed a love of playing hide-and-seek. It was his new favorite activity, and even when Esmée couldn't join in, he played hiding games with his toy animals.

His interest in Echo turned Esmée's thoughts toward the future. Maybe it was time to put down roots. Her own nomadic childhood had been happy, but she wasn't sure she wanted the same thing for Rhys. And if they settled in one place, they could get a dog of their own. She was becoming drawn to the concept of a pet as a form of therapy.

How about a tall, handsome cop? Was there a therapeutic role for one of those in her life? She shook aside the thought as soon as it appeared. There was no room for *any* man in her life. Period. She had messed up in a big way with Gwyn. The only thing she didn't regret about that part of her life was that it had brought her Rhys. Her son was everything to her. Even though her relationship with his father had gone horribly wrong, she could never wish it hadn't happened.

The experience had changed her in so many ways. She supposed the blithe, pleasure-loving person was still inside her somewhere, but that part of her remained well-hidden these days. Rhys was her priority. Even if she had any inclination to start dating again, there was no way she would risk unsettling him by introducing a new father figure into his life. It was just as well she had no interest in men.

Or she hadn't…until Brayden Colton had appeared on her horizon. And that was yet another reason not to contact him. Esmée couldn't be sure, if she did get in touch with him, that she would be doing it for the right reasons. Yes, she wanted to talk to him about Demi, but she was honest enough to admit to a strong desire to see him again. It was an unexpected and dangerous attraction, one she wasn't willing to pursue. It was probably a good idea to steer clear of Brayden and take her research in a different direction for the time being.

With that in mind, she had pursued a few other leads. One of those had been an interview with the owner of Bea's Bridal. The store, located among the fancy boutiques and restaurants of Rattlesnake Avenue, had been temporarily closed. It was another sign of the Groom Killer's impact on the town. No one wanted to be seen ordering wedding gowns in Red Ridge right now. Grooms-to-be were not safe.

Just a few miles away from Rattlesnake Avenue, there was another, very different side to Red Ridge. Located in a run-down part of town, the Pour House was the notorious bar owned by Rusty Colton, Brayden and Demi's father. Hester had watched Rhys the previous night while Esmée made a visit to that interesting establishment. It had helped clarify a few aspects of her potential story.

Rusty was a large, loud personality who had four children, all with different mothers. Although the half siblings had been raised near each other in the poorer part of town, their mothers didn't get on and the kids hadn't been close as they grew up. Observing Rusty as she sipped her soda in a quiet corner of the bar, Esmée couldn't picture him as a loving father.

She would need to speak to him, of course, but she hadn't approached Rusty for his views about his daughter's guilt and her disappearance. Part of her preparation was about getting a feel for the key characters in her story. Even so, word had already gotten out about who she was, and a few people had come forward to give her their opinions. If she went with what she had so far, she would be on her way out of town already, the story of Demi's guilt all neatly packaged up.

What had surprised her was that most of the people who were keen to give her their theories about Demi's involvement were members of the Gage family. It hadn't taken much research to uncover that there was a century-old feud between the Coltons and Gages. In the Groom Killer case, the first victim had been a Gage, the suspect a Colton. These new murders were a fresh wound on top of an older hurt.

Esmée wasn't an investigator. When Demi was found, it would be up to the legal system to determine her guilt or innocence. Esmée's story would be about the people, the town and the impact of the murders. It was about Jack and Sarah and the other couples whose hopes and dreams had been torn apart by a killer who didn't want to see them make it down the aisle. It was about the Gage-and-Colton feud and why this place couldn't move on from that. It was about the welcome she had received from the people of this pretty mountain town and the contrasting raw pain she could feel beneath.

She and Rhys took their cereal out onto the porch of their tiny bungalow. The Red Ridge Bed-and-Breakfast was situated right on the edge of town, close to the winding trail that led to the lower slopes of the Coyote Mountains. Comprising eight wooden guest cabins arranged around a grass lawn, the place had been the most comfortable of those Esmée had viewed. The owner, Wendy Gage, was a distant cousin of Bo, the first victim of the Groom Killer, and a firm believer in Demi Colton's guilt.

Although breakfast was provided each morning in the main house, Esmée and Rhys had only tried it once.

Rhys wasn't a picky eater, but faced with a plate piled high with sausages, eggs, bacon and muffins, he had struggled to finish. Wendy had made a comment that her kids would have been made to sit at the table until the last mouthful was gone. It had taken every ounce of diplomacy Esmée possessed not to respond. Instead, she had informed Wendy that she and Rhys would make their own arrangements for breakfast in the future. The proprietor's initial outrage had been appeased when she realized Esmée was still prepared to pay the full bed-and-breakfast rate.

It was a beautiful day, and the view was perfect.

Across to her right, rolling fields of farmland and ranch land stretched away into the distance. To her left, up close, thick trees bordered the Coyote Mountain range.

She wondered what it would be like to grow up in a place like this. Esmée's own upbringing had been unconventional. Her father had died when she was seven and, from then on, her mother had followed the stories she needed to write her bestselling books. If they stayed anywhere long enough, Esmée attended a regular school. If not, she was homeschooled. But Portia wasn't a traditionalist. Esmée learned as much from the outdoors as she did from her lessons. The long hikes her mother had taken her on when she was a child meant walking was in her blood.

No matter where she was, no matter what the weather, Esmée still got the cravings. Those mountains were calling to her now. There were a few people she had planned to call, a couple of locations she wanted to visit. Nothing that couldn't wait.

Rhys was at an in-between age. He enjoyed walking, examining every leaf, bug, rock and stick, just the way Esmée had once done. Because he wasn't capable of a sustained level of exercise, Esmée had a carrier so she could lift him onto her back when he started to tire.

"Shall we go for a hike?" She pointed to the trail that led toward the trees.

"Boots." Rhys pointed to his bare feet. "Hat, screen, water..."

Esmée laughed. He was listing the items she always told him they needed for a walk. Her insistence on telling him every little detail had paid off. "Yes, we need all of those things. Especially the hat and sunscreen on a day like today."

As they went inside to get ready, she thought about the different emotions this place brought up. She had faced heartache from the first instant she had arrived in Red Ridge, with Jack's death. Even so, she felt more at home here than in any other place she had stayed. Was it time to think about staying in one place for a while? She looked back at the tranquil view. Even with the undercurrents, Red Ridge had plenty to recommend it.

Brayden's role was straightforward. He was the lead search-and-rescue, or SAR, officer. If Frank Lanelli, the Red Ridge Police Department dispatcher, got a 911 call indicating a person, or group of people, may be lost or in danger, he immediately liaised with Brayden, who then took charge of the mission.

The situation dictated the response. The Coyote Mountains were an attractive tourist destination and most calls were about hikers who had wandered off the trail. Brayden and Echo could deal with those alerts without any additional assistance. Sometimes things were more serious. All the K-9 teams had a basic level of search-and-rescue training and, now and then, it was necessary for Brayden to mobilize a larger force. That usually happened if the weather conditions were poor, or the search continued for several hours.

There were occasions, of course, when the problem was just too big, or too dangerous. It didn't happen often. When it did, he needed to call in other emergency agencies. Brayden and Echo went on regular training courses with other SAR teams, as well as medical services, the National Guard and helicopter rescue crews.

Brayden spent a few hours at the start of each day in the training center. Together with Danica Gage, he had devised a program that kept Echo's skills up-to-date and the dog's fitness in peak condition. They reviewed the activities each month, looking at how Brayden and Echo worked together, analyzing the success of recent missions and comparing what they were doing to the work of SAR teams elsewhere.

When training was over, if Frank hadn't been in touch, Brayden checked in at the police-department building. Half a mile closer to town than the training center, the pleasant, one-story, redbrick building was the headquarters for twenty-four officers, plus the twelve officers of the K-9 team. When he wasn't out on an SAR case, Brayden was a regular cop. The only difference was, he kept Echo with him at all times so they were ready to go as soon as a SAR call came in.

The chief's message had gotten through to

Brayden. If he was going to keep a clear head, he needed to stay away from the Groom Killer case. That meant he was free to focus on the PD's other big headache—the Larson brothers.

For the past year, the RRPD had been trying to pin something on the dangerous, wealthy and influential Larson brothers. Finn Colton believed the identical twins, Noel and Evan, who were blessed with good looks and easy charm, were running a growing crime empire in the city. Although they had busted a few low-level crooks, whom they suspected of working for the Larsons, the police hadn't been able to get any of them to name their employers. So far, they had also been unsuccessful in their efforts to find out where the gang stashed their guns, drugs and laundered money.

Lorelei Wong greeted him from the front desk in her usual way, peering at him over the top of her silver-framed glasses as her fingers continued to fly over her keyboard.

"Anything on Richie Lyman?" Brayden asked.

Lorelei flipped through a notepad at the side of her desktop computer. "Nothing."

Brayden frowned. Richie Lyman was bad news. The worst kind of thug for hire, the guy had a violent streak and enjoyed using it in his work. A known associate of the Larson brothers, the last time Richie had vanished was after a bar fight in the Pour House had landed his opponent in the hospital. When the other guy refused to give evidence against Richie, there were rumors he had been paid off by the Larsons. Richie was valuable to his bosses. The Larsons would rather send him out of town until the heat died down than have him end up in a prison cell. Finding another paid attack dog of Richie's caliber wouldn't be easy.

If the Larsons were planning something big, Richie would be in on it. When Brayden had called at the run-down apartment in the poorest part of town to question him, there had been no sign of Richie. Perhaps it wouldn't have raised alarm bells except for the fact that Richie's on-and-off partner, Lulu Love, was due to have a baby within the month.

"When you find him, tell him to get his sorry ass back here in time to see his kid being born." When Brayden had busted Lulu for receiving stolen goods a few months earlier, she had listed her occupation as "exotic dancer." There had been nothing exotic about her expression as she slammed the door in his face.

That had been almost four weeks ago. Brayden had put an alert out within the PD. Richie wasn't wanted for a crime, but Brayden wanted to be informed of any sightings of him. Lorelei's answer had been the same every day.

Brayden couldn't find any reason for Richie's current disappearance. Not that anyone within the Larsons' inner circle was likely to confide in a police officer, of course. He found it strange that Noel and

Evan would be without one of their most trusted operatives at a time when they seemed to be stepping up their activities.

A glance at the clock told Brayden it was close to noon. He tried not to involve his father, Rusty, in his job. There were too many personal conflicts arising from being a cop whose father ran the bar where the town's lowlife criminals congregated. Now and then, a quiet word over the bar was the best way to find out what was going on. This seemed like one of those times.

"If anyone is looking for me, I'm heading out to the Pour House."

Talking to Rusty about the Larson brothers and their hired thugs was not the way Brayden would have chosen to spend the next few hours, but at least it gave him a focus. And he could guarantee it would be a challenge. Something to keep his mind from straying toward the Red Ridge Bed-and-Breakfast. Because ever since he had met her at the dog show, Esmée had invaded his thoughts. He didn't want her there, had done everything he could to force himself to concentrate on other things. It wasn't like he had nothing else going on in his life right now.

The newest *Red Ridge Gazette* story had everyone talking about the latest rumor. Groom Killer Suspect Demi Colton Pregnant! Her Motive Grows Clearer!

Even with that headline setting the town alight, Brayden had been unable to entirely tear his attention away from Esmée. Telling himself it was because of her involvement in the case hadn't worked. He wanted to see her again. It was a simple truth that made his heart race with a combination of excitement and fear. He had even taken the trouble to find out where she was staying.

It was years since he had last felt this way. That had ended in disaster and public humiliation. He wasn't naive enough to believe that, having been burned once, he was incapable of feeling attraction again. He just didn't understand why, after lying dormant for so long, his wayward emotions had to choose such an unsuitable target. Whatever the reason, he knew he had to do a better job of fighting it.

The most important thing he could do was stay out of Esmée's way and hope she would soon be gone. Every time he told himself that, various reasons to drop by the bed-and-breakfast kept occurring to him. What harm could it do to take Echo to see Rhys? Find out how the little guy was getting on with his talking?

*Do the words* lame *and* excuse *mean anything to you, Colton?*

Undeterred, his mind found another motive for a visit. He should stop by the bed-and-breakfast to see how Corey Gage was doing. The sixteen-year-old son of the proprietor had landed himself in some trouble a few months back after driving his mom's car into a wall in the early hours of the morning. No one had been hurt and Corey had gotten away with a caution. Privately, Brayden thought facing his mom would be a whole lot worse for Corey than dealing with the law. Wendy Gage was not known for her warm personality.

"Maybe I should forget the excuses. Just turn up with flowers and candy and ask her on a date instead," he muttered, as he opened the rear door of his car.

Echo jumped inside, his tail thumping loudly in the confined space as he looked up at Brayden with shining eyes.

"I was being sarcastic."

Echo gave a single, enthusiastic bark in response. Shaking his head, Brayden closed the door and walked around to the front of the car.

*Great. Even my own partner thinks I'm a sad loser who needs to be pushed to make a move.*

# Chapter 4

Esmée paused at the top of a steep incline, breathing hard as she took in the view. When they started out, Rhys had been walking, but he had tired after an hour. It was about two months since she had used the carrier, and she was amazed at how much he had grown in that time.

"Talk about giving your mommy a workout."

"Down now." He wriggled to indicate his eagerness to be free again.

Esmée checked out the area. Although they were on a ridge above the forest, they were still on the gravel trail. On one side, the ponderosa pines soared above her. The sheer rock face rising high above the trees resembled cathedral spires. If Esmée tilted her head back far enough, she could just about see the blue sky beyond the rugged peaks. This must be the point known as Eagle's Nest. In which case, Esmée estimated that she was standing right on the rooftop of the famous Red Ridge cave system.

On her other side, there was an expanse of brush and shrub before the ground fell away in a sharp drop down into the valley. She had packed bottled water, sandwiches and cookies in the pockets of the carrier. Beneath the trees on the wooded side of the trail there was a large, flat rock. It looked like a good place for a picnic.

"Okay. But you have to keep close to me." She undid the straps on the carrier. "Stay away from the edge."

Rhys eyed the drop warily. "Long way down."

"It's okay," Esmée reassured him as she pointed to the trees. "We'll be safe over there. Are you hungry? I sure am after carrying you all that way."

She brought their food over to the rock she had chosen as a table, doing what she always did. Talking, explaining what was happening, soothing him with her voice. She watched Rhys carefully, happy when she saw signs that he was relaxed.

Although the sun was high overhead, it barely penetrated the canopy of branches that shaded their picnic spot, and Esmée didn't object when Rhys removed his bright yellow baseball cap. When Rhys had finished eating, he began to investigate the area around the rock. Soon, Esmée's lap was filled with a variety of stones, leaves and sticks. She leaned back against a tree trunk, content to watch him as he explored. There would need to be some serious negotiations about how much of this forest treasure trove they could carry home with them.

"Play hide-and-seek?" Rhys deposited another handful of pebbles in his stash as he asked the question.

Esmée looked around. They were in a circular clearing, surrounded by trees. As long as they stayed within these clear boundaries, there was no reason why she shouldn't indulge Rhys in his favorite game. Besides, he was wearing a brightly colored, dinosaur-print T shirt. She would spot him easily in this natural setting.

Carefully she explained the rules to him. "You can't go past that fallen tree trunk over there and this stone where I'm sitting now."

For a two-year-old his understanding was good, and she didn't need to spoil his fun by telling him she was going to do a little mom-cheating. As he skipped away to find a hiding place, Esmée counted out loud. She pretended to cover her eyes while watching him through her fingers. Rhys cast a quick glance around before ducking under the fallen tree stump that rested up against the face of the rock.

"Here I come, ready or not!" Placing Rhys's precious new possessions in a pile on the flat stone, Esmée got to her feet.

Although she knew where he was, she made a big performance out of the hunt. "Fee-fi-fo-fum. Mommy's gonna get you Rhys-baby." His squeals of laughter rang through the trees. "Ain't no hiding place good enough to keep you from me…"

After calling out a few fairy-tale-style threats, she eventually ducked her head under the stump. "Gotcha!"

Catching hold of Rhys around the waist, she started to tickle him until they both collapsed onto the ground, rolling around helpless with laughter. Rhys scrambled to get away from Esmée and back to his hiding place. The layer of dried leaves and pine needles under the fallen tree trunk had already been churned up and his sneakers were kicking up the loose dirt. Esmée paused as she caught a glimpse of something shiny close to his right foot.

It couldn't be what she thought it was…

If it was, she didn't want Rhys anywhere near it. Setting him on his feet, she gestured for him to stay behind her. "I need to check this out."

"Snake?" His voice was half hopeful, half afraid.

Esmée laughed. "No, it's not a snake. It's just something Mommy needs to get a closer look at."

Once he was safely out of the way, she kneeled and cleared the ground around the object, taking care not to touch it. Her heart began to pound as it became clear that her suspicions were correct. It was a knife.

It was a large fixed-blade knife with an overall length of close to twelve inches. The wooden handle had carved finger grooves and the blade looked like it was made from stainless steel. There might be any number of innocent reasons why this knife was here, half buried in this wooded area off the Coyote Mountain trail, but Esmée's instincts were ringing alarm bells.

This wasn't a big-game hunting area. It was too close to the town for anyone seeking deer, antelope, elk or mountain goat. But this was the sort of knife hunters used to skin their kill, and it looked new. The blade was lethally sharp, shining bright even in the shade of the trees. Except, of course, for the areas where it was covered in dried blood.

That was the main reason for her apprehension. Until Rhys had disturbed it, this bloodstained knife had been shoved under a tree trunk, hidden away in the remotest part of this secluded glade. Now that she had cleared the leaves away, Esmée could also see that the whole patch of ground beneath the fallen stump appeared odd. There was a deep rectangular area that looked as if it had been recently dug up.

At the very least, it all merited a call to the police. Her thoughts turned to Brayden. Not to any of the other two dozen or more officers in the Red Ridge PD. No, she had to turn this grisly discovery into a reason to call the very cop who had been on her mind anyway.

Before she did anything else, she needed to explain to Rhys that everything was okay. Reaching a hand behind her, she prepared to draw him to her side. Except when she felt for him, he wasn't there. She got to her feet, whirling around in a panicky circle. Her eyes widened as they confirmed her worst fears. There was no sign of her son anywhere.

"Rhys?" Her voice sounded high-pitched, seeming to echo back at her within the circle of trees, confirming that she was alone.

But that couldn't be the case. Rhys had been at her side mere minutes earlier. He couldn't have gone far. Taking a few steadying breaths, she told herself it must be another game. He was hiding from her.

"Here I come. Ready or not…"

There were no answering squeals this time. Just that continuing, unnerving quiet. Esmée swallowed the hard lump in her throat and started to look around, her eyes searching desperately for his brightly colored T-shirt.

Just as the feelings of panic were becoming overwhelming, leaves crunched behind her and a twig snapped. She prepared to release an exclamation of joy, but the hairs on the back of her neck prickled, cutting her feeling of relief short. The footfalls were too heavy, the breathing too hard. She knew before she turned that the person right behind her wasn't Rhys.

Sure enough, when she swung around, she found herself face-to-face with a man. Not just any man. With his shaved head and broken nose, this guy was huge. And he was holding a gun—a gun that was leveled directly at her.

Esmée's nerves were already on high alert. She wasn't going to wait around to see if negotiation was an option. Fear and anxiety gave her an extra burst of speed. As she darted to her left, seeking the cover of the denser trees, the man fired. It could have been her imagination, but she felt the bullet part the air close to her head before it hit a tree.

She heard a grunt and a curse before he came crashing after her. Her heart was doing its best to break free of her chest as she raced over the uneven ground, leaping over tree roots and pushing aside branches. She had no idea who this man was, or why he was shooting at her, but she had to get away from him. Most important of all, she had to find Rhys.

The guy was big and heavy, and Esmée used her smaller size to her advantage. He might be the one with the gun, but she was faster and more agile. Not daring to take a look over her shoulder, she ducked low and swerved in and out of the trees, hoping he wouldn't be able to get a shot at a moving target.

She heard the crash of wood breaking and the sound of a large body falling. The curses became louder and angrier. Risking a look behind her, she saw her pursuer had stumbled over a tree root. He was clutching his ankle as he struggled to get up.

She couldn't assume he was incapacitated. He still had a gun…and her baby was still missing. Slowing her pace just enough to pull her cell phone from the pocket of her jeans, Esmée breathed a sigh of relief to see she had a full signal. With fingers that were almost steady, she called 911.

Brayden pulled into the parking lot of the Pour House. Like its owner, the bar was at its best during the hours of darkness. Daylight wasn't kind to the uneven porch and wooden boards that were in dire need of a coat of varnish. The wagon wheels decorating the upper floor were almost rusted away and the advertising posters plastered one on top of the other along the front facade were faded and unreadable.

Occasionally, travelers passing through would stumble across the Pour House and comment on its authentic charm. Rusty, fired up with dreams of fame and fortune, was forever predicting a new dawn. So far, it had never happened and he continued to scrape out a living from his regular customers.

It looked like Brayden had overestimated Rusty's ability to get himself out of bed by noon. The bar was definitely closed and the drapes in Rusty's apartment were drawn tight across the grimy windows. He knew from experience nothing short of a brass band marching through his room would wake his father, who slept like the dead. He was weighing his options when an SAR call came through.

"It was hard to catch the details because the caller was keeping her voice low," Frank Lanelli explained. "Said she was hiding from a shooter."

"A hunter?"

"Not the way she told it. The guy fired at her and she took off through the trees."

Not a regular search-and-rescue case. "Location?"

"The way she described it, she's in the trees on the ridge below Eagle's Nest."

Brayden went into organizational mode, listening to Frank at the same time that his mind processed the details and formulated a plan. He backed out of the parking lot, his route already plotted.

"The missing person is her two-year-old son, Rhys da Costa. Approximate height, three feet, weight about thirty pounds. Dark curly hair and dark brown eyes. Wearing a brightly colored T-shirt with a dinosaur pattern, blue jeans, white sneakers."

*Da Costa?* Brayden tried to ignore the extra beat his heart had developed. He concentrated on pushing the personal feelings aside and keeping it professional. Even so, he spared a thought for the agony Esmée must have been feeling as she gave Frank that description. Her eye for detail shone through.

His own training kicked in. So many hazards to take into account. Put a two-year-old in any unknown outdoor situation and there would be danger.

In this case there was a cliff top, a complex cave system and…*a shooter*? Frank had said Esmée was hiding from a gunman as she made the call. That meant she was also in danger. A guy whose first instinct when he encountered a woman on her own in the woods was to fire at her didn't sound like a rational, law-abiding citizen.

"We could be looking at a hostage situation here," he said, explaining his thinking to Frank. "Mom, kid or possibly both." That was, if he hadn't killed them by the time Brayden got there. It was an image he didn't want inside his head.

"You want me to mobilize a team of K-9 officers?" Frank asked.

Brayden weighed it up. He didn't know what he was dealing with. This wasn't like a guy with a gun who was confined within a building. It wasn't even the same as closing down a few streets to limit the movements of a rogue gunman. Both those scenarios were familiar procedures to the PD. But the area Frank had described was covered in dense woodland. Although the main cave system was lower down, there was another, more dangerous cave close to the place from where Esmée had called. The unknown shooter had a choice of hiding places. If he did grab Esmée or Rhys and the police turned up in numbers, things could get messy.

Brayden and Echo knew that terrain. They could cover the ground fast and do it stealthily. On the other hand, once he got out there and did an initial assessment, he might find he needed backup. Esmée had told Frank she had seen one gunman. That didn't mean he was alone. If there *were* others…

"Put them on standby. Esmée da Costa is staying at the Red Ridge Bed-and-Breakfast." He didn't enlighten Frank about how he knew so much about Rhys's mother. "I'm guessing she started her hike from there. I can get to her faster if I approach from the opposite direction. Have a team of six officers assemble at the Eagle's Nest rest stop. My vehicle will already be there. Tell them to wait by my car until they hear from me."

No matter how fast he drove, Esmée and Rhys were still up on that ridge in a dangerous situation. If she was hiding, he couldn't risk calling her and alerting the shooter to her location. "Send Esmée a text message. Tell her to keep her cell on silent. Give her my number and tell her I'm on my way."

He ended the call, knowing he could rely on Frank to follow his instructions.

Because the Eagle's Nest area had become increasingly popular in recent years with hikers and cavers, the town council had built a rest stop a few years ago. Located on the main highway between Red Ridge and Spearfish, it was at a point where the road dipped close to the beauty spot. On foot, it would have taken Esmée close to two hours to reach the ridge from the town. Longer with a two-year-old for company. Brayden pulled in at the rest stop twenty minutes after Frank had called him.

It was twenty minutes during which anything could have happened on the ridge below him. He opened the back of his vehicle and took out his backpack, which contained essential safety equipment. As Echo jumped out, he checked his cell.

Please hurry

The unknown number from which the message had been sent must be Esmée's. He sent a reply.

Describe your location

In a situation like this, Echo's scent-specific skills couldn't be used. Brayden didn't have anything belonging to either Esmée or Rhys to give the dog to guide him. Instead, he would have to send Echo on an air-scenting search. This was a harder skill for a dog to learn, one that was taught after the animal had become proficient in trailing. Echo would probe the whole area, seeking human scent particles. He wouldn't be detecting a precise scent. The dog would lead Brayden to *any* person he found.

It was a useful tactic because Esmée and Rhys had been separated, but it was also a dangerous one. There was a guy down on that ridge with a gun. He could be the first person Echo encountered and

Brayden didn't want his partner face-to-face with a potentially volatile shooter.

His decision as to which direction to send Echo in once he reached the ridge was crucial and it depended on how much information Esmée could give him. Her reply came as he started his descent.

Two large rocks. Shaped like angel wings. Near cave entrance

"Perfect." From that description, Brayden knew exactly where she was. The Angel Cave, named for the distinctive rocks at its entrance, was located above the main cave system that was so with popular tourists. Although the limestone cavern was spectacularly beautiful, it was also deadly, with deep sinkholes and convoluted tunnels.

Stay there

The path down from the rest stop to the ridge was steep, but he and Echo knew it well. In the summer months, they came out this way several times a week. Even in the winter, the Coyote Mountains were popular with hardier visitors.

Brayden paused at a point where he knew he would have a view of the stones Esmée had described. Trying to see anything through the canopy of the trees would be impossible, but Esmée had described a location close to the rock face. The stones were known as the Weeping Angel rocks and were said to guard the entrance to the caves. From his vantage point, he might just be able to catch a glimpse of her. Even, possibly, catch sight of Rhys.

He saw her straightaway. Esmée was standing to one side of the Weeping Angel rocks. Even from an angle high above her, Brayden could see she was ducking down as though searching for something in the undergrowth. Rhys. Of course she would never stop looking for her son.

What Brayden saw next chilled his blood. Although he was still some distance away, a man was moving slowly toward Esmée. He was dragging his left leg as though injured. He held a gun in his right hand and his arm was already extended in front of him.

Esmée had her back to the guy, oblivious to his approach. Brayden was too far away to fire off a shot of his own and he couldn't call out a warning. If he did, he risked startling the shooter into breaking into a run and grabbing Esmée or shooting when he got within range. The only thing he could do was get down there as fast as he could. He couldn't even spare the time to send her a message.

The rest of his descent was a half run, half slither. He hit level ground at speed, hurtling in the direction he had seen Esmée. Echo kept pace with him as he reached her just as the gunman got within firing range. Esmée gave a little cry of surprise as Brayden sprinted past her. Keeping his head down below the shooter's extended arm, he wrapped his arms as far as he could around the guy's waist and slammed him to the ground. As they fell, he registered his opponent's size. He was built like a tank.

The gunman's bellow of fury rose to the treetops. Because of the guy's size, Brayden had to keep the momentum of the surprise attack going. Conscious the whole time of the gun, he pinned his opponent down and punched him hard on the nose. Bone crunched beneath his fist and the shooter made a gurgling noise as blood welled.

Brayden grabbed the attacker's wrist, bashing it hard against the rocky surface until he released the gun. Out of the corner of his eye, he saw Esmée dart forward and grab it. With a burst of strength, the gunman broke free of Brayden, staggering to his feet. Spraying blood from his broken nose, he swung a punch at Brayden. Although he saw it coming and dodged before it could hit him full in the face, the guy's sledgehammer fist caught Brayden on the side of the head.

Stars danced across his vision and pain bloomed inside his skull. He dropped to his knees, fighting the blackness that threatened to engulf him. A muscular arm tightened around his throat and he clawed wildly at it.

"Let him go or I'll shoot." Esmée's voice seemed to come to him from a long way off.

Without warning, Brayden was free, thrown face-down onto the ground. Spluttering, he struggled to his feet in time to see the shooter running away through the trees. He moved with surprising speed for someone so big and who was impaired by a limp.

"What the…?" Brayden shook his head in an attempt to clear it. When he managed to turn his head to one side, he saw Esmée with her arms outstretched and the gun gripped in both hands. Her lower lip was held tight between her teeth and her face was white as a sheet. He moved carefully toward her. "Shall I take that?"

She handed it over as though it was burning her fingers. "I've never shot anyone…but he didn't know that." Her attempt at a smile went horribly wrong and the tears began to flow. Her next words confirmed that she had been powered by pure adrenaline. "Can we please find my baby now?"

# Chapter 5

Brayden was strong and confident, and Esmée wanted to believe in him so much it hurt. But the fear lodged in her chest was a physical pain, and it was growing by the second. Nothing had ever felt this bad. It was like she was stuck in a nightmare, and no matter what she did, she couldn't wake up from it.

"Echo will find Rhys, but I need you to stay calm and help me. You are the person who knows Rhys best and any information you can give me, no matter how insignificant it may seem, could be important."

She focused on Brayden's voice, would use it to keep herself from curling into a ball on the leaf-strewn ground. His presence was soothing, but she wanted him to get moving, to *do* something. Rhys had been gone for over half an hour…

"Echo works best if he can search for a specific scent. Do you have anything that belongs to Rhys? Something he can sniff to get Rhys's smell?"

Esmée started to shake her head, then she remembered. "Rhys took his hat off, when we stopped to eat a picnic…"

She started to run. But how did she know she was going the right way? Swinging back again, she gave a little sob and hesitated. Which direction was that flat stone where they had eaten their carefree lunch?

Brayden stepped close, catching hold of her shoulders. His hands were big and warm, their touch soothing through the thin cotton of her blouse. "Let's do this slowly, so you can remember. Just take a second to think it through."

"We don't have a second." Her voice quavered—she was on the edge of more tears. "Rhys is out there all alone, and while we stand here talking that guy could be going after him." Her chest hitched as she allowed one of her worst fears to come out. "He could already have him—"

Brayden drew her close, just briefly. The contact was barely enough to be called a hug, but it steadied her. For an instant, her cheek was pressed against the hard muscles of his chest and she felt the strong, steady rhythm of his heart. "Rhys is going to be fine. We're going to find him. Now take me to where you left his hat."

This time, she didn't hesitate. Although she'd run in a zigzag path to get away from the shooter, she hadn't run far before he'd fallen. Within a few minutes, she was leading Brayden into the clearing where she and Rhys had stopped for their picnic. His cap was on the flat stone alongside his collection of stones, leaves and twigs and the abandoned carrier. The sight made her knees buckle and she caught hold of Brayden, clinging to his arm for support.

"Please…"

"It's over to Echo now. He loves this part of his job." Brayden pulled a disposable glove out of his pocket and put it on before he picked up the baseball cap. "If you or I touch Rhys's cap before Echo sniffs it, the scent can become muddled. When that happens, it's no longer a viable scent article."

He crouched and snapped the fingers of his ungloved hand. Echo obediently came to sit in front of him. Esmée watched as Brayden held the yellow cap out to the dog. Echo sniffed it, almost with a look of concentration on his face. After a moment or two, the dog's plumy tail began to wag.

"That's a good sign." Brayden looked up at Esmée. "He doesn't always do that. It's an indication that he recognizes Rhys's scent because he's met him before." He withdrew the baseball cap. "Go find Rhys."

Echo took off immediately, nose to the ground.

"We may not be able to keep up with him," Brayden explained. "But we'll follow in the same direction. Echo will give an alert—a bark—when he finds something. And it's fine to call out for Rhys at the same time. It won't distract Echo from his search."

As they followed Echo's orange vest through the trees, Brayden took out his cell. He spoke a series of numbers and letters and she realized he was giving his call sign to a dispatcher. "Shooter located on the ridge below the Eagle's Nest. He has been disarmed, but is still at large… Negative. I don't want backup down here until Rhys da Costa is found. Any additional persons and K-9s in the area could disturb the scent trail."

He ended the call and Echo led them out of the cover of the trees and onto the trail. Esmée called Rhys's name a few times, trying to keep the desperate wobble out of her voice.

"Do you have any idea who that guy was and why he shot at you?" Brayden didn't break his stride as he asked the question.

Esmée shook her head. "No. I never saw him before and he fired as soon as he saw me."

"Could it have something to do with the documentary you're making?" His eyes remained fixed on Echo, who was a few yards ahead, but she saw his jaw tighten. "Not everyone in town is a fan of the idea."

"It sounds like an extreme way to stop me from making a TV series." Her mind refused to stray far from Rhys. They were close to the edge of the ridge and her imagination went into overdrive as she eyed the drop. "I don't think Rhys would come this way. I told him to stay away."

"If he was lost, he may have wandered in this direction—" Brayden broke off as Echo rounded a curve in the trail and uttered a high-pitched bark.

"That's his alert." Brayden broke into a run. "He's found something."

For a second, Esmée's legs refused to work. Then they became supercharged and she was alongside Brayden, passing him. She hardly dared to breathe as Echo came into view. She gave a little cry of delight as she saw Rhys standing right next to him.

"Careful." Brayden caught hold of her arm before she could charge up to her son. His words of caution made her take in the whole scene. She had been so relieved to see Rhys, she hadn't noticed the way his feet were poised on the extreme edge of the ridge.

As Rhys turned to look at her, his tearstained face broke into a smile. "Mommy…"

He tried to take a step toward her, but the gravel beneath his feet slithered away. Rhys made a frantic grab for Echo, missed and slipped over the edge.

"Stand back." Brayden had to speak sharply to Esmée. In her panic, she was in danger of going over the edge after Rhys.

"I have to…" Her eyes were wide, unable to fix on any one thing, her face pale. She could go into shock, but he had to focus on Rhys. From what he'd seen of Esmée so far, she was a strong person. He reckoned if he could get her working with him, he could shake her out of her shocked state.

"You have to help me." Shrugging off his rescue pack, he handed it to her. "I'm going to take a look over the edge, but I need you to stay back here. We don't know where Rhys is and any sound could spook him. Okay?"

She hugged the backpack tight to her chest as she nodded, her breath hitching. He could see how hard she was working to hold herself together and the urge to go to her and take her into his arms was almost overwhelming. He knew she would understand that the little boy who had just fallen over the cliff was at the top of his list of his priorities.

Brayden crawled on his hands and knees to the edge of the ridge, levering his upper body over the drop. At first, he couldn't see anything. When he pushed himself farther forward, he saw, to his relief, that Rhys was on a narrow ledge about eight feet below him. The boy was curled into the fetal position with his hands over his head. It was impossible to tell if he had sustained any injuries in the fall and, if so, how serious they were.

Brayden didn't want to call out to him in case the sound triggered him into moving closer to the drop. He got to his feet. "I can see him."

"Is he…?" Esmée choked back a sob.

He took his rescue pack from her, placing a hand

briefly on her shoulder as he did. "I'll know more when I get to him."

Opening the largest compartment of the rescue pack, he withdrew climbing rope, a medical kit and a harness that he would be able to use to strap Rhys to him for the climb back up the rock face.

Luckily, there were plenty of tall trees around and Brayden was able to secure the rope to one of them. He put on his climbing harness as he explained what he was doing. "I'm going to rappel down and check him over. If he's not badly injured, I'll bring him up with me."

"What if he is—" he could see Esmée was struggling to get the words out "—badly injured?"

"Then I'll call the National Guard and we'll get a helicopter to airlift him out of here. We're not there yet." He gripped the rope and kept his gaze on her as he eased over the edge. He didn't feel good about leaving her alone with the shooter on the loose. "You have the gun and you have Echo."

It only took him a minute or two to descend the rock face. Using his body as a barrier between Rhys and the longer drop to the valley floor, Brayden kneeled. A quick check showed him Rhys was breathing and he couldn't see any blood—which was all good—but that didn't mean there weren't any broken bones. He had fallen a long way and even though there was a theory that little kids bounced, it didn't always work out that way.

"Hey, Rhys, it's Brayden. Echo's friend."

A tiny whimper greeted his words.

"You must have been frightened when you fell, but you are a brave boy." Rhys had uncovered his head, but kept his hands over his face. He was watching Brayden through his fingers, as though assessing the situation. "Did you hurt yourself?"

"Sore knee."

Relief surged through Brayden at the sound of his voice. It was tearful, but he didn't appear too badly shaken up. The resilience of young children always amazed him. "Can I take a look at it? I'm good at making sore knees better."

Rhys took his hands away from his face. "I got lost."

"I know you did." Brayden slid an arm around him, easing him into a sitting position with his back against the rock. One knee of Rhys's jeans was torn and there was a nasty graze on his leg. It wasn't deep, but Brayden didn't want to risk getting any dirt in it. He undid a flap on his vest and took out the portable first-aid kit. "I'm going to use one of these antiseptic wipes to clean your leg."

Rhys gave him a wary look. "Want Mommy."

"Mommy's waiting with Echo just up at the top there and as soon as I've covered up this cut, we're going back up that rope to see them."

His words had an almost magical effect. Rhys extended his leg. "See Mommy and Ko."

Brayden worked quickly, cleaning the graze and covering it with a waterproof dressing. Rhys watched him with interest, his big brown eyes— so like Esmée's—following Brayden's every move.

"Okay. Now I have to get you into this so we can climb back up to the top." Brayden showed Rhys the harness he was going to use to carry Rhys on his back.

"Like Mommy's carrier," Rhys said. The first sign of a smile glimmered. "Mommy says, 'Oh, Rhys! Too heavy for me.'" The boy reached around and placed both hands at the small of his back as though trying to ease an ache.

Brayden laughed. At least the fall hadn't affected his talking. From their brief interaction at the dog show he guessed that would be important to Esmée. Although he also figured her priority would be to get him back safe and well. She would be half out of her mind with worry at the top of that ridge right now. He held out a hand to Rhys.

"I need you to stand up and step away from the rock."

His words wiped any trace of a smile from Rhys's face. The little boy scooted farther back against the cliff. "Stay away from the edge. Mommy said." He pressed his fists to his eyes. "I fell."

Brayden considered the situation. Clearly, Rhys was making the connection between what his mommy warned him against and the fall. If he tried to lift Rhys into the harness against his will, he risked a struggle on the narrow ledge. Even if he accomplished it, he would traumatize a kid who'd been through a bad experience. As he was contemplating his next move, Rhys lowered his hands.

"Story."

Brayden regarded him in surprise. "You want me to tell you a story while you get into the harness?"

Rhys nodded. "Mommy tells stories."

*Great.* Esmée no doubt had a repertoire of stories at her disposal. Brayden's mind went blank. Aware of Rhys's gaze fixed hopefully on his face, he searched for something—anything—to tell him.

"Uh, once upon a time—about nineteen years ago, to be exact—there were these two kids. A boy and a girl. They were brother and sister, but they didn't know each other very well back then. The only thing they had in common was that they loved the outdoors. And what they loved best of all was these mountains." He watched Rhys, seeing signs that the boy was starting to relax as he talked. His little body was less tense and his eyes, instead of darting toward the drop, remained fixed on Brayden's face. Gently, Brayden took one of the boy's hands in his. "They were still too young to come out here on their own, but they'd spend full days out here with their dad any chance they could. Then, one day, their dad went to, um, answer a call of nature. But he forgot his kids were with him and he didn't go back for them. Instead, he went home without them."

"Was he a bad man?" Rhys let Brayden draw him to his feet.

"I'm not sure he was a bad man. I just don't think he was cut out to be a dad." Brayden fastened the harness around Rhys's waist and legs. "Kids don't come with instructions and some men don't know until it's too late that being a dad isn't for them." He decided a two-year-old wasn't the best audience for the rest of his theory on that subject.

"Did they get lost?" Rhys asked as Brayden lifted him onto his back and fastened the harness into place.

"Yeah, they got lost. They wandered around for hours. They were frightened and cold. Night was falling. They clung to each other as they tried to find their way back down the mountainside." Brayden started to use the rope to haul his way back up the cliff. "I can still remember... I mean, the boy suddenly heard screams from his eight-year-old sister as she lost her footing and fell from the rocks down a steep slope."

"Like me?"

"Just like you. The boy was only ten, but he rescued her. She had a broken ankle, so he carried her home on his back." Brayden crested the edge of the ridge, catching sight of Esmée sitting with her arms wrapped around Echo's neck. She leaped to her feet when she saw him. "That was when he knew what he wanted to do for a career. And his sister? She chose the outdoors as well. Just in a different way."

"Good story." Rhys's voice over his shoulder sounded approving.

"Yeah? I'm not sure it has a happy ending."

Once they reached level ground, Esmée came racing over to them. Echo followed at a more sedate pace.

"Rhys-baby, are you okay?" Her attempts to smother him with kisses were hampered by the harness that held him fixed to Brayden's back.

"Hi, Mommy. I'm a brave boy." Rhys sounded almost pleased with himself.

"Is he really okay?" Esmée watched in amazement as Brayden unhooked himself from the rope and then released Rhys from the harness.

"He has a graze on his knee and I expect there will be a few bruises tomorrow, but he's fine." He couldn't help grinning as he watched her reaction. The pure joy in her eyes that spilled over into tears of relief… That was what being a parent should look like.

After she'd finished hugging Rhys—because she was doing it so hard he started to protest—Esmée turned back to Brayden. "I don't know how to thank you."

He was never much good at this part and somehow it was even harder today. The shining gratitude in Esmée's eyes did something to his insides that was definitely not work-related. "You really need to thank Echo." He reached into his pocket and drew out a handful of treats. "This is how to do it."

Esmée and Rhys took the treats and fed them to Echo, who accepted them with pleasure, his tail thumping on the gravel. Brayden caught the glimmer of fresh tears in Esmée's eyes as she pressed her cheek against the dog's silken head.

He stowed his equipment in his rescue pack. "I know it's been a tough day, but I need to take some details from you while it's fresh in your memory."

"Anything I can do. Just tell me what information you need."

"Let's start with where you were when you first encountered the shooter." Brayden shrugged his pack onto his shoulders.

"It was in the trees. Right after I found the blood-stained knife—" She bit her lip. "I've been around crime scenes and police procedures my whole life. You'd think I'd know better than to casually introduce an unexplained potential murder weapon, wouldn't you?"

"It's certainly an interesting new development." Brayden's mind was racing. Guns, knives, a suspect loose in the woods...what the hell was going on? "Do you think you can describe the location in which you found the knife?"

"Better still, why don't I take you there?"

# Chapter 6

Brayden had made a call to the police dispatcher outlining the entire incident. The shooter's description had been circulated and a team of two K-9 officers and their partners had commenced a search of the area.

Esmée led Brayden back along the trail a few hundred yards. She knew the place she was looking for. The point where she had stopped and looked at the view below her and then up at the rocks was unmistakable. Although her mind was partly preoccupied with Rhys and the danger he had been in, she knew how important this was.

Rhys appeared remarkably unscathed by his ordeal. When he complained a little at having to do more walking, Brayden had offered to carry him. To Esmée's surprise, Rhys had agreed. He wasn't exactly shy, but he had reached an age where he was starting to weigh up strangers before he made a decision about whether he liked them or not. Possibly Brayden's success was linked to the rescue, or maybe it had something to do with Echo. Whatever it was, Rhys looked comfortable nestled in the curve of Brayden's arm.

Thinking about nestling into Brayden's arms wasn't doing her composure a whole lot of good. Telling herself she was still coming down from the shock wasn't helping. It was only natural to see Rhys's rescuer as some sort of superhero. Brayden and his fellow K-9 officers must get this all the time. They probably had training in it—how to deal with citizens who develop a crush.

The idea stiffened Esmée's spine a little. Even though the thought was only in her own head, she refused to be a problem. A crush? That was easy. She could get over that. Just as she made the decision, she turned her head to look at Brayden. He gave her a reassuring smile and she almost groaned out loud.

*Who am I kidding?*

This wasn't a crush. This was an annihilation of everything she knew about herself. And, beyond the whole rescue thing, she didn't understand why. Yes, he was handsome, with curly black hair and those hard-to-read, blue-green eyes. Tall and muscular, with skin that was tanned dark bronze by the sun, and a body that filled his uniform in all the right places. But…what was that all about? She had been around good-looking men in uniform many times, without this sort of extreme reaction. The desire to throw herself into the arms of a cop had only arisen in relation to Brayden. Thank goodness…

"Here." Relieved at the distraction from her own thoughts, she gestured toward the trees. "This is where we stopped. I already showed you the rock where Rhys's hat was. That's where we ate our lunch."

"Hide-and-seek." Rhys added his voice to the explanation.

"Yes, we played a game after we finished eating. Rhys hid under a fallen tree trunk—" Esmée looked around "—that one over there." She led Brayden toward it. "When I found him, I noticed his feet had disturbed something. That's when I saw the knife."

She stooped, preparing to point at the place where she had seen the knife. But there was nothing there. The knife had gone.

"You're sure this is the tree?" Brayden set Rhys on his feet, but kept a restraining arm around him as he squatted beside her.

"This is the place. I know it was. When someone shoots at you, you remember the details." She pointed at an indentation in the soil. "Anyway, you can see the outline of the knife. Look. And this area is unmistakable. It looks like someone has been digging here." She shivered. "It's like a shallow grave."

Brayden didn't answer. Getting out his cell phone, he took a couple of photographs of the impression the knife had left in the soil. He also took a picture of the rectangular, dug-out area and the tree trunk. "Rhys, go to your mommy while I do some digging in this soil."

Although Rhys started to laugh at the idea of a grown-up digging in the dirt, he obediently swapped Brayden's hold for Esmée's. She slid an arm around his waist and pressed her cheek against his hair. It was going to be hard to strike a balance in the future, but she would have to avoid becoming overprotective. Right now, all she wanted to do was wrap him up and never let him out of her sight. She knew that wouldn't be a healthy outcome for either of them. Although Rhys wasn't having such a hard time getting over it as she was. His interest soon wandered in Echo's direction.

Brayden shrugged off his backpack and opened one of the compartments. "This is my rescue pack. It's not about police business," he explained. "But I do carry smaller items that could help with an investigation." He took out a plastic evidence bad and a small trowel. "I can call Forensics out, but if they don't get here until tomorrow this ground could be disturbed overnight by animals or rain."

Carefully, he scooped up the dirt from the indentation and the area around it and placed it in the bag. Sealing it tight, he tucked it in a pocket of his rescue pack.

"Do you think that's why the shooter was out here? He wanted the knife?" The thought sent a sudden thrill of fear through Esmée and she glanced over her shoulder.

"I think it's a strong possibility. He either wanted the knife, or he wanted to keep you away from it. You were here and he fired at you without any warning. Now the knife is gone."

She swallowed hard. "He was prepared to kill me rather than have that knife handed over to the police and taken in for processing. There must be a very important reason for that."

Images crowded in on her. Might-have-beens. *What if I'd been shot and Rhys had been all alone out here? No Brayden to rescue him...*

She became aware of Brayden's gaze fixed on her face. "You've had quite a day. These situations are usually harder on the adults than the kids. Maybe it's time we got you home?"

Esmée got shakily to her feet, momentarily unsure her legs would support her. She tried them out and they were wobbly, but functioning. Wearily, she turned toward the rock where she had left Rhys's carrier. "I am not looking forward to walking back down that trail."

"You don't have to." She raised her eyebrows in

a question and Brayden pointed upward as he explained. "There's a rest stop at the top of the Eagle's Nest. My vehicle is up there. It's fitted with a child's safety seat, so Rhys will be okay to travel in it. I'll take you home."

"I think those are the sweetest words anyone has ever said to me."

He laughed as he swung Rhys up into his arms again. "If that's true, you really need to get out more."

That was when it hit her. Hard and fast. Yes, she was grateful to him. More than words could say. But that wasn't what this attraction was about. This wasn't hero worship. It was about *him*. She'd have felt it if he'd been in a suit behind a desk, or riding a horse out on a ranch.

She picked up her carrier, and a few select items from Rhys's treasure trove of pebbles and leaves, and followed Brayden up the steep slope. Looking up at the tall, broad-shouldered figure ahead of her, she wondered if a gratitude crush might have been preferable. The reality was a whole lot scarier and harder to deal with.

The afternoon light was starting to fade by the time Brayden pulled into the parking lot of the Red Ridge Bed-and-Breakfast. Despite every warning prompting her to keep her distance, Esmée felt she owed Brayden *something* for what he'd done. She turned in her seat to face him.

"Rhys and I are having pasta for dinner. I made

the sauce before we went out on our walk. Would you like to join us?"

The tiniest flare of light in his eyes was the give-away. It told her everything she needed to know. This attraction was mutual. She didn't quite know what to do with that information. On one hand, it was nice to know he felt the same way. On the other, since nothing was ever going to happen, it made it so much harder. Brayden's momentary hesitation told her something else… He was going to fight it just as hard as she was. As hard as he would fight her request for an interview about his sister.

She wanted to explain that she wasn't going to use this as an opportunity to try to get information from him, but she sensed she didn't have to. Brayden was tough and powerful, but he was also empathetic. He had proved that with his behavior toward Rhys. She guessed he would know the offer of dinner was nothing more than a way of thanking him. Even so, Esmée was preparing herself for a rejection. His next words took her by surprise.

"I'm dusty and sweaty after this afternoon's exertions. Why don't I go home and shower while you cook? I'll come back in an hour."

"Sounds good." She'd get dinner started before showering and changing her own clothes. Rhys could have his bath and get into his pajamas. She suspected he'd be asleep soon after dinner. Placing her hand on the door, she prepared to get out of the car.

Brayden's voice halted her. "There's just one thing…"

She turned back, looking at him over her shoulder. There it was again. Stronger this time. A definite spark that made his eyes more green than blue. *Oh, dear Lord.* How was she ever going to resist *that*? "Yes?"

"Is Echo included in the invitation?"

"Rhys wouldn't have it any other way." She smiled. "Actually, nor would I."

"I know what you're thinking," Brayden said, as he filled Echo's bowl with food. "I can tell by the way you're looking at me." Echo tilted his head as though attempting to understand what he was saying. "The sensible thing to do would be to keep my distance, right?"

Apparently feeling some reaction was required of him, Echo gave a bark. Unsure whether the response was a demand for his dinner or a reply to his comments, Brayden placed the dog's bowl on the floor. Relationship advice from a golden retriever? That about summed up the state of his dating experience over the last eight years.

*This is not a date.*

So why the hell did he feel so nervous? Why, for the first time in as long as he could remember—*in his whole life*—had he stepped out of the shower and wondered what to wear? He had settled on jeans, a T-shirt and boots. Because that was what he wore when he was off duty.

When Esmée had invited him to dinner, Brayden's first thought had been to refuse. Not because he didn't want to spend more time with her. On the contrary. He was alarmed by how rapidly his feelings toward her were developing. That was the reason why he had intended to turn her down. He had actually opened his mouth ready to say the words. *Sorry, I can't.* That would be the spoken part. The unspoken message? *Because I have no intention of getting involved.* What had come out had been something else entirely. His heart had done the talking instead of his head.

And once the words had been uttered, he found he was looking forward to it. In a restless, excited, what-the-hell-have-I-done? kind of way.

When Echo had finished eating, Brayden headed for the door. Remembering the bottle of wine that had been sitting in the fridge since a guy he had rescued last summer gave it to him, he went back.

"White wine goes with pasta, doesn't it?" Echo wagged his tail. "Oh, yeah. I forgot. You're a beer man like me. We'll take it anyway."

It was a beautiful evening and, because they weren't working, Brayden broke the rules and let Echo sit in the passenger seat. They had been partners for close to six years and it hadn't escaped his attention that his closest bond was with a dog. It was his only meaningful relationship.

The challenges of search-and-rescue were made

easier because of his connection with his K-9 partner. Handling the difficult physical and emotional situations—extreme heat, harsh cold, sleep deprivation, enclosed dark spaces and hostile vegetation—could take a toll. Having Echo at his side helped Brayden recover after long days and difficult missions.

*Yeah, I talk to my dog.*

"Sometimes you even listen." He reached over and ruffled Echo's ears.

He pulled up at the bed-and-breakfast, aware that he wouldn't receive a warm welcome if Wendy Gage caught sight of him. Brayden had been the officer who'd brought her son, Corey, home after he crashed her car. Since then, Wendy seemed to feel Brayden was out to get her precious son. It was a Colton thing, she was fond of telling her friends. Poor Corey was being set up because he was a Gage.

Luckily, Brayden made it to Esmée's front door without encountering the fearsome proprietor. Instead, he was greeted by a far pleasanter sight. Esmée opened the door looking incredibly pretty, with her long hair hanging loose and slightly damp. She wore black jeans and a red T-shirt that emphasized her dark coloring. Her feet were bare and she appeared to have relaxed after the afternoon's ordeal. As Brayden passed her and walked into the little cabin, her delicious fresh-from-the-shower scent filled his nostrils and made him feel a little giddy.

She took the bottle of wine from him. "I don't

often drink, but this feels like one of those days when it's almost compulsory."

The layout of the cabin was an open-plan square. There was a small living area on one side and a kitchen and dining area on the other. While Esmée went to prepare the food, Brayden joined Rhys, who was playing on the rug with his toys.

Rhys looked up with a shy smile. "Hi, Bray…" He frowned as though realizing the name wasn't quite right.

"My friends call me Bray."

"Hi, Ko. Paw." Echo performed his hand-shaking trick, then rolled onto his back. Rhys went off into peals of laughter as the dog waved all four legs in the air.

"He wants you to tickle his tummy," Brayden explained. "When Echo isn't wearing his orange jacket, he's off duty. That means he can play."

"Do the same rules apply to his master?" Esmée asked.

"Pretty much, although I'm not usually as blatant asking for a tummy rub." He joined her in the kitchen. "Rhys seems fine."

"He really is. I'm hopeful there won't be any ill effects." Brayden helped her as she placed plates, knives, forks and water glasses on the table. As she turned back to the counter, she frowned. "That's strange."

"What is?" Brayden paused in the act of opening the bottle of wine.

"I cooked some sausages to add to the spaghetti sauce. There were four of them on this chopping board." Esmée's expression was mystified. "Now there are only two."

"Ah." Brayden poured wine into two glasses. "Perhaps I should have mentioned that."

"You steal sausages?" Esmée raised her eyebrows as she accepted her glass.

"Not me." Brayden pointed to Echo, who was sitting nearby. He was doing his best innocent dog impression...while licking his lips. "When the vest comes off, his inhibitions disappear along with it. He loves sausages and he's fast."

Esmée laughed. "I guess he's earned a couple of sausages. And I'll be more careful next time."

*Next time.* Brayden liked those words. Being here with her and Rhys felt good. Easy and natural. "I speak from experience when I say he's sneaky."

"Then we'd better eat now while we still have two sausages left." Esmée turned away to finish serving the food.

As Rhys clambered into his booster seat, he pointed to the chair next to him. "Bray here."

Esmée raised her eyebrows as she sat opposite. "You get the position of honor."

"Does it come with any additional duties?" He regarded Rhys's plastic plate and water cup warily.

Esmée laughed. "Don't worry. Rhys has beautiful table manners."

*Beautiful* might have been an exaggeration, but Rhys was an independent eater. The day's adventure seemed to have given him a hearty appetite, and he tucked into his food without talking. Although he occasionally used his hands instead of his fork, Esmée didn't comment so Brayden guessed it must be a two-year-old thing. When he dropped bits of food on the floor, Echo—who, particularly after the sausage stealing incident, should have known better—cleaned them up. On this occasion, Brayden was prepared to relax his own rules. Echo deserved a little downtime, too.

In Red Ridge, it was impossible to have a conversation that didn't at least skirt around the edge of the Groom Killer case. Esmée was unselfconscious about it. "I got a call from Hester just before you arrived. Sarah is home from the hospital."

"How is she?" He still hadn't quite figured out Esmée's connection to Sarah, fiancée of the Groom Killer's latest victim, and Hester Mull. It clearly went deeper than an acquaintance that had been formed since her arrival in town.

"Hester said she's improving a little each day. I'm taking Rhys to see her tomorrow." Esmée bent her head over her plate. "I think it's harder because she can't say goodbye to Jack until the coroner releases his body. There are still some technicalities to do with the case. Waiting for the funeral is difficult for all of us."

Brayden frowned. "You knew Jack?"

She looked up. "He was a very good friend. Probably the best I had."

There was a depth of emotion that went beyond her voice and seemed to resonate through her slender body. It intrigued Brayden. He understood how her path might have crossed Jack's in the course of her work, but he couldn't put the two of them together as friends. Jack was one of the good guys, but he was old enough to be Esmée's dad. Brayden had met him a few times in the Pour House. Jack had been a man of few words. Those he did use were blunt. Mild-mannered Sarah had clearly seen beyond the gruff exterior and fallen in love with him, but Esmée's association with the former cop surprised Brayden.

Her grief was clearly still raw, and he searched for a way to deal with that. "I hardly knew him. He'd only come back to town recently."

Esmée managed a smile. "Jack worked with my mom, helping her with her research. When I started out as a true-crime vlogger, he was the person I turned to for help. He even traveled back and forth to Wales when I spent two years making a documentary. He and Sarah had been childhood sweethearts, but they split up and he left town after she married Barry Mull. We were in Wales when he learned she was a widow. He was so happy to be back in touch with her after all those years apart. I'd have to fight like a tiger to get my laptop away from him." There was a light of reminiscing in her eyes. "We were in the mountains and the phone signal was poor, but the house we were staying in had a dial-up connection. Jack wasn't great on the computer when he arrived in Glanrafon, but by the time he left, he was the king of internet chat."

Brayden liked listening to her as he ate. He liked watching her even more. She was an animated talker. Her eyes sparkled and she gestured with her hands, smiling and laughing a lot as she described Jack's technological mishaps. The food was good, and even though he wasn't a wine drinker, his glass was soon empty. He reached for the bottle and refilled it.

"Is Rhys a Welsh name?" This came under the category of keeping his distance, but the urge to find out more about her was nagging at him.

"Yes." It was like he had flicked a switch. Just like that, all the liveliness was gone and she fell silent.

How to wreck an enjoyable evening the Brayden Colton way. Clearly, the subject of her past was off-limits. He searched around for another topic of conversation, something they had in common. There was always the obvious...but he wasn't going to talk about Demi. That left one other thing. A pretty important one. "The team searching the ridge found no sign of the shooter."

Esmée paused in the act of lifting a forkful of pasta to her mouth. "Did you think they would?"

"I guess not. But it's possible he's still around."

He took a breath, knowing she wasn't going to like what he was about to say next. "Which means you should leave town."

Her eyebrows drew together sharply. "I don't see why. He shot at me because I found his knife. He got it back. I'm no threat to him."

"You still don't think this could be connected to your documentary? It wasn't a warning to you to stay away from this story?" By taking this route Brayden was laying himself wide-open to questions about Demi, but he couldn't ignore it. If there was a chance Esmée and Rhys were in danger from this guy, he had to get her to face it.

"What? You think he is either the Groom Killer, or he was paid by the murderer to scare me off?" Esmée's incredulous tone told him she didn't think much of that idea. "Your sister has become so unhinged, she's gotten herself a paid accomplice?"

"My sister is not a killer." He had said it so many times and in so many ways. Maybe it was the wine and the food, but this time some of his usual fire was missing. He didn't care who Esmée was or why she was in town. He couldn't let it pass. In his presence, no one was going to call Demi a murderer.

He braced himself for the questions. He had just opened up the barrier to the interview she wanted. She would be crazy to let this opportunity pass. But, to his amazement, she did. Deliberately, she sipped her wine and appeared lost in thought.

"No." When she finally spoke, her expression was determined. "I know the guy on the ridge had a gun—and that's the weapon of choice for the Groom Killer—but his focus was that knife. I honestly think Rhys and I were in the wrong place at the wrong time." She reached out an impulsive hand and placed it on his wrist. "Trust me. Even if I was stupid enough to put myself in danger, I would never do that to Rhys."

The words were important. *Really* important. His brain registered them and filed them away, along with the way she hadn't seized on the Demi story. In that instant, something else was taking precedence. His body was responding to her touch. Awareness of her fingertips on his wrist spread along his nerve endings, triggering a series of pleasurable shock waves. It was like nothing he had ever experienced before and, as their gazes caught and held, he could tell Esmée was feeling it, too.

"Done." When Rhys held up his plate to show them, Brayden couldn't decide whether the kid's timing was good or bad.

"So you are." Even though Esmée withdrew her hand as she turned to see to Rhys, Brayden could still feel the lingering warmth of her touch. "He's really tired, I'm going to take him to bed."

Rhys's eyelids were drooping as Esmée lifted him from his chair, but he looked at Brayden over her shoulder. "Bray do story."

"I usually tell him a story," Esmée explained.

"Want Bray. Want the girl who fell down. Like me."

"I have no idea what this is about." Esmée sounded bewildered.

"I told him a story when we were on the ledge together," Brayden explained.

"Ah." She carried Rhys through to his bedroom and Brayden followed her. "That was good thinking. He loves stories."

"It wasn't my idea," he admitted. "Your son ordered me to do it."

She laughed as she tucked in Rhys. "He can be quite forceful." A hint of mischief lit her features. "I don't know where he gets that trait from."

"Story." Although Rhys was almost asleep, he patted the bed next to him.

"Over to you." Esmée stepped back, allowing Brayden to sit down.

A story about the girl who fell down? He searched his memories. "This story takes place about eight years after the last one. Her brother...you remember him, the one who carried her home on his back when she broke her ankle?" Rhys nodded sleepily. "Well, his truck got washed off the road one day during a storm. It hit a tree and slid down a bank into the river. Her brother was knocked unconscious and was in danger of drowning in the fast-flowing water. Without giving a thought to her own safety, his daredevil kid sister took off her boots and handed them to one of the men who were standing in a group hesitating about what to do next. She waded into the water and dragged him free of the vehicle."

He thought Rhys was asleep and made a move to stand up, but a small hand slid into his. "Brave. Like me." Brayden had to lean closer to catch his next words. "Was her name?"

Brayden was aware of Esmée's eyes on his profile as he answered, "Her name *is* Demi."

# Chapter 7

The offer wasn't fully formed, but, after what she'd heard in Rhys's bedroom, Esmée didn't want Brayden to leave until she'd said something about Demi. What she'd seen in his expression when he told Rhys the story of his sister had moved her. There had been love there, but so much pain as well. It was clear that the mix of emotions was eating away at him.

"Let me help."

He paused in the open doorway, looking down at her. "What do you mean?"

Esmée leaned against the door frame, facing him. The April night was mild with only a light breeze stirring the trees. A full moon hung low in the sky, illuminating the other cabins and Wendy Gage's house, which was already in darkness.

"You said your sister isn't a killer. Let me help you prove it."

Although his expression didn't change, she sensed him withdraw slightly. She was used to that reaction. Some people worked with her. Others were suspicious of her motives. Brayden had every reason to be wary about what sort of damage she could do with a story. He was probably wondering if this was just an angle, another way of finding out everything she could about Demi. She had to convince him her desire to assist him was genuine.

"I've been a true-crime documentary maker for a long time, but I don't usually get involved in an investigation. Unlike my mother, I don't uncover injustices, or look into unsolved crimes. I tell stories about the impact of murder. But the difference is subtle, and no one around here will notice if I change my focus. They assume I'll ask questions about the Groom Killer killings. They expect me to poke my nose in where you can't."

"Are you offering to give up your story?" Brayden's voice was openly skeptical. "Don't you have to make a living?"

"I do, but I'm in no hurry to make this documentary." She didn't know why she was about to confide personal information to a man she'd only recently met, but she felt she could trust him. Saving her son's life gave him that level of credit with her. "My mother left me some money. I'm not superrich, but I have a cushion against being out of work. Yes, I'll make my documentary, but I won't make it in real time. Like the one I made in Glanrafon, I'll set it after the case is solved."

"Why would you do that?" He still wasn't letting down those barriers, still wasn't prepared to believe she would do this. For him. She wondered what had happened in his life to cause him to have so little belief in his own worth.

"It wouldn't even come close to what you did for me today, Brayden. You rescued my son. I can't promise to rescue your sister. I can only try to find the truth." She did her best to infuse the words with the sincerity she felt. It must have had an effect, because some of the rigidity went out of his frame. "In my experience, the truth always comes out in the end. Maybe that will be the final focus of my story."

He stared down at her for a moment or two as though he was doing a silent recalculation. "I'll give it some thought."

He couldn't actually stop her from doing what she proposed, but she decided against pointing it out to him. Although she hoped he'd agree to her proposal, Esmée wouldn't go against his wishes when it came to Demi's story. She had a simple rule. The people and places she visited had already been damaged.

She couldn't promise to make things better, but she would do her best not to make them worse.

"I should go." Brayden jerked a thumb over his shoulder in the direction of Echo, who was snuffling along the edge of the lawn. Even though he said the words, he made no movement.

That awareness of each other was growing and building, causing the air around them to crackle. Instinct told her he wouldn't make the first move. The damage he'd suffered—whatever it was—wouldn't allow him to risk rejection. And Esmée wasn't ready to act on these feelings…no matter how compelling they might be.

Placing a hand on his shoulder, she rose on the tips of her toes and brushed her lips against his cheek. It was intended to be a chaste kiss. Instead, when her mouth made contact with his skin, it instantly became the most decadent thing she had ever done. A jolt of desire shot through her and she had to force herself to step away instead of gripping the front of his T-shirt and pulling him closer.

"Good night, Brayden." It was hard to breathe, let alone speak.

He stared down at her for a moment or two, the look in his eyes stealing the remainder of her breath. "Good night."

Brayden paused when he reached his car. Too many thoughts were competing for dominance in his head and he needed to get some clarity. He wasn't convinced by Esmée's arguments about the shooter. She might feel the guy posed no threat, but it was a risk Brayden wasn't prepared to take. Even if the man who attacked her up on the ridge had no link to the Groom Killer case and her documentary, he could have a lingering grudge from a previous story she'd covered.

And the way she'd hushed up when he asked about Rhys's name? It wasn't conclusive proof of a relationship that had ended badly, but it had given him an uncomfortable feeling. The shooter clearly wasn't Esmée's ex, but what if he'd been sent to Red Ridge by him?

"What do you think?" He stooped and gently pulled Echo's ears. It was one of the dog's favorite caresses and Echo's expression became dreamy. "Looks like a nice night for a stakeout."

He figured if the attacker had targeted Esmée—instead of shooting at her because she had stumbled on the knife—he must have followed her up the Coyote Mountain trail. Which meant he knew where she was staying. If the gunman was after Esmée, Brayden reckoned he would strike again soon. Watching her place every night wasn't a realistic option, but it seemed like a good cure for his current restlessness.

Scanning the area, he decided on a location just inside the trees. From that vantage point, on an incline, he would be able to see the whole the bed-and-breakfast, from Wendy Gage's house to the farthest cabin.

Feeling slightly furtive, he watched Esmée's cabin as the living area went dark and a light came on, presumably in her bedroom. He should probably get his mind off Esmée, but that was proving an almost impossible task. Although she was gorgeous, it wasn't just her looks that attracted him. Everything about her appealed to him, and the feeling grew more powerful as he got to know her better. Although she was clearly a strong person, raising Rhys and holding down a tough job, her generosity and understanding about Demi showed a sensitivity that amazed him. He'd never encountered another person with that level of empathy.

She was also easy to talk to. He found himself relaxing with her, smiling with her and Rhys, enjoying their company. If making their acquaintance had been the start of a new friendship, it would be fine... Only it wasn't. His feelings for Esmée were just about as far removed from friendship as it was possible to get.

Brayden was twenty-nine years old and he had *never* felt like this. Not even when he had been engaged. That was something he preferred to push to the back of his mind. His fiancée hadn't loved him. It was the Colton name that had attracted her. Once she found out Brayden wasn't from the rich side of the family, she hadn't stuck around. The baby she'd told him she was expecting turned out to be a lie, her way of trapping him into a proposal. It had been a devastating experience for a reserved twenty-one-year-old. That old saying—Once Bitten, Twice Shy—didn't go far enough. Brayden had always been withdrawn and he would never put his heart out there again. It wouldn't survive another rejection.

Since then, he'd had occasional encounters, but nothing more. Brayden was too honest to turn his back on the truth. His brief dalliance with romance, even though it had ended in disaster, had taught him a lot about himself. He wanted it all. Love, marriage, a family, a home. He wouldn't settle for less, but he didn't believe it would happen for him. The damage had gone too deep. Knowing it didn't mean he could do anything about it.

He had accepted that he was meant to be single. His one attempt at being anything else had convinced him never to try again. Now Esmée had come along and shaken that conviction. Not only had she set his body on fire, but she'd also had him imagining a series of what-ifs. What if they dated? What if she stayed in Red Ridge for a while? What if there were more nights like tonight, cozy nights with her Rhys and Echo… Ones that didn't end with a kiss on the cheek.

*You sad, lonely man.* He gave a soft groan and Echo, clearly feeling some response was required, placed a paw on his knee.

"Never lonely while I have you, hey, buddy?" He ruffled the dog's fur, grateful for the distraction.

Night settled like a cloak over the surrounding trees and the air grew colder. Brayden's thoughts inevitably turned to Demi. Where was she? Yes, she knew how to take care of herself. They had both chosen to make their living outdoors. It hadn't happened by chance—they had been drawn by their love of the mountains. They also had strong survival instincts. Rusty Colton's kids learned early how to stand on their own two feet. But the idea of his kid sister hiding out, alone, afraid, possibly pregnant…

A movement on the path below him drew his attention and, moving silently, he leaned forward to get a closer look. *There!* Someone was approaching the bed-and-breakfast. A glance at the illuminated figures on his watch face told him it was almost 2:00 a.m. Not exactly the time for a social call.

It wasn't easy to see in the dark, but the tall figure was dressed all in black and wore a sweatshirt with the hood pulled up. Hardly daring to breathe, Brayden got to his feet, moving swiftly and stealthily along the path. Echo stayed close to his side.

He kept the target in his sights the whole time. From the height, he got the impression it was a man, but he couldn't say for sure it was the shooter. As the guy drew level with Esmée's cabin, he gave Echo the command to take him down.

"Hold."

Echo and Brayden were the Red Ridge PD search-and-rescue unit, which meant their priority was saving innocent lives. Sometimes they were called on to hunt for criminals who went on the run in the mountains and forests around the town. On those occasions, when Echo alerted Brayden to a find, there was a possibility they could both be in danger. To avoid that happening, Echo was trained to grasp the target's leg in his mouth. It wasn't a bite…but the person on the receiving end didn't understand that. The outcome was usually a quick surrender. On the few occasions when that hadn't happened, Brayden only had to threaten that he would order Echo to tighten his grip to get the desired result.

On this occasion, the guy started screaming hysterically and dropped to the ground as if he'd been shot. Echo stood patiently over him, his jaw clamped lightly around his calf.

"Help! Somebody help me! I'm being attacked—"

Lights started to go on in the cabins and in the main house. As doors began to open and people spilled out onto the lawn, Brayden recognized the high-pitched wails.

Wendy paused at the top of her front step as she surveyed the scene. At the same moment, Esmée stepped out of her cabin. Despite the seriousness of the situation, Brayden took a moment to appreciate how good she looked in pale blue pajamas with her hair in a long braid. Then the guy on the ground stopped yelling long enough for him to get a glimpse at his face, and he recognized him immediately.

"Corey? What the hell are you doing sneaking around at two in the morning?"

Corey Gage gave a whimper. "Call your dog off."

"Release." Echo let go of Corey's leg immediately and returned to Brayden's side. Brayden gave him a reward for following instructions, and a feeling of dread grew inside as he viewed the scene. Corey was lying on the grass clutching his leg, his face as white as a sheet as he snuffled out a few comments about police brutality and harassment. The occupants of the cabins clustered on their porches and steps, watching silently as events unfolded.

Esmée disappeared briefly and reemerged wearing a sweater over her pajamas and sheepskin boots. She held something in her hand and, as she approached him, Brayden saw it was a baby monitor.

"What's going on?" She kept her voice quiet so the occupants of the other cabins wouldn't hear.

Brayden ran a hand through his hair. There was no way he could make this sound good. "I thought he was going to break into your cabin."

Her eyes widened. "Have you been out here all night?"

*Stalker. That's what she's thinking.* "I was worried the shooter might come after you."

Just when the situation looked about as bad as it could be, it got a whole lot worse. Wendy bore down on them like an avenging angel in a flowered bath-robe. "What have you done to my son?"

"Get up, Corey." Brayden offered his hand to the teenager, who shrank away, covering his face.

"Did you see that, Mom? He got his dog to attack me, then he tried to hit me."

"He was helping you!" Esmée's indignation was apparent in her tone. At least she seemed to be on his side.

Wendy's attention momentarily shifted to her son. "Do as he says. I'll deal with you later."

The words had a remarkable effect on Corey, who bolted upright as though electrocuted.

Wendy moved in on Brayden, stopping just short of jabbing a finger into his chest. "This is victimization and I'll be reporting you for it."

"Really? So I got my dog to drag Corey here out of his bed, did I?" Brayden turned to Corey, who was trying to slink away toward the house. "Not so fast. Just where have you been until this time?"

"Just hanging out with some friends," Corey muttered, scuffing the grass with the tip of one sneaker. He cast a sidelong glance in Wendy's direction. "Lost track of the time."

Brayden weighed his options. Now that Corey was on his feet, there was a definite smell of alco-hol about him. Although he was underage, he wasn't falling-down drunk and he wasn't doing any real harm. If Brayden hadn't been watching the premises, no one would have known anything about this nocturnal adventure. And it was obvious that Wendy was going to give him hell when she got him indoors.

"It looks like you were in the wrong place at the wrong time." Corey's shoulders drooped with relief. "But before you go, show me your left leg."

"What...?"

"Now." Brayden spoke with sharp authority. He wanted this over and he was tired of Corey's whining.

Giving him a look of dislike, Corey rolled up the leg of his jeans to his knee. Brayden took his cell phone out of his pocket and started filming.

"Is that the leg that my dog clamped on to?" He stepped closer, making sure he got a clear view of Corey's unmarked flesh.

"Yes."

"And can you confirm that you sustained no injuries during the encounter?"

"He scared the hell out of me, man..." Corey broke off, glaring at him. "No, I wasn't injured."

"Thank you, Corey." Brayden looked around at the people who were watching from the cabins. "I think we have enough witnesses to corroborate that. You can go now." As Corey weaved toward the house, Brayden turned to the onlookers. "Nothing to see here, folks. Just a misunderstanding. Sorry for the disturbance."

Doors began to close as the residents returned to

their cabins, but Wendy, her face red and her eyes narrowed, clearly wasn't done. "This has gone too far. Lying in wait for my son to come home so you could set your dog on him? I don't care if the chief is your cousin. I'll see to it that you lose your job over this—"

Wendy was like a geyser, and Brayden's preferred response was to let her blow. All the rage and poison would come spilling out, then she would stomp off to bed. Whether she called Finn in the morning to file a complaint would depend on what she discovered from Corey. If, as Brayden suspected, he and his friends had been up to no good, Wendy might decide not to stir up trouble. If she did call this in… well, Brayden would already have his report on the chief's desk in the morning.

This time, Wendy's tirade was halted in midflow when a small figure unexpectedly inserted itself between her and Brayden.

"Please stop shouting." Esmée's voice was calm and quiet. "You'll wake my little boy. And you're wrong. I can vouch for Officer Colton's actions. He wasn't here because of your son. He was protecting me."

Brayden was torn between two reactions. He was delighted at the way Esmée had allied herself with him and sprung to his defense. It caused an enjoyable new warmth to fill his chest. But Wendy was a vindictive woman and he couldn't see this ending well.

Sure enough, her expression changed. In an instant, the hissing rage had been replaced with a sly smile.

"That changes everything. I'm sure you'll understand my position." Wendy's sugarcoated tone was as fake as her bright gold hair. "I'm a businesswoman and a commotion like this, upsetting my guests in the middle of the night…" The smile widened. "Well, I just can't take the chance of it happening again."

Brayden could guess where this was going. He stepped up closer to Esmée. "It won't."

"You expect me to take the word of a Colton? That's never been good enough for a Gage." Wendy's features hardened as she stared at Esmée. "I want you out by noon tomorrow."

Brayden sensed Esmée was about to protest, but he placed a hand on her arm. "They'll be gone straight after breakfast."

## Chapter 8

"We'll be gone straight after breakfast?" Esmée closed the cabin door behind her and stared at Brayden with a combination of astonishment and dawning rage. "I can't believe you just said that. You made me and my son homeless without bothering to consult me?"

"She was throwing you out at noon anyway." Once Wendy had stomped away, they had come back inside and were now facing each other across the kitchen table. "Can I get Echo some water? It's been a long night."

She scrubbed a hand across her face as she watched him take a bowl from one of the cupboards. His actions gave her some thinking time. He was right, of course, but *he* was the reason for Wendy's decision.

If Brayden hadn't decided to sit out all night watching over her, none of this would have happened.

*Watching over me.*

The thought sent her anger into reverse. Whether his instinct was right or wrong, Brayden had believed she and Rhys were in danger. He had been prepared to stay up all night to keep them safe. A warm feeling wrapped itself around her. Esmée had been eighteen when her mother died and, since then, she had taken care of herself. If anyone had asked her, she'd have said she liked it just fine and she didn't need anyone to look out for her. Most of the time she didn't. Caring for herself and for Rhys…that was what she did. But the thought of Brayden as her protector? Well, that was a whole new level of comfort.

He stooped to place the water on the floor, pausing to pat Echo's head as the dog began to drink. As he straightened and met Esmée's gaze, there was a wary look in Brayden's eyes.

"I'm sorry."

"You should be." Her lip quivered.

"Oh, hey—" He was at her side in two swift strides. "Please don't cry."

"I'm not." As he took her hand, she lifted her face to his to prove it.

"Go to bed, Esmée."

He didn't release her hand and she faced him, a slight frown wrinkling her brow. "How can I when I have nowhere to stay?"

"We'll talk about that in the morning?" His gaze, like the clasp of his fingers, was warm.

*We?* She should tell him it was none of his business, but at 3:00 a.m., *should* didn't seem as important as his reassuring tone.

"What will you do? Do you still think the shooter will come back?"

"I don't know, but while there's even a fraction of doubt I'm not taking any chances." *My goodness.* It must have been tiredness that made her go weak at the knees when this big, strong man said those words to her.

"You can't stay in the woods all night." Her voice had taken on a new and husky note.

The grin was back, this time accompanied by a hint of mischief. "This time I was planning on moving my stakeout to your sofa."

"Oh." She looked from him to the sofa and back again. "It's not big enough." A blush, the first she'd felt for a very long time, stole into her cheeks. Would he think she was offering an alternative? Now that the idea had been planted in her mind it was all she could think about…

"I've slept in worse places." Brayden was smiling at her in a way that told her he might just have figured out exactly what she was thinking. "And Echo will be a lot happier to exchange the damp leaves for your rug."

As if to demonstrate, Echo gave a heavy sigh and, curling up on the rug, closed his eyes.

"I'll fetch a blanket." Glad for something to shift the focus from her embarrassment, Esmée went into her bedroom. When she returned, Brayden was removing his boots.

His blue-green eyes gleamed as he took the blanket from her. "Get some sleep."

She moved toward her bedroom, pausing as she reached the door. "Brayden?"

"Yes?" When she turned, he was lying on his side, watching her.

"Thank you."

"For getting you thrown out?"

"For taking care of us."

He nodded, his gaze still fixed on her face. She should move now. Turn away. Go to her room. Her mind was relaying a series of instructions, but her body was refusing to listen. Every nerve was on high alert and the message being sent out was in direct opposition to that of her brain. *Go to him*. It was getting harder to resist by the second.

Eventually, she managed to get her mind and body working in harmony again. Her mind won, but it was close. It could have been her imagination, but as she went back to her bedroom, she thought she heard Brayden sigh. It was exactly the same sound Esmée made as she shut her door and leaned against it.

Brayden came slowly awake to the smells of bacon, toast and coffee, and the sound of a child's laughter. The realization that his long limbs were cramped into a space that was way too small made him groan out loud.

"Good morning."

Turning his neck at a sharp angle after being curled onto the small sofa should have been a mistake, but the sight of Esmée took the ache away. Dressed in denim shorts, thick black tights and a plaid shirt, with her hair tied back in a ponytail, she was serving breakfast to Rhys and Echo.

"I didn't know if it was okay for Echo to eat human food, but he seemed to think it was."

The dog was tucking into a bowl of eggs and bacon, his tail thumping appreciatively.

"Echo is a con artist. Don't ever believe anything he tells you, especially when it comes to food." Brayden stretched as he got to his feet. "But it's okay for him to have the occasional treat."

He took a seat at the table, gratefully accepting the coffee Esmée poured for him.

"Bray!" Rhys greeted him like a long-lost friend, before returning to his own breakfast of cereal and juice.

As Esmée slid a plate of food in front of him, Brayden reflected on the difference between this morning scene and his regular start to the day. Since that generally involved grabbing a bite of toast as he ran out the door, then buying a coffee before he reached the training ground, he knew which he preferred.

Esmée's laptop was open on the counter, and she returned to it now as she sipped her own coffee. "The problem with Red Ridge is that there aren't many child-friendly places. I already did this search before we came to town. I won't have Rhys staying in a motel room." She sighed as she scanned the screen. "I really don't want to give up on this story and go home."

Brayden cleared his throat. It was now or never. "I know somewhere you can stay."

"You do?" Her big, brown eyes fixed eagerly on his face.

"It's a little out of the way, but it has three bedrooms and a modern kitchen and bathroom. There's plenty of outdoor space for Rhys to run and play safely." *Stop trying to sell it to her and give her the truth.*

"It sounds like heaven. Why isn't it listed on any of these websites?"

"Because it's my place."

"Oh." It wasn't an outright refusal, which was something. Turning away from the laptop, she leaned against the counter as she finished her coffee. "Why are you offering to let us stay at your house?"

"Because you need somewhere to stay and it's better than anywhere you'll find on there." He jabbed a finger at the computer. "But the main reason is that it's safe. I had a break-in a few years ago and I installed a new alarm system with security cameras. Also, if you are under my roof I can make sure you and Rhys are safe if that shooter does decide to come after you again. And, if you're going to help me prove Demi's innocence, it will be a lot easier if we are able to talk the case through each evening."

She raised her eyebrows. "You're okay with me helping?"

"I have one condition." He'd given it some thought as he tried to get to sleep on the uncomfortable sofa. "While you are out investigating, we find someone we both trust to take care of Rhys." He knew Esmée would never expose her son to any risks, but the shooter on the ridge had unsettled Brayden. He would do everything he could to take care of them both, but he'd feel better if they could keep Rhys in a secure setting.

"I'm one step ahead of you. I was going to ask Sarah and Hester about it today," Esmée said. "If they agree, he could go to them while I'm working during the day."

Sarah was a part-time teacher and Hester was a retired police officer. That sounded like a safe and nurturing environment to Brayden. "Do we have a deal?"

He knew the real reason why Esmée was hesitating. It was the same issue that had kept occurring to him when this solution came to him last night. The two of them living under the same roof? In such close proximity, would they be able to resist an attraction that was already close to being out of control? Part of him wanted to say to hell with it. What did it matter if they didn't resist? What if this investigation also became a fling? He knew he was debating with something other than his brain when he thought that way.

Because the reasons against getting into any sort of short-term relationship were stacked up about a mile high. In reality, there was only one reason he could think of for such an arrangement...but it was a compelling one and it had been responsible for some interesting new fantasies.

He had a feeling, from the faint blush that tinged her cheeks and the sparkle in her eyes, that Esmée's thought process might be mirroring his own. "Okay."

Brayden wasn't prepared for the rush of pure elation that hit him. He had expected to feel mildly relieved that the task of protecting Esmée and Rhys would be made easier if she agreed to stay under his roof. Now he knew he had been practically holding his breath, desperately looking forward to having them close simply because he enjoyed being with them.

Since his happiness was something he didn't want to analyze, he quickly finished his breakfast. "While you pack up your things, I'll call my chief and explain why Echo and I will be doing our training this evening."

"I don't want to mess up your schedule." Esmée leaned across him as she picked up Rhys's empty dishes, and Brayden caught a whiff of her delicious scent.

"I can think of worse disruptions."

There was that blush again. A tiny indrawn breath accompanied it. He had wanted Esmée where he could protect her and he'd gotten what he wanted. Now he just had to figure out how he was ever going to concentrate on anything else.

Esmée turned a full circle in the large family room, admiring the polished wood floors, huge windows and mellow color scheme. Rhys's footsteps rang out as he dashed from room to room with Echo following him. Each time Rhys stopped, the dog nudged him gently in the back with his nose and Rhys, shrieking with laughter, would break into a run again. It seemed safe to say that the bond established at the dog show looked likely to develop into a lifelong friendship.

"Brayden, this is amazing. Are you a secret millionaire?"

He had been grinning as he watched Rhys and Echo, but her words wiped the smile from his face, which was replaced by a bleak look. "I like working with my hands."

"You did all this?" The single-story house was incredible. Every authentic feature had been lovingly enhanced, every item of furniture chosen to highlight the beautiful scenery beyond the windows. "You have a real talent."

"The original house belonged to my grandparents. My mom and I lived here until she died when I was eighteen. We didn't have much money when I was growing up. I don't know if you've met my dad?"

"I've seen him." She already knew she needed to be careful around the subject of his family. His expression told her that went double when it came to Rusty. Having observed his dad, she could understand some of Brayden's reticence.

"Yeah. He wasn't great at helping out. By the time my mom died, this place was about ready to fall down. I thought about selling the land and renting somewhere in town." His gaze went to the view, and Esmée caught a glimmer of emotion in his expression. "But this is my home, so I decided to restore it instead."

She could see why he hadn't wanted to swap this location for a place in town. Close by, rolling grassland sloped down to meet tall trees. The mountains were a distant backdrop and Esmée had glimpsed a field of horses near the rear of the property. "It must have taken years."

"It's not finished. Every time I think a job is done, I find a new thing to do. And the land has remained untouched since my Grandpa Colton's day. I don't suppose I'll ever get around to doing anything with that." Brayden carried one of her bags along the hall toward the bedrooms. He held open a door. "This room has its own bathroom. I thought you could

take this one and Rhys could have the one across
the hall. Unless you want him to share with you? I
could move another bed in here."

Esmée shook her head. "Rhys is used to being in
his own room. I have the baby monitor and as long
as he knows I'm close, he'll be fine."

"I'll get the rest of your things from your car."
He plucked at the front of his shirt with a grimace.
"Then, while you settle in, I need to shower and
change out of the clothes I slept in."

Esmée watched as he dodged the dog-and-baby
chasing game that was still dominating the hall. The
room was charming, with a pretty mirror over the
dresser and a patchwork throw on the bed. There was
a feminine air about it and she suspected it might
once have belonged to Brayden's mom. The possibility brought a weight of responsibility with it that
sent a little shiver down her spine. This very private
man had invited her to share his space.

Her cell phone rang as Brayden returned with
more of her belongings. She checked the display and
gave a little exclamation. "It's Sarah. I almost forgot
I was supposed to visit her and Hester today."

"Ask them to come here. I'm sure they'd love to
help you and Rhys settle in." A mischievous smile
lifted the corners of his mouth. "And, from what I
know of Hester, I'm sure she'd love the opportunity
to be the first to get the gossip about you moving
in here."

"You don't mind?" Squeals from the other bedroom were followed by a crash. Brayden pointed at her cell, gesturing that he would deal with the other problem. While she returned Sarah's call, Esmée reflected that Brayden might soon be unable to recognize his tranquil home.

"Sarah? Hi." She watched in fascination as Brayden marched past the open door with Rhys under one arm and a lamp base in his other hand. Since they were both smiling, the situation didn't look too serious. "Look, this is a long story and I can explain it better when I see you. Do you know where Brayden Colton lives?"

An hour later, Brayden emerged from his bedroom to find Sarah and Hester Mull at his kitchen table drinking coffee. Esmée was taking her stuff out of boxes and putting it into cupboards or the fridge. Rhys was seated on the floor playing with his toy animals and talking to Echo, who was lying next to him.

Brayden had spoken to his chief and explained the reason why he and Echo hadn't turned up for training that morning. He had also mentioned Sarah and Hester's visit. While he had no intention of interrogating Sarah so soon after her discharge from the hospital, where she had spent time recovering from the shock of her fiancé's murder, he thought it wouldn't hurt to speak to her if she seemed well enough. There was probably nothing more she could tell him about Jack's death, but sometimes the little details mattered. Finn had agreed that Brayden should stay home and talk to her.

He took a seat at the table as Esmée poured coffee for him. Although Sarah was more restrained, Hester, as he had predicted, was clearly bursting with curiosity about Esmée's presence in his house. Her eyes flickered from him to Esmée and back again with obvious excitement. Catching Esmée's gaze, Brayden bit back a smile. Clearly, she was aware of the reason behind Hester's bright-eyed interest, too.

"How are you?" He spoke quietly to Sarah and she raised red-rimmed eyes to his face.

"I'm still struggling to believe it." Bravely, she attempted a smile. "Tomorrow would have been our wedding day."

Brayden took her hand. "I'm sorry."

She nodded, clasping his fingers in return. "And I'm sorry you have to put up with the things people are saying about your sister. No one should be judged before they have been tried in a court of law."

"Thank you."

Hester, never one to tolerate silence for long, soon came up with a piece of juicy scandal to share. "Have you heard that Lulu Love had her baby last night, but the no-good father still hasn't bothered to put in an appearance?"

For once, Brayden was happy to encourage her to

develop the gossip a little further. "So Richie wasn't at the birth?"

It was an interesting snippet of information. So far, his attempts to track down Richie Lyman had proved useless, but Brayden had figured even a low-life like the Larson twins' right-hand man would want to see his baby being born.

Hester snorted. "At the birth? He isn't even in town. Lulu was screaming the whole time about what she was going to do to Richie next time she got her hands on him. Seems she hasn't seen him for weeks."

No matter how poor Brayden's opinion of Richie might be, he was surprised to hear the man had missed the birth of his own baby. It made him wonder exactly what was going on to keep Richie away from Red Ridge.

"Is it important?" Sarah's quiet voice intruded on Brayden's thoughts. Her gaze was fixed on his face and he remembered how hard it had always been to hide anything from her when he was a little kid and she was his teacher. "It seems to matter to you that Richie has gone missing."

"I've been looking for him," Brayden admitted. "That's often a good enough reason for him to avoid me, but it seems strange that he wouldn't turn up for such an important event."

"This may be nothing." He got the impression she was having some kind of internal struggle. Her next words explained why. "But Jack knew Richie Lyman."

Hester leaned across the table, grasping her sister-in-law's wrist. "Sarah, you don't have to talk about this if it's too difficult…"

Sarah shook her head, pressing her lips together firmly before continuing. "I want to. If I can help the police in any way, I will."

"Okay." Brayden was unsure how a link between Jack Parkowski, who had left the Chicago PD five years earlier, and Richie was going to help him, but he wasn't going to tell Sarah that. "Do you know how Jack knew Richie?"

"Not exactly. You know that Jack only returned to Red Ridge recently, right?" Brayden nodded. "We were out one night. We'd had dinner and Jack was walking me back to my house when we heard raised voices from across the street. You know what Jack was like." Sarah turned her head to look at Esmée.

Esmée's smile was affectionate and sad at the same time. "Only too well. Let me guess… He intervened?"

"Yes. He went over to find out what was going on. It was Richie and Lulu. They were having a big argument. I think they were both drunk." Sarah's voice grew stronger as she talked. "Jack gestured to me to stay back, but I could hear most of what was going on. As Jack approached them, Lulu shouted at him to get the hell away and mind his own business, but Richie went very still and just stared at Jack. Almost as if he'd seen a ghost."

Brayden frowned. He'd encountered Richie when he was drunk. He doubted if stripping the guy naked and turning a fire hose on him would sober him up. Yet it seemed one look at Jack had worked wonders.

"As Jack reached them, Richie said, 'You!' Just that one word. I couldn't hear Jack's reply. He spoke really quietly. Whatever he said, it had a dramatic effect on Richie. He grabbed Lulu's arm and dragged her away. It was like he couldn't get out of there fast enough."

"Did Jack tell you what he said to Richie?" Brayden asked.

"No. When he came back to me, all he said was that the guy was trouble and I should stay away from him."

"He was right about that." Brayden leaned back in his seat as he drank his coffee.

"Could this be linked to Jack's death?" Sarah's eyes anxiously scanned his face.

"I don't think so." There was only so much he could tell her about the case, but he was conscious of Hester listening avidly to every word. Sarah's sister-in-law was one of the most kindhearted women he knew, but she was addicted to gossip. Red Ridge already had its fair share of rumors. Brayden didn't want to be responsible for starting another. He certainly didn't want to alert the Larson brothers that he was checking up on their associates. "We're sure that Jack was killed by the Groom Killer and there's no suggestion that Richie is linked to those murders. Even so, I'd like to find out how Jack knew him."

"Jack kept detailed notes of every case he worked on," Esmée said. "We used to joke about it because I'd ask him when he thought he was ever going to need them. But he'd just say you never knew when they might prove useful."

Sarah smiled. "That sounds like Jack."

"Do you know where his notebooks are now?" Esmée asked.

"All his stuff from Chicago is mostly in the apartment he was renting over Andy's Liquor Store." Sarah's shoulders drooped again. "He'd started to move a few boxes into my garage ready for when we were married, but he hadn't gotten very far."

"If it's okay with Sarah, I'd like to look for those notebooks." Esmée looked at Brayden. "I could go through them to see if there's any reference to Richie Lyman."

Brayden nodded. "Sounds like a good use of your research skills."

"It's fine with me," Sarah said. "Anything that helps."

"Can we keep this between us?" Brayden looked around the table. Hester liked to talk, but she had once been a police officer. She wouldn't ignore a direct appeal for discretion… At least that was what he hoped.

"Of course." Hester nodded as she rose from her seat. "You can count on me."

Brayden decided not to look in Esmée's direction. That mischievous sparkle in her eyes had a tendency to draw him in and make him laugh at the most inappropriate moments. "Thank you." He kept his voice and expression suitably grave.

They wound up the visit by making arrangements for Rhys's care during the times when Esmée would be working. It was good to see the animation on Sarah's features when she talked about her plans for looking after the little boy.

"There's one thing he will *really* love," Hester said.

"Oh, good Lord, yes." Sarah smiled. "Seems my old Bella-cat must have found herself a gentleman friend. She went missing a few weeks ago and I wondered if I'd ever see her again. Then, I heard a noise at the back of the garage and found Bella and her four babies."

"Kittens? Rhys may never leave." Esmée laughed. "Although, after a few hours spent with a two-year-old, the cats may pack their bags."

"I think it will do Sarah as much good as it will Rhys," Brayden said, as they waved Hester's car out of sight.

"It's probably the best form of rehabilitation," Esmée agreed. "Kittens and kids. What could go wrong?"

As they went back into the house, he noticed it already had a different feel to it. There were toys on the kitchen floor, cups on the counter, a bowl of fruit on the table, chairs out of place, windows open wide… It looked like a home.

"I have to take Echo for his training." He clicked his fingers and the dog moved to his side.

Esmée was already loading coffee cups into the dishwasher. "I'll have dinner ready for when you get back."

For the first time in a long time, it *felt* like a home.

## Chapter 9

After Brayden and Echo returned from their training session, Esmée served the chicken casserole she had prepared.

"Ignore Echo's puppy-dog eyes," Brayden said. "He ate dinner at the training ground and he's developing way too many bad habits lately."

Seated around the large, scrubbed pine table, there was an unspoken accord between them. The temptation to discuss the Groom Killer, Richie Lyman and any potential connection between the two was there, but they ignored it. Instead, they had focused on Rhys, who wanted to talk about his toy animals and the different sounds they made.

Later, Brayden cleared away the dinner dishes while Esmée gave Rhys his bath and put him to bed. With his familiar toys around him, Rhys had no problem with being in a different room. Once she was sure he was asleep, she joined Brayden in the family room.

Placing the baby monitor on the oak coffee table that dominated the center of the room, she curled into a corner of the sofa that was at a right angle to his seat. "He seems to have settled in just fine."

"He talks really well for someone who had a problem. Was there a medical reason for the delay?"

Esmée leaned her head back against the cushions. It was a simple enough question and she had never been averse to providing a superficial answer. For the first time, she felt a desire to confide the full story. She already knew she could trust Brayden, but this went beyond her belief in his reliability. It was about a feeling that she could unload some of her burdens onto him. And that was a little bit frightening. Because she had never felt that way. Even with Jack, who had been the closest thing she'd had to a protector.

She could feel Brayden watching her profile, so she turned her head to look at him. His gaze was steady and nonjudgmental. Would that change if she told him the truth?

"No, there was no medical reason." Her hands twisted in her lap as she remembered that awful night. "It was my fault."

"Hey…" Brayden was at her side as the first tear slid down her cheek, his arm slipping around her shoulders. "I don't know what happened, but I already know that's not true."

She leaned against him, grateful for the strong muscles of his chest beneath her cheek. "I've never told anyone this story. The only person who knew what happened was Jack, because he was there at the time."

"I'm here now if you want to tell me," Brayden said. "I've always preferred listening to talking."

She moved slightly away, not breaking the contact between them completely, but giving herself space to concentrate. Brayden's nearness wasn't good for maintaining a clear head.

"Rhys was born in Wales. His father, Gwyn Owen, owned a farm just outside the town of Glanrafon, where I was making my documentary. We began our relationship almost immediately." Looking back, it was so easy to see the warning signs. At the time, she'd been blissfully unaware. "I'm not making excuses, but I was dazzled by Gwyn. He was so attentive, so—" She searched for the right words and failed to find them. "He seemed too good to be true. Turned out he was. I'm sorry, I don't know if I'm making any sense."

"I don't have any wine, but if this is a conversation that would go better with a beer, I can oblige."

She nodded. "Beer would be good."

He went through to the kitchen and returned with two bottles of beer. Esmée's heart gave a little skip of pleasure when he returned to sit beside her instead of resuming his former place. She tried telling herself it was because his presence was comforting, but her own honesty wouldn't allow that deception. She just liked being close to him.

After taking a swallow of the cool liquid, she felt refreshed enough to continue. "Having a baby was the last thing on my mind, but once I knew I was pregnant, it felt like an important reason to make things work with Gwyn. I was trying hard to convince myself I was in love with him when things started to go wrong."

"In what way?"

"Gwyn was very controlling. It started out with little things. He began by criticizing the way I dressed, telling me I shouldn't draw attention to myself by wearing tight jeans or short skirts. Then he'd get annoyed if he saw me talking to other men, even when I was doing it as part of my job. He hated Jack, especially as we shared a house whenever Jack came over to Wales. I mean, Jack was my *friend*. When Rhys was born, Gwyn barely looked at him. All he was interested in was keeping me to himself. I could see it, but I was going along with it because I wanted a stable relationship for my baby's sake. Finally, Jack intervened. He made me confront what was happening. The documentary was over, Jack was coming

home to America and I realized I wasn't happy." She
drew in a shaky breath. "It was when I tried to leave
that things got really bad."

Brayden took her hand, placing it on his own knee
and holding it there with his own hand over it. "Take
your time."

"I'm okay. It's just hard, even after all this time,
because it was so unexpected." She closed her eyes
briefly, remembering the rage on Gwyn's face, the
first blow. Her own instinct had been to protect
Rhys… "Gwyn attacked me."

Brayden's fingers gripped hers a little tighter. "He
did what?"

"He beat me." It was easier to say out loud than
she'd expected. Over a year had passed. The physical injuries had healed quickly, but the emotional
hurt had taken much longer. The feelings of guilt,
that she was to blame, and the fear that, through
her actions, she had caused harm to her son…those
things had lingered. *Still* lingered. "Jack found out
later that Gwyn had previous convictions for similar offenses. There is a law in the UK that allows
you to check if a partner has a violent past." She
gave a shaky little laugh. "Gwyn was on the register of offenders, but because I didn't know about it,
I hadn't checked."

Brayden exhaled, long and slow. "I don't know
what to say except how sorry I am that you went
through that. How did you get away?"

"Jack came home at just the right time. He heard my cries, burst into my bedroom and pulled Gwyn off me. But Rhys was in his crib in my room. He saw it all. And he stopped talking." She took another slug of beer. "Jack took over then. He did all the practical things, while I focused on Rhys. Jack helped me deal with the local police, got us to the American embassy in London, organized a passport for Rhys and brought us home within a few days. I had a couple of broken ribs and some interesting bruises, but the real damage? That was done to my baby."

A little sob rose in her throat as she said the words. She choked it back and tried out a smile instead. "It's in the past. I'm fine. More important than that, Rhys is okay. Thanks to you and Echo, he's talking again."

"You said it was your fault he stopped talking, but you're wrong. You couldn't have foreseen what would happen, Esmée." The gentleness in Brayden's tone was like a hug, almost undoing her composure. "There was only one person to blame and that was the lowlife who used his fists on you."

"Rhys stopped talking because I made the wrong choices. I knew Gwyn was bad news, yet I stayed with him." She had been over and over this in her own mind. "That makes it my fault. I can't turn the clock back. All I can do is make sure it never happens again."

"You think he'll come after you? Because if he does—"

Esmée shook her head. "Jack took care of the legalities. Gwyn had been serving a prison sentence for a previous offense and had been released early. Attacking me violated the terms of his parole and he went back to jail. He's still there. I took out a restraining order against him and Gwyn has agreed that I should have sole custody of Rhys. If he follows us once he's released, my lawyers will be ready for him." She gave a grim smile. "As for me, I've been taking self-defense classes. If anyone comes at me with their fists in the future, I'll know how to fight back. No, I mean I will never put Rhys in that position again because I won't allow another man into our lives."

"Esmée—" Brayden ducked his head to get a closer look at her face "—I understand how much this must have scared you, but the chances of the next man you get involved with being an abuser are pretty much nonexistent."

"No, you don't understand. I don't think all men are abusers. I wouldn't be scared of getting into another relationship for *that* reason. I'm well aware I probably wouldn't pick a bad guy next time, but I'm not going there. All that matters to me from now on is my son's well-being."

Her hand shook slightly as she raised the bottle to her lips again. She'd never said that out loud. Never voiced the weight of guilt and responsibility that had gone along with what had happened. Not even to Jack, who had been there and seen it.

"What about your well-being?"

She blinked at the slightly harsh note in Brayden's voice. "What do you mean?"

He ran a hand through his hair. "I understand why you want to protect Rhys, but you have a life as well. Don't lock yourself away because of a bad experience."

"I'm a woman, so I need a man to complete me?" She threw the challenge at him, her mood changing swiftly. Just because she'd confided in him, it didn't mean she'd given him permission to analyze her.

Brayden didn't appear to be intimidated by her scowl, or the way she folded her arms across her chest, establishing a barrier between them. "That's not what I meant. If you choose to stay single, do it because there is no one you want to be with, not because it's something you've imposed on yourself as a punishment for what happened to Rhys."

Esmée's initial reaction was to flare back at him with an angry reply. But as she glared at him, she saw the answering concern in the depths of his eyes. She might not have asked for his opinion, but he was giving it for the right reasons. In the short time she'd known Brayden Colton, she'd come to depend on his integrity. He wouldn't sugarcoat a message if he thought she needed to hear it. And maybe it was time she heard this one.

She huffed out a breath. "I thought you said you were better at listening than talking? I'm supposed to be the interviewer around here."

"I guess some things need to be said." His smile triggered a chain reaction deep inside her, a slow, melting sensation that left her feeling lethargic yet tingling all over. "Just one more thing before I get us another beer and you decide what we watch on TV."

She regarded him in fascination. "Another insight?"

"Possibly. You said Rhys was the only one who sustained any lasting hurt that night." The brief touch of his fingertips on her cheek was comforting and disturbing at the same time. "Are you quite sure about that?"

Once he and Echo had completed their morning training the next day, Brayden headed toward the police-department building on foot. He had left his car there earlier, having spent an hour searching through records in an attempt to identify the shooter in the mountains. The guy's size was his main identifying feature. Other than that, there was nothing about his appearance that made him stand out. So far, his quest had proved fruitless, but he was determined to keep trying.

Although his stride was purposeful, his thoughts were distracted. He didn't have to do any deep soul-searching to find the reason for his preoccupation. Just lately, no matter what he was doing, there was only one thing on his mind... Esmée.

A week ago, if he'd been offered the choice of having strangers living in his house, he'd have run a mile in the opposite direction to avoid it. Throw in the complication that those strangers were a woman and a child? A mile wouldn't have been far enough. Then add that the woman was beautiful and that he was attracted to her... Well, the distance he'd have gone to avoid their current situation just kept growing.

But circumstances had taken over. He'd gotten to know Esmée and Rhys. He'd grown to like them both. Already, he liked having them around. Instead of being a hardship, their company was pleasant. The attraction he felt for Esmée may have started with her looks, but it went so much deeper. They shared a sense of humor. A dangerously silly enjoyment of the ridiculous that threatened to spill over at the most inappropriate moments. He knew if he found something funny, she would, too. Just this morning, sitting at a desk in the office, he had overheard a remark and stored it up for later, knowing she would appreciate it. *I must tell Esmée...* He'd never felt so in tune with another person in his life.

The previous night, Esmée had confided in him, opening up to him and allowing him to see her at her most vulnerable. Later, in the darkness of his own room, Brayden had lain awake thinking about the responsibility that came with her trust in him. He didn't have many friends. That was his choice. He certainly didn't have people who shared intimate details of their lives with him. Not because he couldn't be trusted, just because he didn't invite that sort of closeness.

*It's not what I do.*

Esmée had come into his life and changed that. What she'd told him about her experience in Wales had heightened his desire to protect her, even though he'd already seen at firsthand how strong she was. The knowledge that he wasn't able to make the man who had hurt her pay for what he'd done nagged at him, but he was forced to let it go. Jack Parkowski had been there to see justice done on her behalf. Brayden felt a pang of sadness that he hadn't known the ex-cop who had been admired by everyone who knew him.

As she'd talked, Brayden could see how much she was hurting, even though she clearly couldn't see it herself. That vow she'd made to stay single for Rhys's sake? It was so transparently a shield behind which she could hide. She could use it to keep herself safe and never get involved again, never risk getting hurt by another man. Maybe he should have been more tactful, but he had been determined to try to make her see that. He might be new at this whole friendship thing, but he figured that was part of it. Be honest and support each other.

Alongside his resolution to be a good friend to Esmée, he had experienced a new feeling…a desire to confide in her in return. The fear that he couldn't trust her was long gone. They hadn't known each other very long, but just as Esmée had entrusted him with the story of what she had endured at the hands of her violent ex, Brayden knew he could open up to her about his family. He was certain she wouldn't use what he told her as part of the documentary.

His only worry was that, once he started talking, he wouldn't be able to stop. Esmée and Rhys would probably flee the house before he'd even reached the story of his sixteenth birthday party and Rusty's antics with the stripper.

*Yes, my dad thought his shy, sixteen-year-old son would enjoy having a stripper at his party.* Growing up as Rusty Colton's son hadn't been easy.

He had reached the police headquarters when a bark from Echo drew his attention. Looking up, he saw a plume of smoke rising into the air. He judged it to be coming from the area close to the Pour House.

He stepped inside the building. Lorelei was always the best and fastest source of information. "Looks like there's a fire in the downtown area. Any idea what's going on?"

"From the calls coming in, it looks like it could be the apartment over Andy's Liquor Store—"

Brayden didn't wait to hear any more. He ran out of the building and headed for his vehicle with Echo at his heels. When he left the house that morning, Esmée had said she would be dropping Rhys at Sarah's house and collecting the keys to Jack's apartment. The one he had been renting above Andy's Liquor Store.

Esmée had dropped Rhys at Sarah's place. As expected, the kittens had proved to be a huge success. Rhys was so entranced by the tiny, mewing creatures, she didn't think he even noticed when she left.

She had called the liquor-store owner, Andy Coulson, the previous day, explaining that she was a friend of Jack's and that she was going to start sorting through his belongings. When she arrived, he hailed her as "that filmmaker" and kept her talking while he gave her his opinion on the Groom Killer case.

"Demi Colton? Pretty as a picture, but wild as an untamed colt. She was one to avoid." There was a wistful note in his voice that suggested he'd have liked to get closer to Demi, but had never been given the opportunity.

When she finally got away—having stopped in Andy's kitchen to take him up on his offer to make use of his coffee maker—Esmée unlocked Jack's apartment and reflected on how quickly a place could acquire an unlived-in air. There was a steep flight of stairs up to the apartment. The accommodation consisted of a square foyer, with a window over-looking the rear delivery yard, a living room with a kitchen area to one side and a bedroom with an en suite bathroom. Briskly, she had put aside the feeling of sadness that assailed her at the thought that her friend had once lived here. She hadn't come here to grieve for Jack. That was for other times and places. She was here to help Brayden find information on Richie Lyman.

Jack had clearly been ready to move out of this place and into Sarah's neat little house. Most of his things were packed into boxes that were stacked in the sitting room. Esmée pulled up a chair and began to go through them. She had barely started when there was a sound of breaking glass and a loud thud. The noises came from the direction of the hall.

Looking over her shoulder, she took in the broken window at the top of the stairs and the brick lying on the carpeted floor. Jumping to her feet, she was just in time to see a bottle with a burning rag stuffed into its neck follow the brick. The bottle had smashed on impact and a strong smell of gasoline filled the air. Flames immediately licked along the carpet and up the drapes on either side of the window, blocking Esmée's access to the stairs. She slammed the door shut. The action stopped the flames from entering the room she was in, but it left her trapped.

Reaching into the back pocket of her jeans for her

cell phone, she came away empty-handed. A frown furrowed her brow. She never went anywhere without her cell. Then she remembered. While she had been making coffee in Andy's kitchen, Sarah had sent her a message to see if Rhys had any allergies. An image of her phone came to her. She had placed it on the counter in the kitchen downstairs, but she couldn't remember picking it up again.

*The one time I really need it...*

Going into the bathroom, Esmée gathered up towels and soaked them in water. Although she'd stopped the fire from spreading to these rooms, the blaze was blocking her path to the only staircase. Returning to the sitting room, she placed the damp cloths along the bottom of the door.

Throwing up the casement window, she looked down onto the street below. It was too far to jump, and there was no one around. She had to hope someone would see the smoke, maybe even that someone had witnessed the arson attack. Although he was on the other side of the building, it was possible Andy had heard the window breaking. Hopefully, he was already aware that part of his premises was burning, and had alerted the fire department.

Even though there was no one on the street below, she leaned out of the window and shouted for help. Her mind was working overtime as she did. Had Brayden been right all along? Could this fire have been started by the same man who shot at her? It was hard to see how this attack could be connected to the bloody knife Esmée had found up on the ridge. But the possibility that someone had decided to set fire to Jack's apartment on the very day she came to check out his belongings? Within minutes of her arrival? That was stretching credibility to its outer limits.

She still found it hard to believe someone was trying to drive her out of Red Ridge to stop her from making a documentary about the Groom Killer. First, because she hadn't even started on the details of her story. Apart from a few interviews, she hadn't put anything together. Anyone wanting to stop the truth from coming out would be better off going after the editor of the *Red Ridge Gazette*. The newspaper was publishing increasingly lurid articles delving into the past lives of everyone involved. Second, Red Ridge was the sort of town where everyone knew each other's business anyway. Unless Demi Colton was innocent and the person trying to scare off Esmée was the real killer?

When her cries for help didn't attract any attention, she viewed the door. Knowing better than to open it, she went over and held her hand close to it. Sure enough, she could feel the heat through the painted wooden panels. The fire must have taken a strong hold on the other side. Tendrils of smoke were beginning to seep through the gap between the door and the frame. Esmée knew how it went. It wasn't fire that killed. It was smoke.

She bit her lip. The window was the only way. Since jumping was out of the question, she would have to see if she could climb down. As she moved toward the window, a heavy thud hit the side of the building and a familiar head and shoulders appeared in the opening.

"Brayden?"

Momentarily, she wondered if, while she was seeking a way out, her imagination had run wild and conjured up the very rescuer she'd wished for. But Brayden was real. Sitting astride the window ledge, he assessed the situation.

"It doesn't look like we're going to get out through the door." The paint was starting to blister and Esmée could feel the increased heat. "This ladder is a bit shaky, but Andy is holding it at the bottom. I'll be right behind you."

She gave a nervous laugh. "Brayden, you always say the sweetest things."

He stepped into the room. Standing to one side, he helped her climb onto the window ledge, then held on to her until she was steady on the ladder. "Just take it slowly. You're out of danger now."

A glance down told her it was a long way. She could see Andy, his face pale, gripping the base of the ladder. A fire engine had pulled up across the street. Taking a deep breath, she started a slow descent. When she was halfway down, Brayden started to climb down behind her. Although his increased weight made the ladder move around more, his presence steadied her nerves and she moved faster.

When her feet hit the sidewalk, her knees refused to hold her upright. Before she could sink onto the wooden boards, strong hands gripped her waist. Brayden scooped her up into his arms and carried her across to the opposite side of the road.

"We need to get away from the building."

His car was parked behind the fire engine and he lifted her into the passenger seat. Echo was in his specially adapted compartment in the back and all the windows were open to ensure the vehicle was properly ventilated. The dog gave a bark of greeting when he saw Esmée and she reached around to pet him. There it was again. That soothing feeling that came from contact with Echo. Canine therapy. There was definitely something to it.

The apartment above Andy's Liquor Store was now blazing out of control with flames clearly visible within the room Esmée had just left. The image made her feel slightly sick. If Brayden hadn't arrived when he did...if she'd waited for the firefighters...

"Hey." Brayden was watching her face. "It's okay. You're safe."

"Thanks to you." Her chin wobbled. "Again."

"Yeah. Rescuing you is becoming a habit with me." His voice was light, but there was a deeper emotion in his eyes. They stared at each other for a moment or two before the fire drew Brayden's attention again. He watched as the firefighters prepared to turn a hose on the building. "Somehow, I don't think there's much chance of us finding Jack's notebooks now, do you?"

# Chapter 10

Even after giving Brayden the details of what had happened, Esmée was still shaken. She decided to go home instead of spending any more time working, but Brayden suggested going for coffee before she went to pick up Rhys.

"I don't know." She held up a trembling hand. "I'm not sure I could handle it if anyone approached me with a Demi Colton anecdote this morning." She grimaced as she realized what she'd said. "Although they probably wouldn't try it if you were with me."

His jaw muscles clenched. "Don't be so sure about that. Some of the Gage family are only too happy to tell me what they think about my sister. Luckily,

I know a place where we can get a great cup of coffee and some privacy."

A few minutes later, he turned onto Main Street and pulled up outside Good Eats. Intrigued, Esmée got out of the car. From her research into the town, she knew this was the catering business of his older half sister, Quinn. Echo, jumping down from the rear of the vehicle, clearly knew his way and bounded eagerly toward the door.

When they stepped inside, the interior of the store was quiet, but a delicious smell permeated the entire space.

"Kitchen." Brayden jerked his thumb toward the back.

They found Quinn poring over a recipe book while stirring a large pot on the stove. She greeted Brayden with a smile. No hug, Esmée noticed. Maybe that wasn't so strange. They hadn't been brought up together.

When Quinn observed her brother's companion, she frowned. "I don't want to talk about my sister."

"Nor do I," Brayden said. "Esmée knows that. But she's had a nasty shock and I told her you make the best coffee in town." He turned to Esmée. "And I didn't mention the gluten-free lemon cake."

"Do you have brothers?" Quinn asked.

The unexpected change of subject threw Esmée off balance. "Um, no."

"They will say anything for food." Quinn smiled. "Or is that just men?"

Esmée laughed. "I have a son. It's men."

They were soon seated at a table and Esmée discovered that Brayden hadn't exaggerated about either the coffee or the cake. Even Echo was provided for with a healthy dog treat and a bowl of water. As the immediate shock of the fire began to recede, she took the time to observe the interaction between brother and sister. The first thing she noticed was that Brayden and Quinn didn't behave like a brother and sister. Despite Quinn's joke, there was none of the closeness she'd have expected to see from siblings. It was almost as if they were friends because that was what they were supposed to do.

"How's business?" Brayden asked.

Quinn's shoulders drooped. "Awful." She turned to Esmée. "Most of my work used to come from catering weddings. But, you know…" She trailed off, apparently remembering to whom she was talking.

Esmée decided to try to alleviate Quinn's suspicions. "If it helps, Brayden and I have an agreement. I won't make my documentary until after the Groom Killer is found and brought to justice."

"Why would you do that?"

"It's a long story, but Esmée and her son, Rhys, are staying with me for the time being."

"Oh." Quinn looked first at Brayden and then at Esmée. "Are you two—"

"No." Brayden and Esmée said the word together. She recognized the flash of pure mischief in his eyes and threw him a cautionary look.

"I had some problems with the last place I was staying and Brayden stepped in to help."

Quinn gave a sigh. She cast a sidelong look at Brayden. "Don't you sometimes wish you *could* talk about Demi?"

He frowned. "What do you mean?"

"I don't know." She crumbled a piece of cake on her plate without eating it. "It's like the whole town is talking about her and I feel like I should be the one person who knows the truth. But I don't. Isn't that horrible of me? She's my sister and I don't know whether I think she's guilty or not because I don't know her well enough."

"She's not guilty." Brayden's voice was grim.

"What does Shane think?" Quinn asked.

"Shane knows how easy it is to frame someone." Brayden turned to Esmée to explain what he meant. "Our brother was wrongly convicted of murder when he was eighteen. He spent a year and a half in prison before he was released after being fully exonerated. The cop who framed him was a Gage." It was more evidence of the chasm that divided the two families. "I haven't spoken to Shane recently. He's been out on the road on an investigation."

"He's a cop?" Esmée was confused. Even if Shane had been cleared of any crime, she would be surprised to learn he'd joined the police after such a devastating experience.

"He's a private investigator."

An idea entered Esmée's head. It saddened her to see how much this family was hurting. Brayden had done so much for her—maybe there was something she could do in return. He would probably veto the suggestion, so she jumped right in without consulting him.

"You and Shane should come to dinner. That way, you can all talk about Demi without worrying about what other people might think."

Brayden flicked a scowl her way, but Quinn clasped her hands together. "I'd really like that. And I've never seen your house, Brayden."

"Then it's settled. I'll cook and you can bring dessert." From under the table, Echo gave a contented sigh. "And dog treats." She turned her head to look at Brayden as he got to his feet. "You could get Quinn a deal with the K-9 training center."

"I'll bear it in mind." He placed a hand under her elbow. "We should go."

She studied his profile as they returned to the car. "You do that really well."

He glanced down at her. "What?"

"The mean, moody look. Do you practice in the mirror?"

His lips twitched. "You are shameless."

"I can be." She stopped walking and swung around abruptly to face him. "Brayden, look at me."

He did as she asked, his expression perplexed. "What are you—"

She placed a hand on the back of his neck, drawing him down to her until their faces were only inches apart. It had started as a joke, but the temptation to kiss him suddenly became overwhelming. The answering flare in Brayden's eyes made her regret her sudden impulse. She felt so comfortable with him, she had acted without stopping to think about the consequences. In the future, she would have to remember to limit any playfulness to verbal teasing.

With a smile, she touched a fingertip to the corner of his mouth. "Cake crumbs."

Quick as a flash, he caught hold of her around the waist. Leaning closer, he brushed his lips lightly over hers before running his tongue along her lower lip. Perhaps she could blame the delayed effects of smoke inhalation for the way the breath left her lungs in a single dramatic whoosh? Or the way she had to press both palms flat against his chest to stay upright? Even the way her eyelids fluttered closed?

"Delicious."

"Hmm?" She opened her eyes to find Brayden smiling down at her.

"You had cake crumbs on your lips as well." The smile deepened, became wicked. "They tasted like heaven."

She was left staring after him as he turned his back and walked away. When he returned from getting Echo into the rear of the car, his expression was serene.

Her joke had well and truly backfired. Clearly, they were playing a that-wasn't-a-kiss game. "I'll walk back to Andy's store for my car if you need to be somewhere else."

"I'm going back there anyway. I want to talk to Andy and find out if he saw anything before the fire started. Someone threw a brick and then a burning bottle through a second-floor window in broad daylight. I'm hoping he or she was seen."

Esmée slid into the passenger seat. They drove in silence until they reached the smoldering liquor store. Firefighters were still clearing up at the scene and a small group of onlookers were watching from the opposite side of the street.

Brayden viewed it for a few moments before turning to Esmée. "Until we find out who did this, and why, you have to be careful. Two attempts on your life in a few days. That's a hell of a coincidence."

She swallowed hard. "You think the same guy who shot at me did this?"

"I don't know...but I intend to find out."

Esmée decided she couldn't walk away without asking the question that was uppermost in her mind. They might be in the middle of an important investigation—she might even be facing the prospect of someone threatening her life—but she still needed an answer.

"What tasted like heaven, Brayden? The cake crumbs or my lips?"

He smiled and she wondered how she'd ever thought him reserved. "Both."

Brayden found Andy at the entrance to the delivery yard at the rear of the store, gazing up at the damaged building. Firefighters had cordoned off the scene and he wasn't allowed any closer.

He greeted Brayden with an exaggerated sigh. "Fifteen years of my life up in smoke."

"You have insurance, right?"

"Yeah, but starting all over again? I don't know if my heart's in it. At least no one was hurt. If you hadn't arrived when you did…"

Brayden didn't want to follow through on that thought. When he had arrived at the liquor store that morning and seen smoke and flames coming from the window at the rear of the apartment, his emotions had gone into free fall. Powered by fear, he had dashed toward the store. Andy had been standing in the yard gazing up at the building with his cell phone in his hand.

It had taken Brayden only a few quick questions to gather the information he had needed. The fire department had been called, but Esmée had been trapped upstairs. Knowing what he should do in that situation and acting upon it were two very different things. Being professional was all very well, but this was about *Esmée*. Somewhere between his first glimpse of her at the dog show and now, she had become important to him. He didn't know how, or why, it had happened. He had no idea what it meant for the future. All he had known in that instant was that he couldn't leave her in a burning building while he waited for someone else to save her.

Luckily, the rescue had gone smoothly. She was okay and the weight that had lodged deep in his chest felt lighter. But it wasn't gone. Because he genuinely believed that this was the second time someone had tried to kill her. He needed to deal with that and his starting point was to find out if the person who torched the apartment was the same guy who shot at her on the ridge.

"I didn't get a chance to ask you any questions this morning."

"I already spoke to the fire chief."

Andy looked wary. It was his habitual expression when confronted by a cop. Brayden knew why, of course. Although they hadn't been able to pin anything on him, it was an open secret among the teenagers of Red Ridge that Andy's was the place to go to get alcohol "under the counter." Corey Gage and his friends had been heard openly boasting about it, but when pressed for further information, the kids always developed poor memories. So far, Andy had managed to duck the penalty for selling alcohol to minors, but he carefully avoided police scrutiny. From any angle.

Andy was as slippery as a snake, but there was no way Brayden was letting him wriggle out of this conversation.

"Esmée said someone threw a brick through the window that looks over the yard." Brayden scanned the rear of the building. There was only one window that fit the description Esmée had given him. The glass was long gone and the frame was charred and blistered. The walls around the square opening were blackened by smoke. Even to Brayden's un-trained eye, it was clearly the flash point of the fire. "Then, once the glass was broken, he, or she, threw in a bottle containing a liquid—probably gasoline. There was a burning rag protruding from the neck of the bottle."

"A Molotov cocktail." Brayden turned to see Jay Greening, one of the Red Ridge Fire Department investigators, standing just inside the yard. "Much favored among arsonists who like to keep their dis-tance."

"I'm just asking Andy if he saw who did it," Brayden explained. "Esmée da Costa, the woman who was in the apartment at the time it happened, was attacked a few days ago. I'm investigating the possibility the two incidents were linked."

"I didn't know that." Andy's complexion had gone a shade paler.

"Why would you?" Suspicion tickled the back of Brayden's neck.

"Andy here can't tell us anything. In fact, his sudden inability to see or hear this morning is quite shocking." The dry sarcasm in Jay's tone wasn't lost on Brayden. "He was doing some paperwork in his office and was concentrating so hard it seems we could have driven our fire truck through the room and he wouldn't have noticed. Fortunately, it looks like we have footage of our guy taken from the security cameras on the electronics store across the street."

"You do?" Andy's voice was a faint squeak.

"I hate to be the one to tell you this, Andy, but that's good news." Brayden turned back to Jay. "Can I see this footage?" Andy appeared to be hiding something and he would deal with him after he had viewed the film.

"Sure. We'll need to take it away with us when we finish up here, but you can look at it now. If you think the guy is your suspect, I'll get a copy made for you."

Before Brayden could follow Jay, Andy reached into his back pocket and held something out to him. "This belongs to Esmée." It was her cell phone. "She left it downstairs in the kitchen."

Brayden took the phone from him. He stared at the display for a moment or two before slipping it into his own pocket. "Don't go away." Andy nodded miserably.

Red Ridge Electronics had been subjected to a series of break-ins about twelve months earlier and, on police advice, the owner had installed a new security system around that time. Jay explained that it was only by a lucky chance that one of the cameras had filmed the suspect crossing the street and walking into the yard of the liquor store.

"That camera should be filming the sidewalk in front of the electronics store. Fortunately for us, it's been set at the wrong angle." Jay led Brayden through the store to a small office at the back. "The owner only realized something was wrong when I asked if I could check to see if they had any footage from this morning."

He switched on a monitor and used the timer on the machine beneath it to find the point he wanted on the tape. Although the images were black and white, they were of a good quality. Brayden watched as a man approached the liquor store. He was dressed in dark clothing and the hood of his sweatshirt was pulled up to hide his face. In his hand, he carried something that looked like a large brown paper bag. With a quick glance all around, he entered the delivery yard of the store. A few minutes later, he came out again. When he did, he was no longer carrying anything.

"It's impossible to see his face," Jay said. "But his size should make him easy to track down. He could be a heavyweight boxer."

Brayden remembered the sledgehammer fist to the side of his head. "It's a possibility." He was lucky he'd gotten back up again after that punch when he'd encountered the shooter up on the ridge.

"You think this is your guy?"

"I'm sure of it." He looked at the time label on the bottom of the screen. "Can you rewind this to fifteen minutes before our guy approaches the liquor store?"

Jay did as he asked. The video started with a view of the empty street. Then, in a corner of the screen, he saw the front of a car pull up and stop. After a moment or two, Esmée came into the shot. Walking with her usual brisk, hip-swaying, hair-swinging stride, she went into Andy's store.

"There!" He pointed to a movement at the top of the screen. Right by Esmée's car, just for a second or two, the bulky, hooded figure came into view. The same man who had gone into the rear yard of the store—the *shooter*, there was no doubt in Brayden's mind—had been watching Esmée when she first arrived.

Jay whistled. "You think he was following her?"

"Looks that way." *I know someone who might be able to tell me more.* "Thanks, Jay. A copy of the recording will be a real help. In return, I'll send you a transcript of the conversation I'm about to have with Andy."

When he returned to the liquor store, Andy was sitting on the back step. He looked up nervously as Brayden approached.

Reaching into his back pocket, Brayden drew out Esmée's cell phone and held it up. "Tell me about this."

"I already did. Esmée left it downstairs in the kitchen."

"You told Jay you were in your office. Where is that in relation to the kitchen?"

Andy appeared confused by this line of questioning. "Right next to it. The kitchen is really a part of the office. It's just separated by a curtain. Why?"

Brayden held up Esmée's cell to show him the display. He was doing his best to keep his anger under control. "There are three missed calls on this cell phone, all of them made between the time Esmée arrived at your store and the time you called 911 to report the fire."

"I don't understand."

"Let me spell it out for you. Esmée left this cell phone in your kitchen. The kitchen that is right next to the office where you were working. I think this cell phone gave you a real problem because, even though you heard it ringing, you couldn't take it upstairs to Esmée, could you, Andy?"

"I didn't hear it." Andy scuffed the ground with the toes of his sneaker. "It could be on silent."

Brayden gave him a humorless smile. "Shall we find out?" He took out his own cell. When he called Esmée's number, her own phone immediately started up its loud, pop-music ringtone.

"Okay, okay." Andy held up his hands. "I heard it ringing. I didn't want to take it upstairs and disturb her. She said she'd be busy sorting through Jack's stuff…"

Brayden leaned closer. "We both know that's not the real reason you didn't go upstairs. You couldn't go up there because you knew what was about to happen. Someone was going to torch that apartment…and you were in on it."

"I wasn't! I swear—"

"Save the swearing for the judge, Andy. This is attempted murder."

"No." Andy's shoulders slumped. "When he came to me with the plan, I made him promise me she'd be okay. He said she'd be able to get out in time." He raised pleading eyes to Brayden's face. "And she did, didn't she?"

"What was the deal, Andy? You take the insurance payout while your friend got to scare Esmée?" Brayden was having a hard time keeping his anger in check. The desire to haul Andy up from the step by the front of his sweatshirt was growing stronger by the second.

Andy nodded, seeming pleased Brayden understood. "Business hasn't been good lately. I can't compete with the big stores and their two-for-one offers. When this guy came along it seemed like a good way out."

"Even though it meant putting an innocent woman's life in danger?"

"I told you…he swore to me it was just to scare her. He wanted to get her to leave town." Andy's voice was deteriorating into a high-pitched whine.

"Okay. Two questions. Who is he and why does he want Esmée to leave Red Ridge?"

"I don't know."

"You seriously expect me to believe that, Andy? A complete stranger strolled in off the street one day, offered to torch your store and you said okay?" The last thread of Brayden's patience was about to snap.

"It wasn't like that." Andy heaved a sigh. "Even though I never knew his name, I'd been introduced to this guy by a mutual acquaintance who knew I wanted to find a way to get at my insurance money. We already had a plan in place for him to burn down the store. I was going to give them both a cut once I got the cash from the insurers. It was only when he called me a few minutes before it happened that I knew it was going down today. That was the first time I knew what he was planning for Esmée."

At last, Brayden felt like he was getting somewhere. "What's the name of the mutual acquaintance who introduced you?"

"Richie Lyman."

"Let me get this straight," Brayden said. "You were introduced to this guy by Richie?" Andy nodded. "So that would have been at least four weeks ago, because Richie has been missing for that length of time?"

"That sounds about right."

The time frame sounded right, but nothing else about it did. Brayden's mind was working overtime as he figured out what had happened.

"But at that time, Jack Parkowski was living in the apartment above your store." Brayden observed Andy's expression becoming increasingly miserable. "You must have mentioned that during your discussions about torching the place, otherwise you risked killing the guy who was living there." Andy swallowed hard. *Bingo.* "Or was that the point? Did this start out as a plan between Richie and his pal to kill Jack? It wasn't acted on because Jack was murdered by the Groom Killer—or at least, the MO was the same—but, when Esmée arrived in town, your new pal's focus changed. He told you to look out for her."

Brayden was making connections about what had happened and he knew from the look on Andy's face that he was right. But he still didn't know why the mystery guy who had wanted Jack dead had now switched his attention to Esmée.

"If she turned up here, he wanted to know. Everything was in place for the arson attack, he could be ready to go at a few minutes notice. And, guess what? She gave you a call to say she would be dropping by this morning… Am I getting close to the truth here?"

"I don't want to say any more." Andy folded his arms across his chest.

"I think you and I need to head down to the station now so we can talk about this some more." Brayden waited while Andy got to his feet, his anger colder now but still as dangerous. "Just so we're clear—you are under arrest."

# Chapter 11

"How does news travel so fast in this town?" Esmée accepted a cup of Sarah's soothing mint tea and sank gratefully onto a comfortable sofa.

"It's the Red Ridge effect," Hester said, pulling a footstool over and lifting Esmée's feet onto it. "Plus, I have a friend who works in the shoe store on Main Street. She called me to tell me about it. There's talk of Brayden being given some sort of civic award for saving you from the fire."

Esmée covered her eyes with one hand. "I can't imagine anything he would hate more."

"Are you really okay?" Sarah's kindly eyes searched her face. "It must have been such a shock."

"I was shaken up, but I'm fine now." Esmée lowered her hand and reached out to touch Sarah's knee. "There isn't anything left of Jack's belongings."

"Those are just things." Sarah clasped her fingers briefly, a shadow flitting across her features. "If there's one thing I've learned just lately, it's that people are what matters."

Esmée looked across at where Rhys was sprawled on the floor drawing pictures on a giant sheet of paper. His artistic efforts were constantly interrupted by kittens as they tumbled out of their basket and walked across his masterpiece. Patiently, Rhys picked them up and returned them to Bellacat, who was reclining gracefully on a pile of cushions. Sometimes, he kissed the kittens on their tiny, pink noses. Often, he paused to stroke them. Now and then, he talked to them about what he was doing. Esmée wondered how it was possible to love him so much it actually hurt.

"You're right," she said to Sarah. "A day like today is a reminder about the important things. It looks like Rhys has been having fun."

"He's the sweetest child ever. And he's been telling us all about Bray and Ko." Hester clasped her hands beneath her chin. "It's like they're his *family*."

"Put away that matchmaking face right now, Hester Mull." Esmée studied her friend over the rim of her cup. "You've got it all wrong if that's what you're thinking about me and Brayden. I don't want any rumors that could put Brayden in danger, especially for something that isn't even true."

"Well, if it *was* true, he'd probably be the only bridegroom in town who would be safe. Him and Shane," Hester reflected. "Demi wouldn't come after her own brothers, would she?"

Esmée choked back a laugh. "Possibly not, but since we don't know for sure that Demi is guilty— and there is nothing going on between Brayden and me anyway—we're straying into the realm of fantasy. Why don't you fill me in on the Red Ridge gossip?" Hester's encyclopedic knowledge of the town's personalities might prove useful in her quest for information.

"I'm not sure there's much to tell." Hester gave a discontented sigh. "There have been no new sightings of Demi and nothing new to report on the case. The biggest news right now is the behavior of Valeria Colton and Vincent Gage. They are driving their families crazy with their refusal to listen to reason."

"Why?" Esmée sat back and sipped her drink, allowing the drama of the morning's events to recede in this cozy setting.

"They are nineteen years old…" Hester paused to let that information sink in. "They wanted to get married on Christmas Eve, which happens to be both their birthdays. The Coltons and Gages went wild when they heard the news, but Valeria and Vincent were determined. Then, all of a sudden, it was all off. Valeria publicly dumped Vincent. Except it looks like that was all for show because they've been seen around town together kissing and canoodling."

"Dangerous move," Esmée observed.

Sarah shook her head. "Exactly. They are little more than children. It's no wonder their parents are concerned. If the Groom Killer thinks they are still in love, Vincent could be the next victim."

"Oh, that's not all." Hester was clearly enjoying herself. "Apparently, the two lovebirds have announced that if the stories are true and Demi really is pregnant, they are prepared to bring up her baby if she goes to prison." She sat back in her seat. "What do you think of that?"

Esmée wondered why the story of Vincent and Valeria had brought a sudden lump to her throat. Sarah was right. They were just kids, so it was foolish to think of them as brave. It was more likely they were misguided. But somehow the thought of them falling in love and standing firm against parental opposition—even being prepared to face the ruthless murderer stalking their town—made her feel her own life was missing something. She shrugged the feeling aside. She was twenty-seven, not nineteen. She'd tried romance. It had gotten her a split lip and a black eye.

"I think they need to be careful." She put down her empty cup. "And they should try caring for a baby for a day or two before they make any rash promises."

Before Hester could reply, Sarah suddenly sat up straighter. "Esmée, remember what I said? Jack brought some of his things here when he was preparing to move in. I wonder if his notebooks might be among them?"

"We can always hope," Esmée said. "Can I take a look?"

Sarah led her outside to the garage while Hester watched Rhys. After she had unlocked the garage, Sarah took hold of Esmée's hand. "You will be careful, won't you? We haven't known each other very long, but I couldn't bear to lose you as well. And Rhys needs his mommy."

"I've already promised Brayden I won't take any chances. And I won't," Esmée said. "This is the first time my job has ever felt dangerous. I'm not an adrenaline junkie. Being frightened isn't a feeling I enjoy."

Sarah seemed content with that answer. Jack's boxes were stacked neatly at the rear of the garage. "Do you mind if I leave you to look through them alone? I don't think I'm ready to, you know…"

"Of course. I'll come back inside when I'm done here."

Esmée watched as she walked away, sadness tugging at her. Sarah and Jack would have been so perfect together. Her feelings were stretched tight today. Possibly it was the shock of the fire, but she felt like it went deeper. It was as if, just lately, she was walking an emotional tightrope and she didn't understand why. Temperamentally, she was usually steady as a rock. Since her arrival in Red Ridge she had been shaken out of her calm. She supposed that could be down to everything that had happened lately. Jack had been killed. She had been shot at. Rhys had been in danger up on the ridge. Just a few hours ago, she had been in a fire that was started deliberately.

Yet good things had happened here as well. Despite the threats and the feuds, she felt comfortable in Red Ridge. For a long time, Jack had been Esmée's only real friend. Although the pain of his loss would always be with her, she had made other friends here. She already felt close to Sarah and Hester. But if she was being honest with herself, the person who had become most important to her, and in a dizzyingly short space of time, was Brayden.

Just thinking about him brought an unexpected glow of warmth. Did he feel the same way when he thought of her? The question made her smile. Why would he be thinking of her except as part of the case on which he was working? That could hardly be expected to provoke pleasant feelings. Nevertheless, it seemed impossible that she felt such a strong pull between them while Brayden remained oblivious to it. All she knew was, when she was with him, she felt at home, as though she had known him all her life. When she tried to recall their conversations, the details often eluded her. Even so, they could comfortably talk for hours on any subject.

*It's called friendship.*

Even as she told herself that, she lifted her fingertips to her mouth. It must be her imagination. Her lips couldn't still be tingling from that half kiss. And it had been a *joke*. One she herself had initiated. Brayden had probably forgotten all about it by now. No matter how much she wished he hadn't.

She should forget it as well and get to work. It was with no real expectation of finding anything that she opened the first of five boxes. It soon became clear that Jack had moved his important belongings first. The boxes were filled with photographs, books and family mementos, including an old pocket watch, a locket containing a lock of hair and a bundle of yellowing letters tied with a faded red ribbon. And there, in the final box, she discovered Jack's notebooks, each one filled with his familiar, tight, neat writing. She hugged one to her chest briefly before going back into the house to let Sarah know what she had found. Perhaps Jack had come to her aid one last time.

Brayden arrived home that evening to find the kitchen filled with the delicious aroma of cooking. For some curious reason, the table and chairs were covered by a bedsheet. As he studied this new development with bemusement, Esmée called out to him. "We're under the table."

A few seconds later, Rhys popped his head out from under the sheet. "Bray. In the cave." It was the voice of authority.

Brayden shrugged. Getting under his kitchen table hadn't been uppermost in his mind when he'd pictured how he'd spend his evening, but he was becoming more flexible these days. And there was a first time for everything.

"Hi." It was a bit cramped, so he copied Esmée and tucked his knees up under his chin. He could guess what was coming next. Clicking his fingers, he invited Echo to join them. The dog didn't appear to find anything strange in the arrangement and wagged his tail while Brayden removed his vest. "Uh, do we have to do anything while we're here?"

Esmée gave him a look of mock pity. "Don't you know how play caves work?"

"Clearly my childhood was missing some of the essentials. I know nothing of the cave code of conduct." His neck was bent at an awkward angle. "Will we be in here for long?"

"Only until Rhys gets bored or hungry." She shuffled closer to him so they could talk while Rhys stroked Echo. "I found Jack's notebooks in Sarah's garage. I'll start going through them tonight when

Rhys is in bed. Did you get any information from Andy?"

Just the thought of Andy Coulson fired Brayden's temper all over again. He got it under control while he told Esmée what he'd discovered about Andy's connection to the shooter, Richie Lyman and their attempt to kill Jack.

"The plan was all in place, they just switched targets. Instead of Jack, they had you."

"I don't get it." She had been listening to his explanation with an expression of growing confusion. "Even if he wanted to kill Jack, how can I be this guy's new target? I don't *know* anything. And I've never met Richie Lyman."

"I don't understand it, either, but there's no question about what Andy told me, or about what I saw on the security-camera footage. The shooter arrived at Andy's store at the same time as you because he knew you would be there."

She shook her head. "It's just so hard to believe. Where is Andy now?"

"In a cell. And he's mighty glad to be there," Brayden said. "He realizes his new friend might not be very happy with him, but he's indicated that he's willing to talk in exchange for police protection. Andy's less scared of the cops than he is of the guy who set fire to his store."

"I still can't get this clear in my mind. I was so sure my encounter with the shooter on the ridge was random. I thought he shot at me because I'd found his knife." Esmée shook her head. "You don't think he's threatening me now because I saw his face?"

"That would only make sense if you could link him to something. If you'd witnessed him committing a crime, or you'd heard his description in relation to a suspicious activity. And don't forget that I saw his face as well," Brayden reminded her. "No, there's only one thing I'm sure of."

"What's that?"

"This has to be the craziest place in which I have ever tried to have a conversation."

Esmée laughed. "You have to admit it—there is something to be said for doing the serious stuff in a ridiculous situation. It takes the sting away."

She bumped her shoulder companionably against his and he felt the action shoot along his nerve endings like static electricity. Ever since that not-quite-a-kiss outside Good Eats earlier in the day his senses had been on high alert, with part of his mind fixed on Esmée. Now the switch was dramatic. Every part of him was hyperaware of her. It wasn't only because of her physical proximity. It was as if they were connected by an invisible thread that was getting pulled tighter by the second. Even when she moved away from him, that connection was already so strong Brayden was helpless to fight its lure.

"How about dinner?" Esmée's voice wasn't quite steady as she crawled out from under the sheet.

"Dinner." Rhys clapped his hands in agreement.

Brayden dismantled the cave. "It smells delicious. What is it?"

"My dad was from Ecuador." Esmée was busy taking plates out of cupboards and a large pot out of the oven. "He died when I was seven, so I don't really remember him, but this beef stew was one of his favorite dishes."

This was other people's normality. Setting the table for dinner. Chasing the two-year-old when he ran away with the dog's bowl. Stopping that same dog from stealing the bread from the table. Talking about everyday things while eating. Saving the conversation about how to deal with the scary guy who was targeting Esmée for later.

"Hester has a theory, but I'm not sure you'll like it." There was a roguish smile in Esmée's eyes. "If you follow her line of thinking, you should get married simply because you are the only person in Red Ridge who will be safe from the Groom Killer."

Brayden stared at her. "She said that?"

"Not in so many words, but that was the direction she was taking. Just think about it, Brayden. You could help out the town's ailing economy by giving the wedding business a boost." Esmée laughed at his thunderstruck expression. "Haven't you ever been tempted to try married life?"

"I considered it once and decided it wasn't for

me." He reached across the table and helped himself to bread. "How did Sarah seem today?"

Although she answered his question, he was aware of her gaze lingering on his face as she spoke. Esmée was just a little too perceptive for his liking. He supposed it was what made her good at her job. It also meant she had the ability to recognize a change in conversation for what it really was. An emotional-avoidance tactic. By mentioning it at all he had already said too much. He hoped she wouldn't ask him any more about it. He was an expert at shutting people out, but he didn't want to do that with Esmée.

"Who wants ice cream?" The suggestion received an enthusiastic response from Rhys.

Esmée rose and went to fetch dessert. The moment was lost, but for the first time ever, Brayden regretted his inability to open up and talk about his feelings. It was a tiny shift in his psyche, but was a huge change in his life. In that moment, he didn't know what he was feeling. He was definitely confused. Probably scared. At the same time, there was a ton of excitement buzzing around in his veins.

When Esmée turned and smiled at him, he recognized his chief emotion. It had taken him so long to acknowledge it because it came his way so rarely. No matter what craziness was going on around them, he was happy. That was what Esmée did to him. If he had to stop overthinking and pick a feeling, then happiness was the one he would go with.

* * *

"I thought bathing dogs was hard work." Brayden pulled the front of his wet shirt away from his body with a grimace. "How can one small boy splash so much?"

"You encourage him." Esmée gave him a stern look. "It's a conspiracy in which Mommy ends up being the bad guy for actually trying to wash him."

He grinned. "Sorry. He was just enjoying the submarine game so much."

She placed her hands on her hips, keeping up the stern pose. "Well, you get the job of cleaning up the mess in the bathroom while I put the submariner to bed."

"No." Rhys managed a protest even though he was smothering a yawn. "Want Mommy and Bray." The words were followed by the inevitable. "And Ko."

"Let's all put him to bed, then I'll clean up in the bathroom." Brayden wrapped Rhys in a towel and hoisted him into his arms. The little boy settled his head onto his shoulder.

As Esmée watched them, her throat tightened with something close to tears. That was what her son should always have had. A big, strong man who played games with him, but who lifted him up when he needed support. Although she carried a lot of guilt inside her for what Rhys had seen in Wales, she knew she'd always done her best for him. She'd been his mom and dad, and she'd played both roles well. Being a single mother was hard, but she would always make sure he never missed having two parents. Seeing him with Brayden hurt simply because it reminded her of the hopes and dreams that had never come to fruition.

Rhys was asleep almost as soon as his head touched the pillow. While Brayden set to work restoring the bathroom to respectability, Esmée went to her car and took Jack's notebooks out of the trunk. Sitting on the floor in the family room, she sorted through them until she had them in order by date.

When Brayden came into the room wearing a clean T-shirt and carrying two cups of coffee, she was already engrossed. She glanced up from her task. "Jack kept meticulous records and searching through them for any mention of Richie Lyman is going to be a long job."

"Why don't I help?" He sat next to her, stretching his long legs out on front of him.

"Okay. I started with Jack's earliest cases. If you take the ones from the end of his career we can meet in the middle."

"Sounds like a plan."

They read in companionable silence, the only sounds Echo's heavy breathing and the wind rustling the trees outside. After about an hour, Brayden discarded his second book. "I haven't found any mention of Richie, but I am developing a healthy respect for Jack's ability to take down facts. Some of this would make good material for a book."

Esmée looked up from the ten-year-old notes she was reading. "It's one of the reasons he and my mom worked so well together. When it came to research, she wouldn't trust anyone else with the fine details. Except me, of course. Between them, they taught me everything I know."

"Why did you decide to switch from working for an online news company to working for yourself?" Brayden asked.

"I wanted the freedom to cover the stories my way." Esmée placed the notebook she had been reading facedown on the rug. "I didn't like the way we were encouraged to go for the sensational approach. We were dealing with people's lives and I prefer to do that with sensitivity."

"You are not what I expected." His gaze was intense.

"I never am. People think I'm going to come along and thrust a camera in their face at a funeral, or bug their phones." Esmée stretched her arms above her head, conscious of the way the movement drew Brayden's eyes to her body. She liked the way he watched her. As if he couldn't get enough of looking at her. "*What Remains* was a chance to do it my way, to tell the story of what is left after the police and forensics teams have gone. What happens to a community after the court case is over and the press interest has died down, but the families and friends of the victims and the killer have to pick up the pieces and rebuild their lives."

"I'm not sure Red Ridge can be rebuilt." Brayden's voice was thoughtful. "A town needs a strong foundation to support it after something like this. Too many divisions mean this is a community that is unlikely to come together after the Groom Killer murders are solved."

"Don't be so sure. There are a lot of good people in Red Ridge." She smiled. "People like you."

He looked surprised. "You hardly know me."

"I know everything I need to. I know you have a big heart even though you try to hide it. I know you have a schoolboy sense of humor." Before he could protest, she grinned. "Yeah, just like mine. I know you would do anything to help someone in trouble, even if that person was a stranger. And I know you don't like yourself very much...even though I can't understand why."

He was silent for a moment or two, studying a frayed patch on the seam of his jeans. "I don't recognize that hero you just described." His voice was gruff.

"I told you why relationships weren't for me. Maybe it's your turn now." She ducked her head to look at his face. "I'm a good listener, Brayden."

When he remained silent, she thought he was angry at the suggestion he might want to confide in her. Deciding to let the matter lie, she reached for her notebook again, but Brayden's hand snaked out and closed over her wrist.

"You want to hear it? The whole sorry story?"

"Only if you want to tell me."

He leaned back, rested his head against the sofa and looked up at the ceiling. "I was twenty-one. She was thirty. Her name was Ava and she was from out of town. I couldn't believe this beautiful, sophisticated woman was interested in me. Turns out, she wasn't. Ava was a gold digger. She thought I was from the wealthy side of the Colton family and didn't bother to check any further. We'd been dating a few months when she told me she was pregnant." He gave a mirthless laugh. "I should have known a woman like Ava wouldn't leave anything to chance, but like a fool, I fell for it. I went out, bought the best ring I could find on my rookie cop's salary. Then I took her to meet my dad."

Although the words were lighthearted, Esmée could hear the pain in his voice. She could see the tension in the tightly clenched fist that rested on his thigh. She wanted to close the distance between them and hold him, to soothe away eight years of hurt inflicted by a cold, callous woman who had ruthlessly destroyed a young man's dreams.

"When she met Rusty, Ava realized the truth. She couldn't get out of Red Ridge fast enough. Even then, I hadn't figured it out. I thought it was something I'd done, or said. I tracked her down to a motel just outside Sioux Falls." He closed his eyes briefly. "That confrontation wasn't my finest hour. I pleaded with her to stay with me for the sake of the baby. She laughed in my face as she told me there never had been a baby. As I walked away feeling like my whole world had come to an end, she shouted after me that the only reason she'd been with me was because she'd made a mistake." He turned his head to look at Esmée, his eyes dark with hurt. "There it is. My only attempt at romance and I was on the receiving end of a mistake."

Esmée didn't stop to think. She moved closer to him. Taking his face in her hands, she kissed him. For a moment or two, Brayden appeared stunned. Then his hands came up to grasp her waist and he returned the kiss. It was long, hard and very thorough.

When Esmée raised her head, the bitter look had gone and he was smiling. "More cake crumbs?" She shook her head. "Tell me it wasn't pity?"

In response, she kissed him again. This time, the kiss was hotter, passion flaring and spiraling higher. Brayden probed her mouth, caressing and licking until she moaned softly. He growled when she sucked his tongue, taking him deeper, showing him how much she wanted him. This time, when she raised her head, they were both breathing hard. "Did that feel like pity?"

"No." His voice was husky. "But it felt like something we should talk about."

Esmée shook her head. "No talking. No thinking. We don't have to analyze it. Neither of us wants a relationship. We both know where this is leading. Let's allow it to take us there. Let's just enjoy *this*."

"You're sure?" When she nodded, he stood. Reaching out a hand, he drew her to her feet. "Then I think we should let it take us to the bedroom."

## Chapter 12

Even though he had never been so aroused, Brayden was conscious of the need to get this right. Esmée had said neither of them wanted a relationship, but they were already important to each other. It might not be a romance, it might not be forever, but it mattered. The friendship that had developed between them so rapidly meant this wasn't a one-night stand. They couldn't walk away with a shrug of their shoulders.

*And I don't want that.*

As he lay on the bed, turning on his side to face her, he wasn't sure what the thought meant. He only knew there was no going back from this breathtaking moment. Sliding a hand down Esmée's back, he pulled her gently against him.

"Holding you like this is heaven."

She pressed her lips to the hollow of his throat. "I haven't done this for a very long time…not since before Rhys was born."

"Anytime you want to slow down, tell me. Or stop. We can stop if you need to."

She gave a throaty chuckle. "What if I want to go faster?"

"I'm good with that." He raised his head to look at her. "Just tell me what you want, Esmée."

"You." There was no trace of laughter in her expression now. "I want you, Brayden. I'm aching for you."

Her words made his breath catch in his throat. "Can I touch you?"

She leaned back, creating a slight gap between them. Taking his hand, she guided it over the soft, warm flesh of her stomach and inside the waistband of her jeans. The tight material made it impossible for him to move his fingertips any farther. Keeping his eyes on hers, Brayden reached for the fastening on her jeans with his other hand. He held his breath, hoping nervousness and clumsiness wouldn't ruin the moment. Although his fingers were trembling slightly, he managed to undo Esmée's button and zipper and separate the two halves of material.

He snatched a breath as his fingertips moved inside her underwear and brushed silken curls. His erection pulsed hard, demanding release, and his heart hammered a wild beat. As he ignored the needs of his own body, Esmée caught hold of his wrist, moving his hand lower until he encountered velvet heat.

"Yes. Right there."

He used one finger to spread her wider, probing down and deep. Esmée jerked her hips upward, grinding against his touch, her whole body shuddering. Holding her tight to him, he slowly stroked her, finding her small, firm bud deliciously slick under his touch. She whimpered and arched her back as he circled it before returning to trace the length of her slit.

Esmée's eyes were glazed as he outlined her nipples through her T-shirt and bra with his other hand. "Oh, Brayden, I can't..."

Her voice faded as he crooked the tip of his finger into her entrance. Lifting her hips, she attempted to draw him deeper into her. Her breathing was ragged as moans left her lips in a constant soft murmur. From the way her stomach muscles fluttered and her legs jerked against his, Brayden could tell she was close. He was right.

Abruptly, Esmée stopped breathing. Her whole body convulsed, then she gave a cry as her inner muscles tightened around him. Brayden pulled her into a tight embrace, slowing the teasing movement of his fingers as he stroked along her spine, taking her through each wild aftershock, until she gave a final sigh and rested her head on his chest.

"That was so good," she whispered. "So amazing. I have been dreaming of your touch for days."

He brushed his lips over her forehead, and she made a quiet murmuring noise as she burrowed in closer to him.

"I'm a little out of practice." He whispered the words against the shell of her ear.

"If that was out of practice, I can't wait for what happens next."

He was still, listening to her breathing and remembering the tight heat of her body. Not rushing things. He was achingly hard, and he drew in a shuddering breath as Esmée reached down to stroke him through the cloth of his jeans. His erection twitched and he heard her inhale sharply as she felt the movement.

"Do you know what I want to happen next, Brayden?" Her voice was soft and tempting. "I want all of you. Right now."

She lifted her leg over his, her thigh pressing into his arousal, warm and hard. The temptation to grind himself into her through their clothing was exquisite torture. Instead, Brayden stared into her glittering, dark eyes as she shifted position until she was straddling him. Gripping the hem of her T-shirt, she lifted it up and over her head. Her bra followed, and Brayden gave a groan as he reached to cup her breasts, marveling at her firm, smooth flesh.

"Need to lose the rest of the clothes." He was having trouble speaking.

Esmée shifted back to his side and finesse was forgotten as they removed their remaining garments. "Protection?" The word was a gasp and he was glad he wasn't the only one whose ability to talk appeared to have been affected.

Brayden reached into the drawer of the locker at the side of his bed and found the box of condoms. He'd never brought a woman back to his house, had never planned to do so. He replaced the box when the expiration date was up, taking one out to keep in his wallet. Now and then, he'd considered not bothering. Then he remembered Ava's laughter and the baby that had never been. His encounters since then had been few and brief, but he'd always been prepared. Right now, he was thankful for his own foresight.

Esmée laid back, watching him as he sheathed himself. Her eyes on his body took his arousal to new heights. When he moved into position over her, she wound her arms around his neck, drawing his mouth down to hers in a long, slow kiss. Brayden's control shattered as he claimed her mouth. His fingers dug hard into her ribs, holding her as if he would never let her go. He kissed her like he owned her, as if he was branding that truth into them both forever, not caring if his body was giving a different message to the words they'd spoken earlier. Esmée moaned as she parted her lips, and he slid his tongue into her mouth, relishing the taste of her.

Moving his hand between them, Brayden slid his fingers along her folds, parting her and savoring her heat as he pressed against her.

Esmée whimpered against his lips. "Now, please."

He moved his hands down her smooth thighs and over her hips to her buttocks, lifting her to him as he pushed into her. And it was the sweetest heaven.

"Esmée…" He pressed his forehead to hers, his whole body shaking with emotion. "You feel amazing."

He could see his own wonder reflected back at him in her eyes. Even though every inch of their bodies was touching—even though he was *inside her*—this enchantment he was feeling wasn't just physical. This was about their unique chemistry. For the first time, he truly understood what sex was about. It was an affirmation. It was about showing Esmée, with his body, the meaning of their connection. It was the ultimate expression of what she meant to him. And what she meant to him was…

"Can't wait." Esmée started to move as she spoke, cleaving tighter to him and rocking her pelvis against his. Those tiny incremental motions triggered a fire in Brayden's bloodstream. Her smooth skin, her soft lips, her hard nipples, the tight, welcoming heat of her body… Rational thought deserted him as he drove into her, deep and hard.

Esmée hissed out a breath, her nails tracing the muscles of his back. "Yes. Like that."

Brayden knew he couldn't last long. "Too perfect."

His groans mingled with Esmée's sighs. She lifted her hips in time with his rhythm as he pulled out and slammed into her again, grinding, pushing back against him, driving onward. Esmée reached up a hand, tangling it in his hair and pulling him down so she could kiss him. Brayden felt her start to tremble beneath him.

His own release hit as she was thrashing wildly and calling out his name. His stomach muscles clenched and his vision faded. Ecstasy took hold of him, flinging him into the abyss and locking him into wave after wave of pure, white heat. Aftershocks kept him shuddering as Esmée clung to him.

Eventually, he slumped forward, taking his weight on his elbows as, breathing hard, he kissed up her neck and across her jawline. She murmured softly in response, a wordless, appreciative sound that acted like a soothing balm.

Reluctant to end the sweet moment of intimacy, but wanting to hold her, Brayden eased onto his side and drew her into his arms. Esmée nestled into him. "Seems like we both had a lot to get out of our systems," she said.

He snorted. "You think that was a release of frustration?"

She tilted her head up to look at him. "No. I think it was about us, about something special we created. How about you?"

"It wasn't what I imagined."

She looked disappointed. "No?"

"My imagination isn't that good." He pulled her tight against him. "It was better than anything I could have dreamed. Take my wildest fantasy and multiply it by a thousand."

Her smile was wicked as she kissed along his collarbone. "Next time we should try for a bigger number."

Esmée couldn't sleep. The room was almost completely dark and Brayden's soft, rhythmic breathing was the only sound. Her body was relaxed. She smiled to herself at the thought. *Relaxed?* She felt weightless. As though euphoria had seeped through her pores and into her bones.

Her mind was equally soothed. Like a pond on a sunny day, it was ripple-free, taking her back to a time before she knew what stress felt like.

*So why can't I sleep?*

A tiny voice—that 4:00 a.m. voice—at the back of her mind was insistently trying to tell her the reason and she was doing her best to ignore it. The voice won and she gave a sigh as she allowed it to be heard.

*It was like Brayden had said. It was too perfect.*

She turned her head. Although she could barely see Brayden in the darkness, she could make out his outline. He was lying on his side, facing her. It didn't matter that he wasn't touching her. From now on, she would always feel like he was touching her. There could be no going back from what they had shared.

Esmée had been the one to suggest they should give in to the physical attraction between them. They had been stepping around it ever since they'd first met and the heat had been building and growing until it had threatened to consume them. And it *had* consumed them. Only not in the way they'd expected.

Sex hadn't extinguished their fire. Instead, it had become an inferno, blazing out of control. But it was no longer just physical…and they had both recognized the change. She knew Brayden had acknowledged it to himself as well, even though they hadn't talked about it. *We had other things on our minds.*

She just didn't know what to do with all these new feelings. Maybe she felt this way about Brayden because he was the opposite of Gwyn? Because he was strong, protective and considerate? Especially now, when she was in danger, those traits made him particularly appealing. When she was wrapped in his strong arms, she could pretend there wasn't a man built like a block of granite who had made two attempts on her life.

Even as the thought occurred to her, she dismissed

it. Of course, she found Brayden's strength and ability to care for her and Rhys attractive. She was also drawn to his gorgeous eyes and his smile, but they didn't define him. Nor had amazing sex somehow magically transformed her opinion. It had only confirmed it. She was captivated by everything about him. From the first moment of meeting him, she had seen beneath the taciturn exterior to the warm heart beneath.

*I'm in trouble and getting in deeper by the minute.* If that was the case, why was she moving closer so she could share his warmth and breathe in his delicious, masculine scent? As she did, Brayden murmured something unintelligible. Esmée decided she may as well put her restlessness to good use instead of waking him. Sliding carefully from the bed, she fumbled in the dark for something to wear. Finding Brayden's discarded T-shirt, she pulled it on.

In the kitchen, she snagged a bottle of water from the fridge and took it through to the family room. Switching on a lamp, she curled into a corner of the sofa and picked up the notebook she had been reading earlier in the evening. Within minutes she was back in Jack's world. Ten years ago, he had been investigating a daring armed robbery from a safe-deposit-box facility.

The case appeared to be something of a personal crusade for Jack. He had clearly gone back over time and updated his original record whenever he received new information. His notes included a scathing criticism of the press coverage of the case. Jack seemed to feel that journalists made the criminals appear classy and clever while ignoring the fact that a security guard was killed during the raid. No one was ever convicted for the guard's murder. Items stolen from safe-deposit boxes included gold, jewels and precious stones, along with a collection of rare blue diamonds. Although some items had been recovered, the diamonds had disappeared without a trace.

Although Jack was convinced he knew who the getaway driver was, he had been unable to get the evidence needed for a conviction. The name jumped out at Esmée as she read her friend's account of his attempts to secure an arrest. *Richie Lyman.* No wonder Jack had recognized Richie when he saw him in Red Ridge. And naturally he had warned Sarah about the man he was certain had driven the getaway car for a hardened criminal gang. With all his years of experience, Jack knew better than anyone that, if Richie was mixing with a criminal gang ten years ago, he was unlikely to have fixed his ways and gone straight since then.

Another interesting piece of information caught her eye. Jack had a theory about the name of the man who had killed the security guard. Roper Keene was a thug who was feared even by his fellow gang members. There was speculation that Keene had double-crossed the others and removed the blue diamonds from the heist before the proceeds had been split.

The information that had her reaching for her laptop made her heart beat a little faster. Once again, she said a silent word of thanks to Jack for his meticulous record-keeping. It was just one sentence, but it could make all the difference to their current case.

*Roper Keene, former heavyweight boxer...*

Brayden came awake slowly, aware of a sense of well-being that was like a warm, comforting blanket. The faint light through the thin drapes told him the sun wasn't fully up. The empty pillow next to him told him Esmée was gone.

He sat up, scrubbing a hand across his face to dispel the last traces of sleep. His feeling of happiness disappeared like bubbles popping on the surface in a glass of soda. Why wasn't she here? Was she regretting what had happened? Had he said, or done, something wrong?

He drew a breath, fighting off the demons of self-doubt. When he'd fallen asleep, Esmée had been nestled in his arms. The closeness between them hadn't been his imagination and nothing could have changed while he'd been asleep. What he needed to do now was stop focusing on himself and find out where she was.

For some reason, he couldn't find his T-shirt. Impatiently, he pulled on his boxer-briefs and stepped into the hall. A faint glow from the direction of the family room alerted him to Esmée's whereabouts.

He paused in the doorway for a moment, watching her without announcing his presence. She was seated on the sofa, her bare legs tucked under her and her hair tumbling about her shoulders. Her gaze was fixed on the screen of her laptop as her fingers flew impatiently over the keyboard.

Brayden must have made a sound, because she glanced up, her face breaking into a smile. And that smile undid him. It was as if his heart went on a bungee jump, plummeting wildly toward his feet before swooping up again to lodge in his throat. By the time it had completed its journey, Esmée was on her feet.

"You were sleeping. I didn't want to wake you." Her body was warm and soft against his as she stood on the tips of her toes and wound her arms around his neck.

Any thoughts that she may have changed her mind flew out of his head as he lowered his head and claimed her lips. "Just so we're clear, I will never object to being woken by you."

He made the interesting discovery that she was naked beneath his T-shirt and his hands roamed over the curves of her buttocks. Esmée squirmed with pleasure. "Just hold on to that thought while I show you something."

She led him toward her laptop and Brayden grumbled as she pulled him down onto the sofa next to her. "When you said you were going to show me something…"

Even in the lamplight, he saw the color that tinged her cheeks. "I need you to be serious for a few minutes."

"I was being serious." He encountered a reproachful look and held up his hands. "Okay, I'm listening."

She positioned the laptop so it rested on both of their knees. She had been looking at a boxing site that collated information about fighters and shared it with fans. The page on the screen had statistics about a fighter named Roper Keene. Although he hadn't fought for over twelve years, his record was impressive.

"Keene won every one of his professional fights, most of them through knockouts." Esmée pointed to the information on the screen.

"And this matters because…?"

"I think he stopped fighting when he found a more lucrative occupation." She turned her head to look at him, her eyes sparkling. "I think Roper Keene discovered there was more money to be made from armed robbery."

Brayden draped an arm around her shoulders, leaning closer. "I'm guessing you didn't choose this guy at random?"

She shook her head, the action causing her hair to tickle his cheek. "Keene and Richie Lyman are mentioned in Jack's notes as part of a gang who carried out an armed heist ten years ago."

Brayden sat up a little straighter. "You think Keene could be the shooter?"

"I'm sure of it." Esmée pointed to a small image in the corner of the screen. "This picture doesn't help us at all. It must have been taken around the time Keene started fighting and it's only a head-and-shoulders shot." She opened a new tab. "But this one…"

It was coverage of the buildup to one of Keene's last fights. A picture beneath the headline showed the boxer getting out of a car and posing for the cameras as he dwarfed the people around him. Brayden sucked in a breath. Although the image was twelve years old, there was no mistaking the shaved head, the broken nose, the width of those shoulders or the fists the size of hams.

"This robbery took place when Jack was in the Chicago PD. After I saw Richie's name in Jack's notes, I checked it out on the internet." Esmée had obviously memorized every detail of what she'd read. "It was a break-in at a safe-deposit facility."

"I've heard about that case." Brayden frowned in an effort to remember. "It was huge, and the press reported it as if the gang were celebrities instead of vicious thugs."

Esmée nodded. "They burst into the building and overpowered the security guards, beating them all badly and pouring gas over them to make them give up the combination numbers. One of the guards was killed. The robbers got away with millions in gold bars, jewelry and precious stones. No one was ever caught."

"What made Jack suspect Richie and Keene?"

"Jack knew Richie when he was a juvenile. In his notes, he detailed how Richie graduated from petty crime to bigger things. He had gotten in with the gang who were suspected of organizing this robbery. Jack had an informant who told him pretty much all he needed to know about the heist, including the information that Richie was the getaway driver. But, no matter how hard he tried, Jack couldn't pin anything on any of the guys involved. Richie and Keene had been seen hanging around together in the days prior to the break-in and Keene's description matched that of the guy who killed the security guard." Her mouth turned down as she outlined the details of the murder. "Even though the robbers were armed, he didn't use a gun. He killed the guard with his bare hands. First, he punched him in the side of the head, then he broke his neck." She turned her head to look at him. "That was what Keene was planning to do to you up on the ridge, Brayden."

It was a sobering thought. Even more troubling was the notion that Keene was nearby, waiting for the opportunity to get at Esmée again.

"There was more information in Jack's notes. His informant told him that after the robbery, there was a split within the gang. Part of the spoils included a stash of rare blue stones known as the Angelika diamonds. The gems were worth more than the rest of the haul put together. Keene disappeared immediately after the robbery and so did the diamonds. The rest of the gang were convinced he'd double-crossed them, but there was nothing they could do. According to what Jack's informant told him, the gang's leaders were torn. While they were angry at Keene's treachery, the diamonds were seen as a liability. They were so distinctive, trying to sell them would have attracted attention. In the end, there was a feeling of relief. They were rid of the guy who had killed the security guard and, of course, they didn't have to give Keene his share of the proceeds."

"The Angelika diamonds are legendary in law enforcement," Brayden said. "As time has gone by, it's almost impossible to believe they'll ever be found."

"Exactly. Even the most crooked dealer wouldn't touch such high-profile gems. The leaders of the gang knew that, but it looks like Keene didn't."

"Do Jack's notes hold any clue to where Keene has been for the last ten years?" Brayden asked.

"No. His trainer was Colombian and Keene fought there during his career. I wondered if he could have gone there after the robbery, but it's been impossible to find any information on him from the internet. The only other thing that's interesting is that Keene served in the army and was a survival expert. Hiding out in a cave probably wouldn't be a hardship to him." Esmée set aside her laptop with a sigh. "And, although we know he came to Red Ridge to kill Jack, we don't know why he has hung around."

Brayden gave that statement some thought. "I think we have an idea." Esmée raised questioning eyebrows. "It seems clear that Richie Lyman is a key figure in all of this. He and Keene were associates at the time of the safe-deposit robbery and Andy has confirmed that it was Richie who introduced him to Keene."

"But Richie has disappeared," Esmée pointed out.

"And I wonder how much Keene knows about that?"

"I'm confused," Esmée said. "What is there in Red Ridge to interest the man who has the Angelika diamonds in his possession?"

An image of twin, charming smiles flashed into Brayden's mind. Was it possible? The Larson twins were audacious—believing themselves above the law—but if he was right, what they were planning was close to lunacy. Could they have come up with a scheme to dispose of the Angelika diamonds?

"During your Groom Killer investigations have you encountered Evan and Noel Larson?"

Esmée wrinkled her nose. "Not in person. From what I've heard, I'm not sure I want to."

"Very wise. Those two are responsible for most criminal activity in Red Ridge, but their followers are so loyal, it's impossible to get anything on them. Richie is one of their most loyal gang members."

"You think the Larsons could be the reason why Keene has come to Red Ridge?" Esmée snuggled closer to him, momentarily endangering his ability to concentrate.

"I think it's a possibility. I also think we have to try harder to find Richie." He tightened his arm around her shoulders. "But since it's still early, maybe we should go back to bed?"

She tilted her face up to his. "I couldn't sleep."

"I wasn't suggesting sleep." He slid a hand under her chin, running his thumb over her lower lip.

"Oh." Her indrawn breath sent a delicious shot of heat straight to his groin. "Rhys will wake up in about an hour."

"In that case—" He got to his feet and reached down, scooping her up into his arms and carrying her toward the door. "I suggest we don't waste any more time on talking."

# Chapter 13

"I have to be sure Rhys is safe," Esmée said as they left the house after breakfast.

"And I need to be sure you are both safe." Brayden strapped Rhys into the child seat in his car as he spoke. "That's why I've been talking to my chief for the last half hour and getting some plans in place for how we deal with Roper Keene. All the cops in the Red Ridge PD have been alerted to be on the lookout for him. He's not an easy guy to miss."

"That's one of the things I don't understand. Where is Keene staying? He's an unmistakable figure, yet he doesn't seem to have been seen around town." She wrapped her arms around herself, scanning the open countryside. Surely a man as big as Keene would be noticeable if he tried to sneak up on them?

"The chief is going to interview Andy again himself to see if he can get any more information from him." He ran a finger down her cheek and his touch instantly soothed her. "Finn is the best chief of police there is. He's also my cousin. He'll do everything he can to catch this guy. We all will."

"I know that." She gave him her best attempt at a smile. "Are you sure Sarah's house is the best place for Rhys?"

"Yes. I know Hester comes across sometimes like all she thinks about is gossip, but appearances can be deceptive. She was a good cop. You can trust her to take care of Rhys." His expression was serious as he stared down at her. "It's you I'm worried about."

"I'm not going to get into a fight with a man as big as a bison."

"I don't want you in a position where Keene can get close to you." They had already been through this as they ate breakfast. Although Esmée tried to keep things lighthearted, she was touched at the depth of his concern for her safety. "Which is why I've cleared it with Finn so that I can stay with you as much as possible."

"What happens if you and Echo get called out on a search-and-rescue mission? You can hardly take me along." She rested a hand on Echo's head as the dog jumped eagerly into the back of Brayden's car. "I'd slow you down."

"If I can't be with you, another officer will take over." He drew her into a quick hug, the warmth of his body comforting her while also igniting a series of wonderfully erotic memories. When she drew away, she could see the same residual heat in Brayden's gaze. "Touching may be a bad idea until we can be alone."

She laughed. "We'll just have to try for a little restraint."

"You call it restraint. I call it torture."

When they arrived at Sarah's house, Esmée was relieved to see the way Rhys treated her place like a second home. Greeting Sarah and Hester with a casual wave, he headed straight for the basket where Bella-cat and her kittens were curled up. Since the cats were sleeping, he kneeled close by to watch them.

Rhys wasn't the only one who was fascinated by the feline cuteness. Echo left Brayden's side to go and sit next to the little boy. His expression was entranced as he gazed at the kittens. Every now and then, the large dog turned his head to look at Brayden as though to say, "Have you seen this?"

Rhys draped an arm around the dog's shoulder. "Kitties," he explained.

Since the kittens weren't ready to play, Rhys moved onto the stash of toys Sarah had kept from her time as a teacher. These soon littered the floor as he emptied boxes and threw various toys around in his search for the items he wanted.

Sarah smiled as she watched him. "I can't tell you what it means to me to have him here. After everything that's happened, having a child around the place has been exactly the distraction I needed."

Esmée raised her brow as a building block was thrown in their direction. "Plus you get the benefits of a daily workout as you dodge the toys on your rug and duck to avoid flying playthings."

Brayden quickly filled in Sarah and Hester on the latest developments regarding Roper Keene. "I don't think he'll come after Rhys. I believe Esmée is his target, but we can't be too careful. The chief has placed an alert on this address and on this landline number. I also want you to call the police department and give Lorelei Wong your cell phone numbers so she can make sure they are also included in the alert. That way, if either of you place a 911 call, it will be given the highest priority." He looked directly at Esmée. "This is a precaution. We already have all our resources focused on finding Keene."

"Could this man be the Groom Killer?" Sarah asked.

Esmée could see Brayden battling briefly with his emotions. She could tell he wished more than anything that the answer was yes. But Brayden was a realist. And he was a cop. His instincts and his knowledge of the case overruled his heart.

"Keene has a violent past, but the Groom Killer murders are very personal to Red Ridge. I just can't see a stranger turning up and carrying out these attacks." There was trace of regret in the way he shook his head. "I believe his reason for being here will be connected to the raid he and Richie Lyman were involved in ten years ago. Which is why Esmée and I are going to pay a visit to Lulu Love."

Esmée kneeled beside Rhys, who had found a set of wooden dinosaurs and was arranging them in height order. "Mommy has to go now. Be a good boy for Sarah and Hester."

He turned to wrap his arms around her neck, planting a kiss on her cheek. "Bye, Mommy." Her heart gave a little jump of joy, just as it always did when he called her that. Although it was new, she had a feeling it always would. He waved a hand at Brayden. "Bye, Bray. Bye, Ko."

Esmée got to her feet, watching as he returned to his toys. Sarah placed a hand on her shoulder. "You should be very proud that he's confident to see you go, knowing you'll be back. That's the sign of a child who knows he's loved."

Once they had left the house and were seated in the car, Brayden turned to study her face. "He'll be okay. Trust me."

"I do trust you." More than she had ever trusted

anyone. Even Jack. It was scary how fast it had happened, but she didn't question her faith in him. She knew he would do everything he could to protect her and Rhys. "It's just hard to accept that Keene is out there, lurking in the shadows."

"At least we know he has to look for big shadows."

Esmée chuckled. "Now I have an image of him tiptoeing from one dark place to another like a cartoon character."

He started the engine. "I'd rather you were laughing at him than worrying about him."

"I'll do both. Laugh when I'm with you, but worry until he's caught." She looked out the car window in silence as the scene changed from Sarah's neighborhood to the rougher part of town. "Tell me about Lulu."

"There aren't enough words to do her justice." He halted the car outside a sleazy apartment block. "But you are about to find that out for yourself."

Lulu lived on the second floor of a run-down apartment building. The front door was hanging off its hinges, so they walked straight in. After mounting stairs with a handrail that wobbled dangerously, Brayden knocked on the door. He knew from experience that the buzzer didn't work.

"You may want to stand back," he told Esmée. She raised questioning eyebrows. "Lulu likes to throw things."

Lulu opened the door wide, a scowl descending when she saw who it was. "I have to see to my baby—"

Since she stalked away from them before she'd finished speaking, Brayden took that as an invitation to enter. Wrinkling his nose as the smell hit him, he beckoned for Esmée to follow him. The distinctive aroma was soon accounted for when he saw the overflowing pail of used diapers in one corner of the room.

"I'm here to ask a few questions."

The baby was screaming and Lulu held her over one shoulder as she tried to fix a bottle of formula in the small kitchen area. "You can take that look off your face right now, *Officer*," Lulu snarled as she followed the direction of Brayden's gaze. "I got no one here to help me. Unless you want to take the dirty diapers down to the trash for me?"

Motherhood hadn't softened either Lulu's aggression or her appearance. Her trademark waist-length hair was as eye-wateringly yellow as ever and her silver eye shadow matched her long nails. She frowned when she saw Echo at Brayden's heels. "That animal isn't coming near my baby without a muzzle."

"He's a K-9 officer and he is used to kids of all ages, Lulu." He pointed to the door and Echo laid down next to it, placing his head on his paws. Although the dog's attitude was relaxed, his gaze remained on Lulu as she continued her tirade.

"You know what you can do with your questions, Officer Colton?" Her hand was shaking as she pointed at him, her voice rising over the baby's cries. "Why are you here harassing me when you should be out there looking for Richie? He's been gone four weeks now—"

"Why don't I take your baby while you finish getting her formula ready?" Esmée's quiet tone cut across Lulu's agitation.

For a second, Brayden contemplated grabbing her by the arm and dragging her out of there. Baby or no baby, the full force of Lulu's rage was like a full-on flamethrower and he didn't want Esmée exposed to its blistering effects. To his surprise, when Esmée stepped up close and held out her hands, Lulu blinked at her as though she couldn't believe her eyes and then handed over the baby.

"She's beautiful." Esmée smiled down at the tiny baby in her arms, rocking her back and forth as she walked up and down in the limited space. The motion seemed to have a soothing effect and the baby started gnawing on her fist instead of bawling. "What's her name?"

"Venus."

Brayden could hardly believe it was Lulu talking. It was as if someone had flipped a switch, softening her features and voice.

"Shall I feed her while you talk?" Esmée held out a hand for the bottle and, to his astonishment, Lulu agreed.

Lulu dumped clothes, take-out cartons and baby toys onto the floor so they could sit on a corner sofa. Her eyes remained on Esmée and the baby as she spoke to Brayden. "Make it fast."

"I already know you haven't seen Richie for about a month. I want to ask you about what happened before he went away. Did he say or do anything different?"

Lulu hunched a shoulder. "Like what?"

"Had he talked about any new people? Met anyone you hadn't seen before?" Brayden asked.

Lulu dragged her eyes around to his face. "You mean the cop who was murdered by the Groom Killer? You can't pin that on Richie. He'd already left town when the guy was killed."

"I'm not trying to pin anything on Richie, Lulu. I'm just trying to find him. But since we're on the subject of Jack Parkowski… He knew Richie from a case he was on ten years ago. You were there when the two men came face-to-face again here in Red Ridge. Can you tell me what was said?"

Lulu picked at one of her fingernails. "I was drunk—" She stole a look at his face and sighed. "Okay. Okay. I remember it because it was so strange. We were fighting. Richie wanted to go home and I wanted to stay in the Pour House. The cop came over to us and I started to tell him to butt the hell out, but Richie was just staring at him. Then Richie said, 'It's you' or 'You.' The other guy stepped up real close to

Richie. He spoke in a normal voice, like he was talking about the damn weather or something. It freaked me out and Richie just stood there and listened." She laughed. "That is *so* not Richie."

Brayden smiled. "I know."

"The words themselves didn't make much sense to me. He said Richie better stay away from him and anyone he knew. Then he said if Richie was still in touch with his friend with the stones he should give him a warning. He said real cops never retire. That was why murderers always had to watch their backs."

"That was it?"

"Pretty much. The cop walked away and Richie dragged me back here. When I asked him what it meant, he wouldn't tell me." She shook her head. "But he acted strange from then on. Scared but also wired."

"Wired? You mean he was excited about something?" Brayden frowned. He couldn't find anything in Jack's warning that would fire Richie's enthusiasm. Quite the opposite.

"Yeah. The next day, he said the cop didn't realize what he'd done. He thought he could frighten Richie, but instead he'd given him an idea."

"You don't know what that idea was?" Brayden's mind was racing.

"All I know is, from then on, he was never off his cell. It was driving me crazy. Every time I wanted to go out and get stuff for the baby, he was talking to some guy in Colombia." Brayden exchanged a glance with Esmée. "I know, right? He should have been focused on me and the baby. It got worse when Richie's friend turned up, someone he knew from way back." The corners of her mouth turned down. "He scared the crap out of me. I mean, the guy looked like he'd escaped from the *zoo*."

Brayden was trained not to show emotion during an interview. Even so, it was difficult to contain the exhilaration those words provoked. Determinedly, he kept his voice casual. "Did you ever hear this man's name?"

"Not his real name. Richie always called him Neckbreaker." She picked up one of the baby toys. It was an ugly-looking thing. A huge, heavy rattle that seemed intended more to frighten the child than entertain her. "He brought this for the baby, even though she hadn't been born then."

"I'd be careful with that when Venus gets older." Esmée regarded the rattle with a look of horror. "It looks like it could injure her if she hit herself on the head with it."

"I know, right?" Lulu grimaced. "I wanted to throw it in the trash, but Richie wouldn't let me. He said it was a bad idea to annoy the Neckbreaker."

Since she didn't have any more information for them, Esmée handed back the baby and they got ready to leave. "Let me know if you hear from Richie," Brayden said as they reached the door.

"I'm not going to hear from him, am I? We both know that, Officer Colton." As she closed the door, he glimpsed the fear in Lulu's eyes.

"Remind me to take you along if I ever need to do any lion taming. Lulu would never have talked to me if you hadn't been there to soften her up by feeding the baby," Brayden said as he drove toward the Pour House.

"I felt sorry for her. Bringing up a baby on your own can be a lonely experience." Esmée looked around at the bleak buildings. "At least, thanks to my mother's hard work, both as an example and the savings cushion she left me, I never had to survive in a place like that."

"I think you're doing yourself an injustice." Brayden pulled into the parking lot of the bar. "You wouldn't have let life pull you down the way Lulu has. Even if you had to bring Rhys up in a tiny apartment, I know you wouldn't have let him live in squalor."

"I like to think I also wouldn't have exposed him to a man with a friend called the Neckbreaker."

Brayden grimaced. "Just when you think nothing has the power to shock you anymore, you hear about two slimeballs whose idea of a joke is a nickname linked to the way one of them killed a security guard."

Together with Echo, they exited the car and walked toward the entrance of the Pour House. Esmée looked up at the run-down exterior. "I came here when I first arrived in Red Ridge. I wanted to get a feel for Demi's early life."

"What did you find out?"

She hesitated for a moment. Even though things had changed between them, the unspoken taboo about his family was still in place. Or was it? "It can't have been easy for her. For any of you."

He gave a snort of laughter. "The exterior hasn't changed much, but the interior has had something of a makeover since we were kids. Back then it was more an old-style watering hole and pool hall. Rusty's idea of Saturday afternoons with the kids was to bring us here and sit us at the end of the bar with a soda while he carried on with business as usual. We weren't allowed to step down from our stools in case we got in the way of the paying customers."

Esmée thought of Rhys, of how hard she worked to make sure he had the freedom to run, play and explore. She pictured four little kids forced to sit for hours in a grown-up atmosphere with nothing to do except watch, listen and long for more. Her heart constricted. "I guess, even now, it's not the sort of place you'd come for a family meal."

"You guess right. The core clientele are still cowboys, a few passing tourists who've come down off the Coyote Mountain trail and find it 'quaint' and local traders such as the guys from the tire shop. And the Pour House has always been the go-to place for

Red Ridge's unsavory characters. It's a well-known fact that, on a Saturday night, you'd best have one hand on your wallet and the other on your bowie knife."

"Is Rusty an informant?"

Brayden pushed open the door and they stepped from bright sunlight into the darkened interior. "I ask him a few questions now and then. Only when it's unavoidable."

His voice and attitude spoke volumes. Brayden could turn the same spotlight he had used on her right back on himself. His own start in life hadn't been the easiest. Having met Rusty, she guessed it would have been easy for his son to pick up the same casual approach to morality. Instead, Brayden had turned out to be the opposite of his father in every way. Clearly, Rusty had acted as a role model for everything Brayden didn't want to be.

Her eyes adjusted to the gloom, taking in the horseshoe-shaped bar, the pool tables under their covers, the old-fashioned jukebox in the corner and the tables set around the edge of the room. A poster on the wall advertised a party room with a stage area and karaoke. Those Saturday nights Brayden had mentioned probably got pretty wild.

"Can't you read?" Rusty's voice crackled like sandpaper from somewhere at the rear of the bar. "We don't open till noon."

"I thought you said your door was never closed to

family?" Brayden leaned over the bar and snagged two bottles of soda. He used the metal opener that was fixed to the wall, then handed one bottle to Esmée, before taking a slug from his own.

"Well, if it isn't my favorite son." Rusty's cheery grin didn't match the bags under his eyes or his graying stubble. He carried a giant cup of coffee and the smell told Esmée it was a strong one.

"If you're saying that it must be because you owe Shane more money than you owe me."

Rusty was unabashed. "He's better at keeping a tab than you are."

Esmée watched the exchange, reflecting that Rusty was one of those men who, when he was younger, must have relied on his looks to get him by. There was a resemblance between him and Brayden, but Rusty wore his masculinity as a badge. Strutting, flirting, preening…he tried his charm on everyone he came in contact with. Four kids each with a different mother? That was either carelessness or a desire to prove his virility. Possibly, in Rusty's case, it was both. From what Brayden had said, he hadn't learned from his mistakes when each new baby came along. Just patted them on the head and treated them all the same, letting their mothers do the hard work.

Rusty's gaze rested on Esmée and a gleam came into his eyes. "You here to interview me about Demi?" His grin widened as he opened his arms suggestively. "I'm all yours."

"I can see how worried you are about your daughter, Mr. Colton."

Brayden made a choking sound. "We're not here to talk about Demi. I want to ask you about Richie Lyman."

Rusty laughed and made a walking motion with his fingers. "Word is he finally got up the courage to leave Lulu."

"I'm interested in a man he was seen hanging around with before he left town. A big guy. Richie introduced him to Andy Coulson."

"You mean the boxer?" Rusty shook his head. "That guy wasn't just big. He was *huge*."

"Did you get his name?" Brayden asked.

Rusty gave him a sidelong glance. "I've been in this business long enough to get a feeling for people. Sometimes you don't ask."

Everything they had heard about Roper Keene so far told Esmée Rusty's instincts were right. She wanted to jump in with a dozen questions of her own, but Brayden was in charge here. Although impatience was eating her up, she had to leave it to him. Luckily, he was asking all the right things.

"Have you seen this man since Richie left town?"

"Yeah. He's been in here a few times." Rusty took a moment to sip his coffee. "I know what you're going to ask next. Last time was a couple of days ago."

"Did he meet with anyone interesting?"

"I know where this is going, Bray, but I can't help

you. The Larson twins wouldn't soil their hand-stitched, designer boots in a dive like this. The big guy spoke to a few people. Some of them could have been Larson goons, but I couldn't swear to it." Rusty seemed genuinely regretful.

"Okay. That's been helpful. Thanks." Brayden finished his soda and placed the empty bottle on the bar. He made a move to turn away and then paused. "Do you have any idea where this guy is staying?"

"No, but I know one thing for sure. It's not in town."

Brayden sighed. "That's what I thought. If he was staying in Red Ridge, I'd know about it. He's unmistakable."

# Chapter 14

Before Brayden went into the K-9 team meeting he asked Lorelei Wong to set up Esmée in an office with a laptop. "Even though we now have a name for the suspect, it's worth doing this search in case his image comes up in connection with another crime. He may use an alias, or there may be a facial composite on file if he is wanted but the police department who issued it don't have a name for him."

She leaned back in her chair, smiling up at him. "Tell the truth, Officer Colton. This is a babysitting exercise. While I'm in here, you know what I'm doing."

He grinned. Casting a quick glance around, he leaned over and snatched a quick kiss. "You got me."

He said the words lightly, but their meaning struck deep. *You got me.* It was true. He belonged to her. Completely. So much was going on, but he needed to do something about that. Like maybe tell her?

Brayden left Esmée and went into the meeting room. Most of his colleagues were already there and the last few arrived a minute or two later. The well-trained dogs, familiar with this routine, settled next to the seats of their partners. Finn Colton took up his usual position, leaning against a desk at the front of the room.

"Okay. We don't have much new information on the Groom Killer case. Ballistics reports indicate the person who shot Jack Parkowski was right-handed, the same as with the other victims."

"Same as Demi Colton." It was the voice from the back of the room.

Brayden felt his anger rear up, but it died down just as fast. The thought of Esmée close by calmed him as much as Echo's soothing presence. It was as if he had developed a new immunity to the Gage barbs. He would always defend his sister, but petty comments no longer had the same effect on him. Esmée and Rhys had brought a new dimension to his life. The thought sent a thrill of excitement through him. He had no idea what it meant, or where it was leading. He only knew he was enjoying it.

"Same as almost ninety percent of the population." Brayden's response drew a general murmur of approval from his colleagues.

"We do have another case that's developing fast. Bray, can you bring the team up to speed on your investigation?" Finn stepped aside to let Brayden move to the front of the room.

Brayden quickly and succinctly outlined what he knew about Roper Keene and his links to both Jack Parkowski and Richie Lyman. "This is speculation, but Jack spoke to Richie about 'his friend with the stones' and Richie told Lulu those words gave him an idea. Soon after that Keene appeared in town. It's possible that Richie, now working for the Larson twins, got back in touch with his old friend and told him he had some high-powered new contacts who could help him dispose of the Angelika diamonds."

There was a general groan around the room. "Pinning anything on the Larsons is like trying to catch smoke with a spoon," Nash Maddox said.

"Although Richie has been missing for a month, Keene was seen in town a few days ago. Clearly, he still has a reason to stick around. And he's our suspect in the arson attack on Andy's Liquor Store. We need to find out where he's staying."

Elle Gage raised a tentative hand. The rookie K-9 cop was the sister of Bo Gage, first victim of the Groom Killer. Unlike Lucas Gage, she didn't express an opinion about Demi's guilt or innocence, preferring to get on with the job. "This is about the attack on Andy's store." She paused. "I was wondering about something."

"Go ahead." Brayden was prepared to listen to any theory that could lead them to Keene.

"Andy said in his statement that Richie introduced him to this guy and they planned to torch the store, right?" Brayden nodded. "If it was a plot to kill Jack Parkowski, he wasn't guaranteed to die in the fire. I wonder why Keene, who'd killed before, didn't try a more foolproof method."

"That's a good point."

Brayden's mind raced through the details. Richie wanted Jack dead. Keene wanted a partnership with the Larson twins, who, if Brayden was right, were offering to mediate in the sale of the diamonds. Andy wanted to dispose of his losing business. Jack had been standing in everyone's way.

Although he had never been able to find the proof he needed, Jack knew enough about Richie and Keene and their links to the heist to make their lives very uncomfortable. The Larson twins were always careful to avoid police scrutiny. If they were planning to get rid of the diamonds, they wouldn't be happy if Keene or Richie drew attention to themselves. Yet Jack could have blown the whole thing wide-open with a word to the cops.

Why hadn't Keene gone for his tried and trusted method of breaking Jack's neck? Or use the gun they knew he had in his possession? Brayden supposed the answer to that question lay in the future Keene saw opening up ahead of him. Even taking out the cut he'd have to give Richie and the Larson twins, the Angelika diamonds would be worth billions. Keene would want to be able to enjoy his money without the possibility of a murder conviction hanging over him.

That was why he planned to make Jack's death look like an accident. But he hadn't needed to do anything. The Groom Killer had done the job for him. Keene must have been unable to believe his luck. But how did Esmée fit into all this?

Brayden was still pondering that question when the door opened and Frank Lanelli came in. Finn beckoned him over and the two men exchanged a few words. When the dispatcher left, the chief addressed the team.

"A 911 call has just come in from a couple of hikers. They've found a body in the woods near Lifeless Creek, at the base of the Coyote Mountains." He turned to Brayden. "I want you to lead on this. The body is in bad shape, but indications are it could be Richie Lyman."

Esmée did her best to keep up with Brayden and Echo as they exited the building at a run. "I know you have to do your job, but I don't want to see a dead body that is described as being in bad shape. I don't want to see *any* dead body."

"I need to get out to the scene and we don't have time to take a detour to Sarah's house." He cast a glance in her direction. "You can wait in the car when we get to Lifeless Creek."

"When Neckbreaker Keene could be on the loose in those woods? I don't think so. I'll be glued to your side."

"Then you'll have to be glued to my side with your eyes closed. Unless—" He shielded his eyes as a vehicle pulled into the parking lot. "It looks like the answer to our problems has just arrived."

The man who got out of the car and walked toward them was tall and muscular with sandy hair and blue eyes. A corgi bounced jauntily at his side. When Echo saw the other dog, he gave a bark of delight and bounded forward. The two canines greeted each other with obvious pleasure. First, they bumped noses before progressing to the other end of the body and performing a thorough rear-end inspection. Then they ran around each other, jumping for joy and yapping like puppies.

"Can dogs have friends?" Esmée asked. It certainly looked that way.

"Sure they can. Stumps and Echo are best buddies," the other man said as he reached them. "Quinn called me. She said something about dinner and cake, but I thought she must have the wrong family?"

Although Esmée had already guessed who he was, Brayden's next words confirmed it. "Esmée, this is my brother."

Esmée studied Shane Colton with interest. Although he had suffered the trauma of wrongful imprisonment, she knew the private investigator was on the payroll of the Red Ridge PD. Although he was only a year younger than Brayden, she couldn't immediately see any resemblance between them.

Brayden turned to Shane. "I don't have time to explain it all now, but Esmée is in danger and I have to head out to the location of a body."

When Shane smiled, the similarity between the brothers became more apparent. He caught on fast to what Brayden was saying and turned to Esmée. "I guess that means you, me and Stumps have the rest of the day to ourselves?"

"Got to go." Brayden clicked his fingers and Echo reluctantly moved away from Stumps. As he opened the back of his car, Brayden spoke quietly to Esmée. "For the sake of my sanity, stay with Shane."

She nodded. "Don't worry. We'll see you at dinner."

Shane watched as Brayden drove away. "Was that really my brother?"

Esmée frowned. "What do you mean?"

"Just wondering what's been happening since the last time I saw him. It's like he's been taking lessons in how to be human." He shrugged. "What do you want to do now?"

"Grab a coffee and interview you about Demi." Although she would have an opportunity to observe the half siblings together over dinner, Esmée wanted to hear Shane's thoughts about his sister.

"Ah." He whistled and Stumps, who had been examining the strip of grass at the front of the building, hurried over as fast as his stubby legs would carry him. "You're *that* Esmée."

Shane drove to Main Street and pulled up outside the Hideout coffee shop, a place Esmée already knew was popular with the K-9 cops because dogs were welcome. "I came here instead of Good Eats because I figured you'd probably already spoken to Quinn."

"Will we be able to talk without being overheard?" Esmée asked.

"It'll be quiet at this time of the day," Shane assured her. "And I know which tables are the best for anyone wanting privacy."

Shane was right, the place was almost deserted. While he went to the counter, Esmée slid into the booth he indicated. Stumps took a moment to consider his options. Apparently deciding against curling up under the table, he hopped onto the bench at Esmée's side and rested his head on her knee. She stroked his head and the dog gave a sigh of bliss before closing his eyes.

"How is Bray holding up?" Shane asked when he returned with the drinks. "This whole Groom Killer thing blew us all away, but he has to stare it in the face every day as part of his job."

"The hardest thing is that he's so worried about Demi. He refuses to believe she's guilty."

Shane stirred his coffee, his gaze shifting to the street outside. "She's our sister."

"Look, I've promised Brayden and Quinn that I won't make my documentary until the Groom Killer is caught and convicted," Esmée said. "Nothing you say to me now will impact on the case against Demi."

He frowned. "So what's the point of this conversation?"

"Because these real-time thoughts and feelings are important. After it's all over, it will be easy for people to say, 'Oh, I knew that.' And the three of you are the ones who know Demi best."

"That's just it. We barely know each other at all." He sipped his hot coffee for a moment or two, appearing to gather his thoughts. "Do I think Demi is capable of killing Bo Gage in anger if they got in a fight? I don't like the idea, but I sometimes wonder if that might be possible. Shooting him and stuffing a cummerbund in his mouth? That's not her style. And the idea that she would go on to kill other men—men she doesn't know—just because they're getting married and she isn't?" Shane's expression became more determined. "No, that's not Demi."

"Does that mean you agree with Brayden? You believe she's innocent?"

"She's not acting like an innocent person. By running away, she has the whole town crying out that she's guilty." He ran a hand through his hair. "I wish she'd get in touch. That way, we could help her."

"When you say 'we,' you mean you and Brayden?" Esmée asked.

His eyes were sharp as they scanned her face. "You think she wouldn't do that because of Bray's job? Because she knows he'd have to choose between helping his sister and turning her in? I never thought of it that way. They always were the closest out of the four of us. But that's not saying much."

"You don't think she'd ask Rusty for help?"

He almost choked on the coffee he'd been drinking. "Have you met Rusty?" Esmée nodded. "Well, then. I think you just answered your own question."

"Quinn said you thought it would be easy to frame someone for these murders." She wasn't sure how he'd react to her skirting around the subject of his own past.

Shane didn't seem concerned. "It's easy to frame someone for any murder. But some of these details are pure drama. They're not really evidence. The finger dipped in blood spelling out Demi's initials? The locket? Witnesses claiming to see Demi running from crime scenes—and in one case, actually shooting someone? Witnesses who've both ended up dead? Too easy."

Esmée didn't want to interfere in Brayden's life, but she could see that the wall around his heart had been built during his childhood. Quinn and Shane had similar issues. Demi probably did, too. For some reason, the hurt went deeper with Brayden. Part of it was genetics. He had that built-in reserve. Maybe it was also to do with his first and only experience of love. Was it too late for this group of siblings who were almost strangers to grow closer? Esmée, who had her own unique insight into murder and its impact, thought they might still have a chance. Perhaps something could be salvaged from this situation.

As for her place in it…all she knew for sure was that she had never felt as alive, or as secure, as she did with Brayden. She didn't know what the future held for them, and maybe now wasn't the time to decide. That was what her head said. Her heart was trying to make other plans.

"What do you want to do now?" Shane indicated their empty cups.

"I need to go and get my little boy from Sarah Mull's house, then we may as well go back to Brayden's place and I can start preparing dinner." She prodded the sleeping dog in her lap, who opened one eye. Reluctantly, Stumps jumped down and Esmée got to her feet.

"You're staying with Brayden?" Shane raised his eyebrows as they left their table.

"Yes. Sorry. You got thrust into the role of bodyguard without any information to go with it." Aware that he was regarding her with a curious expression, she frowned. "Is that a problem?"

"On the contrary. It explains something that's been puzzling me." He grinned as he held the door open for her to pass through ahead of him. "I wondered why my big brother was looking so happy."

Lifeless Creek got its name because it was almost dry for most of the year. A narrow channel that ran along the base of the Coyote Mountains, it came to life in spring when melting snow turned it into a stream. Brayden and Echo trudged through the surrounding mud to reach the place where the body had been discovered, close to the bank. Yellow crime-scene tape marked the area and a forensic team was already at work.

A white, protective tent covered the remains. Ordering Echo to stay, Brayden ducked inside. The sweet but pungent smell hit him and he took a moment to adjust. Sadly, his job occasionally brought him in contact with dead bodies. Mostly, the fatalities he encountered had occurred recently. Now and then, he came across corpses that were older. He never got used to the rank aroma of death.

"The hikers who found this guy are waiting to make a statement." Dr. Alice Wilson was photographing the scene and didn't turn her head.

"I wanted to find out what your first impressions were before I spoke to them."

She did look around then. Stepping aside slightly, she allowed Brayden a clear view of the remains. He winced as he looked down at what had once been a person.

"My first impressions? I won't put anything on the record until I've completed my examination, but let me tell you what I think happened to this guy. Whoever killed him thought they could cut him up, presumably to make it easier to dispose of him. But they misjudged how difficult it is to do that, especially as they seem to have tried it with an ordinary knife." Brayden thought of Esmée's description of the hunting knife she had found. "So they gave up and buried him out here. Except the runoff from the melting snow has brought the creek to life and washed the top surface of the soil away. Sure gave those people who came out here for a pleasant walk a nasty shock."

"I don't suppose you can give me an idea of when he died?"

She shrugged. "It's difficult to say because he's been buried and then exposed to the elements. By the condition of the body, I'm going to say weeks rather than months." She reached a gloved hand down toward the corpse, bringing up an item and holding it so that Brayden could see it. "The people who discovered him found this a few inches away."

Although the document was dirty and ragged around the edges, the print on it was clear. It was Richie Lyman's driver's license.

"I know what you're going to say." Dr. Wilson

wasn't known for her sense of humor, but there was a faint twinkle in her eye. "You want this case treated as a priority?"

"I'd appreciate it," Brayden said.

"So much for my quiet life. It's like this town has gone crazy in the last few months." Brayden followed her as she stepped outside the tent. "I'll be in touch when I've completed the examination."

The young couple who had found the body were huddled together on a nearby rock. Their dog, a border terrier, sat at their feet. They weren't local and explained that they had left their car in the town center, had set off early and followed the Coyote Mountain trail.

"We hiked for a couple of hours and came back down into the valley," Steven Halford said. "As we were walking along the edge of the creek, Buddy found something. He kept sniffing at it and wouldn't come away when we called him."

His wife covered her lips with a shaking hand. "It looked like a bundle of old rags, but when we got up close..." Her eyes filled with tears. "How could anyone *do* that to another person?"

Brayden took down their details, but it was clear they didn't have much else to tell him. They had done all the right things, calling 911 immediately and not touching the body. Although the remains were in poor condition, it was clear the dead person had been a victim of violence. Since it was obvious he had also been dead for some time, the Halfords hadn't felt it was necessary to leave the scene to ensure their own safety.

"You're free to go." Brayden couldn't see any reason to keep them there. The forensic team were moving the body and the late-afternoon sky was darkening with the threat of rain. "I'll be in touch if I need any further information."

As the Halfords left, Brayden stepped back to view the scene. From where he was standing, he could see in a straight line up from the creek to the mountain trail. The Eagle's Nest was immediately above this point. Dr. Wilson would determine whether Richie—and it seemed likely it *was* Richie—had been killed here, or if he'd been murdered elsewhere and his body dumped here. But it struck Brayden as odd, or possibly coincidental, that Esmée's encounter with the shooter had taken place on a ridge that was directly above the point where this body had been hidden.

The forensic team was carrying the covered body toward their vehicle, and there was no further reason to stay here. Calling Echo to him, Brayden headed to his car. He may as well return to town and grab a coffee to take out before filing his report.

# Chapter 15

Esmée and Shane left the Hideout and headed for his car. Just as they reached the vehicle, she gave an exclamation of annoyance. "I meant to get some coriander for this meal I'm making."

"You can get that from the Spice Rack." Shane indicated the deli across the street.

"I'll be two minutes." Esmée had already started to cross the road as she was talking.

A quick glance first in one direction, then the other, showed her the street was free of traffic. She was almost in the middle of the road when she heard a dog barking. The sound attracted her attention and she paused. It wasn't Stumps. The bark was too low-pitched. It was definitely Echo's bark. If Echo was close by that meant Brayden was, too. In the same instant that she turned her head, a black car came racing out of a side street opposite to where Shane was parked. It was heading directly toward her.

Esmée spun around just as a pair of strong hands grabbed her by the waist and hauled her out of the path of the vehicle. She took a moment to register it was Brayden and then they were sprawled on the sidewalk as the car, a black SUV, screeched past at high speed. Moments later, Shane had jumped into his own vehicle and was racing after it.

Brayden brushed himself off and turned to Esmée. "Are you okay?"

"Just a little shaken." It was an understatement, but he looked so worried that she wanted to reassure him.

"I need to call this in. Can you walk?" She took the hand he held out to her and leaned on him as he supported her to his car.

Although she wasn't injured, her legs were shaking and she was glad of Brayden's strong arms as he helped her into the passenger seat. Leaning her head back, she tried to fight off the waves of shock. Her insides were cold, her stomach cramping. Her heart was pounding so hard against her rib cage, it felt like it was about to explode with each beat, and her breathing was coming hard and fast. Although her skin felt clammy, she started to shiver and wrapped her arms around herself.

She was conscious of Brayden's eyes on her as he gave quick, concise details of the incident to the PD dispatcher. "A black SUV heading down Main toward Rattlesnake. Shane Colton is in pursuit."

When he ended the call, he leaned across and drew Esmée close to him, using his warmth and strength to comfort her. She melted into his embrace like it was where she belonged, his arms around her restoring a level of peace despite the horror of what had just happened.

"If Echo hadn't barked when he did, I'd have been right in the path of that car." Hearing his name, the dog, who was on the back seat, shuffled forward and nudged her shoulder with his nose. Esmée obliged by turning to stroke him. "You are such a good boy." She raised her head to look at Brayden. "And you…" Her voice quivered and she took a moment to get it back under control. "You saved me. Again. But you came from nowhere. Why are you here?"

"I'd finished up at Lifeless Creek. There wasn't much to do out there. I was driving back here to the Hideout to get a coffee. I saw you and Shane come out and had just gotten out of my car when you started to cross the road." His expression darkened. "What the hell was that brother of mine playing at? I thought I asked him to take care of you?"

"To be fair to Shane, I was only going to the deli to get coriander. He couldn't have known someone would try to run me down." Esmée looked down the road. "And now he's gone racing off in pursuit. Anything could happen to him."

"Looks like he's okay," Brayden said as his brother's car reappeared.

Shane parked behind them and got out, his whole appearance expressing fury. "Lost him." He leaned in the driver's-side window of Brayden's car. "He jumped a red light at the intersection of Rattlesnake and James. Almost caused a three-car pileup."

"Did you get a look at the driver?" Brayden asked.

"No. The vehicle had tinted windows and no registration plates." Shane scuffed a booted foot on the sidewalk. "I'm willing to bet good money that car won't be found."

"I have to go in and file a report about the dead body out at Lifeless Creek," Brayden said. "Is there any chance you two could manage to stay out of trouble for a few hours while I'm gone?"

Shane started to protest, but Esmée laughed. "We can try, but I still need coriander."

"Then Shane will go get it, while I stay here with you."

"You can't treat your brother like an errand boy…"

Shane shook his head. "He's a tyrant, Esmée. Get used to it."

As he strode off toward the deli, Brayden took hold of Esmée's chin, tilting her face up to his. "Do you have any idea how I felt when I saw that car heading toward you?"

She started to speak, but, ignoring the fact that they were in full view of anyone passing by, he bent his head and kissed her. "Groom Killer," she murmured when she was finally able to say something. "I know a public kiss isn't the same as an engagement ring, but we need to be careful."

He raised his head, gazing into her eyes. "I don't give a damn."

"Well, I do. From now on, let's keep the displays of affection behind closed doors."

The smile in his eyes replaced the chill in her veins with sweet warmth. "You give a damn?"

When he looked at her that way, keeping her own rule about no kissing in public was going to be harder than she'd anticipated. "Brayden, I give several."

When Brayden arrived home a few hours later, Esmée was preparing dinner in the kitchen while Shane was slumped in front of the TV. Echo bounced into the family room to greet Stumps.

"Why is the house so quiet?" Brayden looked around in surprise. "Where's Rhys?"

"Taking a quick nap before dinner. He's tired himself out. Kitten overload."

Shane followed Brayden into the kitchen. "Why doesn't your TV remote work properly?"

"Ah." Esmée gave Brayden an apologetic look. "It may have found its way into Echo's water bowl."

"Rhys likes to find out if things can float," he told Shane. "Hang on to your cell phone."

"Thanks for the advice," Shane said. "We still have a few hours before dinner, right?"

"We'll eat at about six. We've turned your brother's routine upside down and forced him to keep two-year-old hours." Esmée and Brayden exchanged a smile.

"I'd come straight from my last job when I met you in the PD parking lot. I'll go to my place, dump my stuff, freshen up and collect Quinn. We'll see you later."

When he'd gone, Esmée moved purposefully toward Brayden, gripping the front of his shirt in both hands. "Now we're alone, what shall we do with all this grown-up time we have?"

"I have several interesting answers to that question, but I've been out in the woods looking at a dead body." He brushed his lips over her forehead. "I need a shower."

"Care for some company?"

Drawing her closer, he slid his hands down over her hips. "I can't think of anything I've ever wanted more."

Brayden headed for his bedroom while Esmée checked on Rhys. A smile touched her lips when she saw him sprawled on his bed with Echo curled up on the rug nearby. Once she reached Brayden's room, she placed the baby monitor on the bedside locker, sparing a thought for how the definition of spontaneity changed with parenthood.

Following the trail of Brayden's discarded clothing through to the bathroom, she removed her own garments along the way. Through the mist that already filled the small room, she could see Brayden behind the glass panel of the shower cubicle. He was already standing under strong, hot jets of water when Esmée piled her hair on top of her head, securing it in place before stepping inside to join him.

"Let me do that." She placed her hand over his as he reached for the bottle of bodywash. The delicious clean, musky scent that she had come to associate with Brayden filled the small space as she coated her hands with the gel before smoothing it over his shoulders and upper arms.

"Are you trying to kill me?" His voice was a despairing growl.

She didn't reply. Instead, she slid her soapy hands across his chest and stomach. His sharp hiss of indrawn breath told her exactly what her actions were doing to his self-control. With a little smile, Esmée glanced up at him as she slowly traced circles in the bubbles around his nipples.

"Esmée…"

"Stop talking and turn around."

Although he did as she asked, the warning glance he gave her over his shoulder told her she was pushing him to the limits of his endurance. Ignoring him,

Esmée ran her hands over the toned muscles of his back. Dipping lower, she kneaded his tight buttocks.

"That's enough."

Brayden swung back to face her. Taking both her hands and holding them behind her back, he pushed her up against the tile wall as he kissed her. Esmée gave a soft moan as she felt him, hard and demanding, pressing up against her.

He released her wrists but kept her firmly against the wall with the weight of his body as he began to caress her. His left hand stroked up her side, brushing her nipples before cupping her breast. The right trailed across her stomach then moved purposefully down.

Parting her thighs, he used his thumb to gently rub her clitoris. Esmée tilted her head back, letting the jets of water wash over her face as she gave herself up to the heavenly sensations triggered by his touch. Continuing the massage movement, he eased two fingers inside her. Almost immediately, convulsions of raw pleasure began to sweep along Esmée's nerve endings.

She could feel him growing harder and she was desperate to feel more, but her hands were still trapped. Brayden smiled as he held her there a moment or two longer. Leaning in closer, he caught the tender flesh between her neck and shoulder in his teeth, nipping it lightly before he released her. The delicious hint of pain sent Esmée's senses into a frenzy and she cried out, digging her fingers into his forearms to stay upright.

Regaining her balance, she reached out a hand to grasp his length. Pumping him slowly at first, she increased her pace as she kneeled in front of him. Planting a soft kiss on his head, she lightly circled the tip with her tongue, applying just enough pressure to have him groaning and tangling his hands in her hair. Moving forward gradually, inch by inch, she took him deeper into her mouth. Raising her eyes to his face so she could enjoy his response, she sucked him hard as she swirled her tongue around his tip.

Brayden threw his head back and groaned, his hands tight in her hair and his thigh muscles tense beneath her cheek. After a minute or two, he eased out of her mouth, placing his hands under her arms to lift her up. He pulled her tight to him and kissed her hard.

Grabbing her by the waist, he turned her so she was facing the wall. Placing her hands flat against the tiles, he moved her feet apart so he could stand between them. She saw him reach onto the shelf that contained soap and shampoo and take down a condom. Muttering a curse as he struggled with the foil packaging under the water, he finally got the condom on.

Slowly, he eased into her from behind.

"You feel divine." His chin was on her shoulder, his lips against her ear. "Warm, tight and all mine."

He teased her. Inch by inch, the same way she had taken him into her mouth. Esmée responded by letting him feel her muscles tighten and contract around him. As he pressed deeper, she began to moan, unable to resist begging for more.

"Please, Brayden."

He started to move, the angle of his erection just brushing the exact place that sent her wild with intense, electrifying bliss. Her knees began to tremble and Brayden wrapped one arm around her waist, holding her upright as he reached around to cup and stroke her breasts. Esmée's moans soon became breathless gasps as he pumped firmly and rhythmically. Her whole body quivered as she felt his full length, hard and thick, brushing that sweet spot inside her with each thrust.

Brayden's breathing was coming faster now, his movements less controlled. She could feel his thighs pressed hard and tight against her own as the tension grew, mounted, became unbearable.

"I can feel how close you are." His voice was a breathless whisper. Her legs buckled slightly and he pulled her closer to him, still pounding into her. "Let it happen."

As soon as he said it, the orgasm started to flow through her. She began to convulse as waves of incredible pleasure radiated out from her clitoris, racing through her body and crashing up her spine and out through the top of her skull. Everything else froze as the sensation ebbed and flowed. Her muscles gave out, her breathing came in short pants and she flopped forward over Brayden's arm.

Even through the storm crashing over her, she was aware of him calling her name as he succumbed to his own release. Although he was shaking, he continued to drive into her, trying to lock them both into the moment of ecstasy for as long as possible.

Eventually the sensations ebbed and they both collapsed against the shower wall, barely standing. The warm water was blissful on Esmée's tingling skin. After a few seconds, she turned to Brayden. He stroked her face with his fingertips before drawing her into a gentle kiss.

"Do you think our dinner guests will notice that I smell of your bodywash?"

"I don't care." He started to laugh. "All I know is I will never be able to use that brand again without getting dangerously aroused."

Esmée was relieved they could lighten the mood with humor. It saved her from the reality of dealing with the depth of her emotions. They had started this knowing they both wanted nothing more than a physical relationship. No entanglements. Nothing long-term. That was what Esmée had sworn her life would look like after Gwyn had treated her so badly.

But that was before she'd met Brayden. Even within such a short space of time, he'd shaken her convictions and changed everything. Every minute spent with him, every exchange of glances, every touch, only reinforced that. It was no good telling herself she could back out at any time. She was already in too deep.

A few hours later, Brayden felt warm and rested, yet curiously energized. He was also intensely frustrated.

"A car has been found on land near Fenwick Colton's energy plant. Although an attempt was made to set it on fire, it looks like the black SUV that was used to try to run you down." Brayden ended the call with his chief, irritation firing through him. Just lately, every lead seemed to take them down a dead end, whether it was the Groom Killer case or this new one. "It has no plates and no prints have been found, so we're unlikely to get anything from it."

"We know it was Keene," Esmée said.

"But we have to either pin something on him, or find him." He didn't add "or he'll do it again." She already knew that. It felt like they were on Keene's agenda, and Brayden wasn't happy about it.

"I may have cooked too much," Esmée confessed, turning his attention away from Keene and back toward the evening ahead. She was right. There would be enough time to focus on finding the man who was trying to kill her.

Brayden eyed the number of dishes thoughtfully. "I *was* starting to wonder if my kitchen table could take the weight."

She flapped a dishcloth at him and he caught her around the waist. Rhys, wide-awake after his nap, ran over and pulled on the leg of Brayden's jeans. "Hug."

Brayden scooped up the little boy and held him between them. Rhys wrapped an arm around each of their necks, planting a kiss on Esmée's cheek, then one on Brayden's. The simple gesture sent a shot of liquid warmth straight to Brayden's chest.

He'd never wondered what it would feel like to hold another man's child in his arms, or considered the prospect of a ready-made family. Esmée and Rhys came as a package, and he didn't have to think about, or question, that. The feelings he had for Rhys were as strong as those for Esmée. He was falling for them both in different ways...and his heart stuttered with fright at the thought. Not because he didn't want it, but because of how much he wanted it.

This was what he had craved all those years ago with Ava. A home and a family. Returning at the end of the day to people who loved him... Warmth. Contentment. Support. His throat tightened as he gazed into the twin pairs of dark brown eyes that were fixed on his face.

He wasn't afraid that Esmée would hurt him the way Ava had. When he looked at her, he saw her honesty and kindness. No, his fears were about the speed with which he was forgetting his cold, cynical shell. After he had closed himself off from the thought of another relationship for all those years, Esmée and

Rhys had burst into Brayden's life. Despite the danger facing them, they'd brightened his existence with their infectious joy and laughter.

*When this is over, and they've left, what then?* Would everything return to the way it had been before? Was that what he wanted?

Esmée took Rhys and placed him on the floor. Taking Brayden's face between her hands, she pressed a kiss onto his lips. "Stop it."

"Stop what?"

"Overthinking. It never did anyone any good."

The front doorbell rang before he could answer and the monitor in the hall showed it was Shane and Quinn. When they stepped inside, Rhys studied them by peeping out from behind Esmée's legs for a moment or two. Although he'd already met Shane earlier, Quinn was a stranger.

Quinn squatted until she was on his level. "Hi, there."

Clearly deciding she wasn't a threat, Rhys took her hand. "I have pigs and ducks." He led her into the room where his wooden animals were scattered across the floor.

Shane shook his head. "None of my pickup lines ever worked that well."

"Try that one next time." Brayden handed him a beer. "Rhys is a generous little guy. He'll let you borrow his toys."

Esmée's chicken pie, baked sweet potatoes and

homemade cornbread were a success, and Brayden was more relaxed in the company of his brother and sister than he'd ever been. There was no denying it—with Rhys in his high chair and the two dogs on the alert for crumbs, there was a family mood in his usually soulless kitchen. He contrasted this to other evenings, when he used to come home from work and fix himself a microwave dinner while pouring Echo's food into his bowl. Some days, he wouldn't even bother to put the light on in this room.

He looked up and caught Esmée's eye. The corners of her eyes crinkled into a half smile and he was lost. Who was he kidding? He could never go back to a time before he'd known her and Rhys. Why would he return his life to its old default setting of loneliness when he'd experienced the alternative? For the first time in his life, he knew what love felt like. He wasn't letting that go.

The conversation drifted naturally into reminiscences about their childhood. Esmée sat back, content to listen to the stories that would have been unbelievable—if they'd been about anyone other than Rusty.

"He was more like a carefree relative than a dad," Shane said. "Sailing into our lives and having a good time, but backing out again super fast if ever he was asked to do anything responsible."

"There were fun things about being with Rusty... no set bed times, no rules about healthy foods, nobody standing over me making sure I did my home-work." Quinn pulled a face. "But I remember the downside as well. Trying to wake him up to take me to school. Looking for him in the audience when he'd promised to come and see me in my school play, knowing he wouldn't be there."

"Remember my bike?" The mood shifted from lighthearted to somber as Brayden spoke.

"I know how much you loved it," Shane said.

"Yeah. My grandpa saved for months to buy it for my tenth birthday." Brayden could still recall the feeling of pride he had as he rode around town on the shiny bicycle. "I left it at the Pour House one day while I was at school. When I went back, Rusty had taken the wheels off and used them to replace the ones that had broken on the cart he used to move barrels from the yard to the bar."

"That's even worse than when Demi was desper-ate for a T-shirt with a picture of her favorite pop star on it. Rusty promised he'd get it for her, but he left it too late, and when he tried to order one they were all sold out." Shane turned to Esmée. "You won't believe this, but Rusty bought a plain white one and drew a picture on the front."

Esmée's expressive face registered her shock and she turned to Brayden. "This is a joke, right?"

"No, this is our dad."

"Nothing beats the jar on the bar." Quinn gave a laugh that had no humor in it.

"What was that?"

"I was eleven," Brayden said. "We were all in the bar at the time…me, Quinn, Shane and Demi. The place was full. All the regulars were there and Rusty was in high spirits. Suddenly, he rang the bell over the bar and asked for quiet because he had an announcement to make. He placed a jar on the corner of the counter. It was a collection, he said. All donations welcome. He didn't want any more 'little accidents'—his exact words—around the place, so he'd decided to get a vasectomy."

Quinn took a long slug of her soda. "The whole place erupted into laughter. I just wanted the ground to swallow me up. When I turned to see if Demi was okay, she burst into tears and ran out."

"Didn't Rusty realize what he'd done?" Esmée asked. "Surely he must have thought about it and recognized the embarrassment he'd caused you?"

"You'd think, wouldn't you?" Shane said. "The jar is still there. It's become a Pour House joke that Rusty's vasectomy has to be the most expensive medical procedure in history."

Esmée gave a horrified gasp and Brayden nodded. "If I thought it was serious, I'd be the biggest contributor."

Shane snorted with laughter. "Don't waste your money. Rusty empties that jar once a week. It's his drinking fund."

"You should all be proud of what you've achieved,"

Esmée said. "And, although you talk about him with indulgence, you did it in spite of Rusty, not because of him."

Those simple words made Brayden stop and take a fresh look at his life, and he could see them having a similar effect on Quinn and Shane. Brayden had always accepted his place in Red Ridge society. It had been mapped out for him by the Colton family hierarchy. Rusty was the poorest of the three cousins, looked down on by wealthy Fenwick and successful Judson. In addition, Rusty's antics made him, and his family, a regular object of ridicule. His kids had been the target of Red Ridge jokes for so long, they'd taken the role for granted.

Despite all of that, Esmée was right. They'd done okay. Brayden had achieved his dream of becoming a search-and-rescue cop. Quinn was running her own business. Despite a terrible setback that could have ruined his life and put him on the wrong side of the law, Shane was making a success of his life.

"Here's to us." He tilted his beer bottle toward his brother and sister. "And that includes Demi."

It was a solemn moment, an acknowledgment of a bond they'd denied until now…and their concern for their missing sister. Had this been Esmée's intention all along? Her expression was serene as she watched them, but he had a sneaking suspicion she wasn't surprised at the way the evening was unfolding.

"I wish she'd get in touch." Quinn's voice was fretful as she served slices of her apple pie.

"Is there anyone, apart from the three of you, she might contact?" Esmée asked.

"The only other person I can think of is Serena," Quinn said. "That's our cousin, Serena Colton. She and Demi had grown close recently and Serena has been one of the few people prepared to say she believes in Demi's innocence."

"Will she talk to me?" Esmée asked. "Even though this problem with Keene has surfaced, I'd still like to try to find evidence that helps Demi's case."

"I'll contact Serena. Maybe if we meet with her together, she'll be willing to give you an interview," Quinn said.

Their guests left soon after dinner when Rhys, who had been allowed to stay up late, started to show signs of tiredness. As she was leaving, Quinn embraced both Brayden and Esmée. "We need to do this more often."

Brayden swallowed a momentary obstruction in his throat. He was twenty-nine. Quinn was thirty. That hug was the first voluntary physical contact they'd shared as adults. It felt good. He grasped Shane's shoulder. "We do."

When they'd gone, Brayden locked the door and turned to look at Esmée. Rhys was in her arms, his head nestled sleepily into the curve of her neck. Just looking at them brought him such deep joy that he was momentarily speechless. He would never get tired of that feeling. Chasing rainbows and searching for dreams…he'd leave that to other people. In the strangest of circumstances, he'd found everything he wanted. Right here, right now, right behind his own front door. His only remaining doubt now was how soon was too soon to tell the woman he'd known for just over a week—the woman with whom he'd agreed there'd be no strings—that he wanted more?

"I don't feel like I'm doing anything to help you find Demi." The note of frustration in Esmée's voice brought him back down to earth.

"Was that what tonight was about?" He quirked an eyebrow at her. "I got the feeling there was a hint of family matchmaking going on."

"Maybe that was the plan as well." Her gaze scanned his face. "I don't want to disrupt your life, Brayden."

"Esmée, you're in my life…and that suits me just fine." He reached out a hand and stroked Rhys's curls, conscious of her bemused expression as she watched him. "Now let's get this little guy to bed."

## Chapter 16

Two days later, the morning started out in a mad rush as they all overslept. Waking in Brayden's arms was heavenly, but the realization that she had exactly half an hour to get herself and Rhys ready and out the door sent Esmée scrambling wildly toward the bathroom. By some miracle, they left the house showered and clothed only a few minutes later than Brayden's usual time.

"Breakfast in the car is not a proper meal." She handed an aluminum foil-wrapped packet of toast to Rhys, who was already in his child seat in the rear of her vehicle, and one to Brayden.

"Totally worth it for an extra hour in bed with you." He was unrepentant as he kissed her. "I'll follow you to Sarah's. If you leave her house for any reason, let me know."

After the drama of the car trying to run her down a couple days earlier, Brayden wasn't comfortable about leaving her, but Finn had called him about an assault that had taken place during the night. The unconscious victim had been taken to the hospital and the chief wanted Brayden to get down there and see what he could discover. Esmée was still hoping to hear from Quinn about an interview with Serena.

"I'll be fine with Sarah and Hester," she reassured him. "I've got my laptop, so I'm planning to start making some notes on what I've got so far. If Quinn talks to Serena and she agrees to speak to me, I'll be at her place with your sister."

She could tell he was still worried and wished they had more time so she could tell him what his concern meant to her. After everything she had been through with Gwyn, to have this man look at her with that expression in his eyes, to put her and Rhys first, to know that their safety was his priority...

"Timing." Brayden appeared to be reading her mind. "Why can't Keene and the rest of the world just take a few days off and leave us in peace?"

She laughed. "We wouldn't be here now if things hadn't gotten a little crazy."

"You're right." He looked stunned. "If it wasn't for the Groom Killer, we might never have met."

Esmée pointed to his car. "We don't have time for

this conversation now. Go." She softened the message with a swift kiss. "I'll see you later."

As she drove, Rhys talked about the kittens in between each mouthful of toast. Esmée indulged in a pleasant daydream. Should she get him a kitten *and* a puppy? Maybe she should concentrate on deciding where they were going to live and then finding them a home. And making sure Roper Keene was safely behind bars. The thought of the man who was targeting her made her shiver. Even though Brayden was following close behind, she felt the loss of his presence. She wanted him right next to her, close enough to touch. *Always.*

When they reached Sarah's place, her friend was waiting on the doorstep with Hester beside her. Esmée pulled up right alongside the property, giving Brayden a wave as she did. Having watched her lift Rhys from the car and go inside, he drove away.

Once they were in the house, Rhys went straight to Sarah's comfortable sitting room. The kittens were becoming more adventurous and Rhys gave a cry of delight to see them spilling out of their basket. After watching him play with them for a few minutes, Esmée placed her laptop bag down.

"You're sure you don't mind both of us invading your space today?"

"Whatever it takes to keep you safe." Sarah put a hand on her arm. "I couldn't believe it when you told us about the latest incident."

"If it wasn't for Brayden's quick thinking you'd have been killed." Hester lowered her voice so Rhys didn't hear.

"I know." Esmée rubbed her rear end reminiscently. Although Brayden had broken the brunt of her fall, she'd still taken a whack when she hit the sidewalk. The bruises on her buttocks were an interesting variety of colors.

"When will this end?" Sarah wrapped her arms tight around her own waist. "It's bad enough that we have a serial killer in town targeting bridegrooms, but now there's someone out to get you…"

Tears sparkled on the ends of her lashes and Esmée placed an arm around her shoulders. This was hard on all of them, but it was doubly difficult for Sarah, who had lost Jack to the Groom Killer. With everything else that was going on, she wasn't even able to grieve in peace.

"This *will* be resolved," she said. "The truth always comes out in the end. The Groom Killer will be caught and the person who is targeting me will be found. In the meantime, maybe we need to teach Rhys that kittens shouldn't be carried upside down?"

Sarah managed a laugh and the three women sat on the rug to play with Rhys and the cats, who were already developing their individual personalities. Some time later, Esmée went into Sarah's small study and opened up her laptop. She had a number of interviews to collate and pictures of different locations to organize. Maybe she was allowing her closeness to Brayden to influence her, but even though she had no real evidence to support her conclusion, she didn't think Demi Colton was guilty.

Perhaps that should be her starting point. A hunch. All the evidence pointed in the opposite direction. Almost everybody in Red Ridge believed Demi was the killer, but Esmée, a stranger in town, who knew nothing about the victims, or the suspect, had a gut feeling that the feisty Colton bounty hunter was innocent. With that in mind, she started to type.

She'd been working for about half an hour when her cell phone buzzed. She checked the display and saw it was Quinn.

"Serena said she'll talk to us, although she wants to make it clear up front that she doesn't know where Demi is."

"That's okay. I just want to get her impression of what's going on." Esmée shrugged her shoulders, releasing her muscles from their cramped position. "I'll meet you there."

Since she knew Brayden was going to the hospital to conduct an interview, she sent him a message instead of calling him. When she returned to the sitting room, the kittens were asleep and Rhys was seated on the sofa next to Hester, who was reading him a story. Esmée stooped to kiss his cheek.

"I'll be back soon. Quinn and I are going to speak to Serena Colton."

"You will be careful?" Sarah looked up from her knitting with an anxious expression.

"I'll drive straight there and back. Promise." She waved as she went out the door. "Back in an hour. Two at the most."

The guy in the hospital bed had been beaten so badly, there was barely an inch of flesh that wasn't bruised. Both his eyes were so swollen he could barely open them, his nose was spread halfway across his face, his bottom lip was split and he was missing several teeth. In addition, he had broken ribs and the fingers on both hands were damaged after the attacker had viciously stamped on them.

Brayden took a seat next to the bed. "Damn it, Ray. I hope you weren't planning on entering any beauty contests."

Ray Findley worked in the tire shop close to the Pour House and Brayden had known him since they were at school together. "Don't make me laugh, Bray. Hurts."

"Who did this to you?"

Ray was the most inoffensive guy Brayden could think of. He was hard-working, friendly, lived at home with his widowed mom and volunteered most weekends at the Red Ridge Animal Sanctuary. The only out-of-character thing he'd done lately was that he'd been seen around town with Hayley Patton, Bo Gage's fiancée. Since Bo's murder, Hayley seemed to be on a mission to work her way through Red Ridge's available men. Brayden could have given Ray some advice about that situation, if he'd asked. Hayley was one of the police department's K-9 trainers and she'd fluttered her eyelashes in Brayden's direction a few times. Even if he'd been interested, he knew trouble when he saw it. Even before her engagement to Bo, Hayley had always been a whole lot of trouble wrapped up in a pretty package.

"Didn't get a look at him. I left Hayley's place around midnight." Ray winced with the effort of talking. "Next thing, something hit me over the head from behind. Guy started beating the crap out of me. I tried to get up…got to my knees once, I think. He kicked me in the ribs and I went back down."

"Did he give you any idea what it was about?" Brayden asked. "Or say anything at all?"

"Not a word. Nothing that I heard anyway. I must have lost consciousness." Ray struggled to sit up straighter and Brayden helped him by raising his pillows. "Next thing I knew a couple of guys who'd just left the Pour House were standing over me. They called 911."

"Can you think of anyone who might have done this? Anyone who might have a grudge against you?" Ray was silent for so long Brayden began to wonder if he'd heard him. "Ray?"

Ray sighed. "I'm not the only guy Hayley's been dating."

"I'd heard that." Since Hayley had taken to flaunting a different guy each night, the whole town had heard it.

"You think I'm a fool?"

"I just want to find out who beat you up, Ray. I'm not judging you." Brayden had long ago given up finding fault with other people's relationship decisions. It had happened right around the time Ava had laughed in his face as she told him their baby was imaginary.

"I suppose you could start with the other men she's been seeing. It may take you some time."

Brayden stayed awhile longer, taking down a few more details. When he left the hospital, he checked his cell and found a brief message from Esmée telling him she was meeting Quinn at Serena's ranch. He tried calling her but her phone went straight to voice mail. From the timing of her text, he guessed she was probably driving. When he tried calling Quinn, he got no answer from her, either. Deciding to try Esmée again later, he drove to the K-9 training center.

When he entered the building, both Danica Gage and Hayley were inside. Although Echo was experienced, there was no such thing as a fully trained dog and it was important to constantly work on his partner's skills and fitness. Over the past few weeks, they had been spending time focusing on Echo's scenting abilities and Danica was walking a random route around the center, hiding a variety of objects in different places.

"Can you take Echo through this morning's routine?" Brayden asked, when Danica finished. "I need to speak to Hayley."

"Sure." Danica held out a treat to Echo and he pranced eagerly alongside her to the start of the training course.

Although Hayley looked like she'd been crying, she had carefully reapplied makeup to disguise her puffy eyes. Brayden held open the door to the office. "Shall we go in here?"

For a moment, she appeared to consider refusing. Then, with a muffled sob, she followed him. Brayden closed the door behind them.

Hayley flopped into the only chair and covered her face with her hands. "I can't deal with this. I don't know anything about what happened to Ray."

"Hayley, a nice man, who you've been dating, got badly beaten as he left your place last night. I know you'll want to help with the investigation any way you can."

She lowered her hands, showing him a tearful face. "Ever since Bo was killed..." She had been using those words about a dozen times a day ever since her fiancé's murder.

Brayden sympathized with Hayley over Bo's death. Up to a point. Like most people in Red Ridge, he wasn't sure how deep Hayley's feelings went. He suspected Demi, who had only been engaged to Bo for a week when he dumped her for Hayley, had cared more for the dead man. Did any of that matter when it came to finding out who had attacked Ray? Probably not.

"Let's start with the names of the other guys you've been seeing. One of them could have done this out of jealousy."

Persuading her to give him the names wasn't easy. "None of them are anything serious."

"They may not know that, Hayley." Brayden handed her a piece of paper and a pen. "How about you write me a list?"

Her expression shifted from sorrowful to sulky. Scribbling down a few names, she thrust the paper back at him. "If I wasn't missing Bo so much…" The tears made a reappearance.

Brayden tucked the list into his top pocket. "Ray will be glad to see you when you get off work."

Hayley dropped her eyes from his steady gaze. "I, um, I have a date."

For a moment, Brayden considered telling her to cancel and make sure she got her selfish little ass down to that hospital. He decided against it. As much as it would hurt Ray if she didn't show, it would do him good to find out exactly how shallow she was before he got too involved.

"If you think of anything that could help catch the person who did this, give me a call."

The conversation had left a bitter taste in his mouth and, as he went in search of Danica and Echo, Brayden's mind turned to Esmée. He wasn't so hard-hearted that he believed the whole world was made up of Avas and Hayleys, but if he hadn't met Esmée he could have gone through life unaware anyone could have so much generosity of spirit. When she entered his world, her agenda had been to find out about his sister. Within days, she had wrapped him in her warmth. She had the biggest heart of anyone he'd ever known, always giving and asking nothing in return.

Just the thought of Esmée made his heart race. He checked his watch and judged she must have arrived at the Double C Ranch by now. She was with Quinn and Serena, and Judson Colton's cowboys wouldn't let anyone near the place without permission. She was safe. He decided to give it another half hour before he called her.

Having checked the GPS on her phone, Esmée took a route that skirted around the center of town toward the Double C Ranch. She was on a quiet stretch of highway when the car began to vibrate wildly. Although the tarmac was smooth, it felt like she was driving across the surface of the moon.

Immediately aware that she had a flat tire, she pulled over to the side of the road. Checking that the doors were locked, she took a moment to analyze the situation. She knew how to change a tire. She'd been in this situation once before and had managed just fine. It was just that she had this crawling feeling down her spine...

Was this a coincidence? Her eyes scanned the area. She really was in the middle of nowhere. All she could see for miles around was grass and a few trees. But that was a good thing. There was nowhere for a hulking ex-boxer to hide.

Cowering in the car wasn't going to get her anywhere. Before she panicked and called Brayden, she should at least check on the damage to the tire. If it was something she could fix herself, she could be on her way in ten minutes, fifteen at the most.

Unlocking the doors, she slid from the car, still unable to resist a quick look around even though she knew there was no one there. When she reached the back of the vehicle, she sucked in a breath, staring in dismay. Both rear tires were completely flat.

*Both?* There was no way *that* was a coincidence. Had someone let the air out while she was in Sarah's house? It seemed the only possible solution.

She was reaching into her pocket for her cell phone when a car approached on the opposite side of the road. Fear gripped her and she momentarily froze before darting back toward her own vehicle. As she pulled open the door, the other car slowed and she registered that the car was bright pink and the driver had long blond hair. There was no way it was Roper Keene in disguise. Relief flooded through her at the same time that she realized she knew the driver.

Lulu Love drew alongside her and slid her window down. "Bummer."

"You could say that." Esmée relaxed slightly. "I only have one spare and both rear tires are flat."

Lulu drummed long, candy-pink nails on the steering wheel for a few seconds. Her eyes were hidden behind designer shades. "How about I drive you into town? That way, you can pick up another spare. The guys in the tire shop can either drive you back out here and change your flats, or they can bring the tow truck out and take your car in so they can do the repairs there."

Esmée experienced an insane rush of gratitude toward this woman she had met only once. It was so strong she wanted to hug her. She actually wanted to go over to the car, lean in and embrace her. Since Lulu didn't look like a hugger, and she didn't want to waste any more time at the side of this road, she nodded. "Let me get my purse and lock my car."

Once Esmée had secured her vehicle, she got into the other car with a word of thanks.

Lulu flapped a dismissive hand. "No problem." She swung into a U-turn and headed back on the road toward town.

Esmée reached for her cell. She was going to be late for her meeting with Quinn and Serena and she wanted to let Brayden know what was happening. Before she could make her calls, Lulu's voice halted her. "Lose the phone."

Frowning, the implication of the words only half registering, Esmée looked up from the screen. Lulu was driving with her right hand on the wheel. Her left arm rested across her body and in it she held a gun. It was pointed at Esmée.

"Now." Lulu took a second to look away from the road so she could nod at the cell phone. "Throw it out the window."

Esmée weighed her options. And decided she didn't have any. The gun was inches from her abdomen. If she tried to grapple with Lulu in a moving vehicle, she risked being shot. The very best she could hope for was that she would cause them to crash. Even if the car didn't have central locking—and she guessed it did—they were traveling at a high speed. Throwing herself from a moving vehicle wasn't an option she liked.

She needed some thinking time, but her mind was racing in time with her heartbeat. Trying to stay calm, she took a second to switch her cell to silent. Using the button on the door to release the electric window, she watched Lulu out of the corner of her eye.

"I guess we're not going to the tire shop?"

To Esmée's surprise, a single tear slid out from beneath the expensive shades and tracked its way through the heavy makeup on the other woman's cheek. "He has my baby."

Esmée held her breath as she dropped her phone between the passenger seat and the door instead of out the window. Lulu appeared not to notice. That first inhalation as she started to breathe again was painful. Slowly, she raised the window. "Are you talking about Roper Keene?"

The gun wobbled slightly and Esmée kept her gaze fixed on it. "He came to my apartment first thing." Lulu's voice cracked and she struggled to get it under control. "Snatched her right up out of her crib."

"Lulu, we can call the police right now…"

The other woman shook her head, her improbable curls bouncing wildly. "If I don't take you to him in the next hour, he'll kill her. He said if he saw any sign of the police my baby girl would be dead and then he'd come after me." The note of anguish in her voice increased. "You didn't see him. He held her head in one of his hands, talked about how he could crush her skull without even trying…"

The tears were coming faster now, pouring down her face, and she lifted the hand that held the gun to her face and swiped the back of her wrist under her nose. Esmée figured that keeping her calm might be more important than trying to persuade her to call Brayden. Given her history, Lulu wasn't going to be inclined to trust the police to rescue her baby and she wasn't in the right frame of mind to listen to reason. Esmée tried to put herself in the other woman's place. If Keene was holding Rhys hostage, would she be capable of rational thinking?

*No, just like Lulu, I would be out of my mind.*

It looked like Esmée would soon be swapping places with little Venus Love. While getting the baby out of Keene's hands had to be the priority, the thought didn't fill her with confidence. She checked the time on the dashboard display. They would be expecting her at the Double C Ranch about now. When Esmée didn't show, Quinn would call her cell. Hopefully, when Esmée didn't respond, Quinn's next step would be to call Brayden.

Instead of trying to engage Lulu any further, she concentrated on the route. They were traveling away from the town, and, as the road began to climb toward the hills, their destination became clear. They were headed toward the Eagle's Nest.

## Chapter 17

When Brayden's cell buzzed as he left the training center, he jerked it out of his pocket, hoping it was Esmée. He'd called and messaged her several times, but she hadn't replied. Although his heart sank when it wasn't her, he was pleased to hear Dr. Wilson's voice.

"These are initial findings. My full report will take longer."

"Anything you can tell me that will help the investigation is appreciated."

"Okay." He could hear papers rustling. "Dental records have confirmed that the body *is* that of Richie Lyman. Although the corpse was badly mutilated, I was able to ascertain that the cause of death was a broken neck."

"Roper Keene." Clearly, Richie had ceased to be useful to his friend the Neckbreaker.

"Pardon?" He could hear the confusion in Dr. Wilson's voice.

"Sorry. Just thinking aloud."

"The other injuries, the cutting wounds, were postmortem. As I told you at the scene, it looks like the person who killed him wanted to chop the body up and dispose of the pieces. When he failed, he buried the remains."

"Was he killed at the same place he was buried?" Brayden asked.

"I'm waiting for the results of further tests." Her voice was cautious. "But on the evidence I have now, I'm going to say he was killed elsewhere and moved to the burial site. There were limestone deposits on his body that are not consistent with the area in which he was found. I also found pine needles and soil that suggest he may have been buried elsewhere first."

Brayden pictured an indentation in the earth beneath a fallen tree trunk, in the place below the Eagle's Nest. The place where Esmée had found the bloodstained knife. He remembered Esmée shivering as she said it looked like a shallow grave. Could that have been the first place Richie was buried? If so, why had Keene decided to move him?

Since Dr. Wilson didn't have any further information for him, Brayden thanked her before ending the call. He needed to update his report on the body. Then he would need to get out to Lulu's place and break the news to her that Richie was dead. His cell buzzed again as he was contemplating that unpleasant task.

"Quinn?" Brayden heaved a sigh of relief when he heard his sister's voice. "Ask Esmée why the hell she isn't answering my calls and messages."

"I'm calling to ask you the same thing." His sister's voice was slightly higher-pitched than usual. "Esmée isn't here, Bray."

"What do you mean? Did she leave already?" *Tell me she left already.*

"No, she never got here. We were expecting her at least half an hour ago—"

"If she turns up tell her to call me immediately and then stay put at the Double C until I get there."

Some extra sense told him Esmée wasn't going to show up at the ranch. As he ran across the training center parking lot with Echo at his heels, he called Sarah. "Is Esmée still with you?"

"No, she left to meet Quinn at Serena's place." He heard her sharp, indrawn breath. "Oh, dear Lord, Brayden. Is everything okay?"

"I hope so." Three inadequate little words that didn't come close to what he was really feeling.

His first thought was that something must have happened to her. That Keene had gotten to her. He told himself he could be wrong. There may be any number of reasons why she hadn't made it to the Double C. Car trouble. Maybe she even got lost. What if she'd actually found Demi?

*Hope.* It was a tiny flicker, but he had to nurture it. If he didn't, the fear that was gripping his insides would paralyze him. If his gut instinct was right and Keene did have her, then he had to rely on what he knew of Esmée. On her strength, her positivity, her determination. His Esmée was a fighter.

*His* Esmée. Why the hell hadn't he told her about that when he had the chance? When he saw her again, he wasn't going to waste another precious minute. Esmée was going to know exactly what she meant to him. The thought propelled him into action. He tried her cell again as he gunned the engine, but it went to voice mail. Driving out of town, he took the obvious road Esmée would have to drive along to get from Sarah's place to the Double C.

And there it was. The very thing he didn't want to see. Her car was on the side of the road…with two flat tires. Two. It was possible that was bad luck, but given everything else that had happened just lately, it was highly unlikely.

Brayden slammed his open palm against the steering wheel. Where had she gone? She wouldn't have walked into town from here—the distance was too great and she knew she was in danger with Keene on the prowl. So why hadn't she called him, or Quinn, or Sarah for help? The answer was obvious. She had gone with someone. And the fact that he hadn't heard from her meant that person was holding her against her will.

He got on his radio, hardly recognizing his own voice as he gave his call sign. "Missing person. Name—Esmée da Costa. Age—twenty-seven."

As he went through the routine of providing Frank Lanelli with the details he needed to alert all officers, Brayden's mind was racing ahead. He had to dredge deep inside himself to find his usual focus, but it was there. Although his feelings for Esmée threatened to drown out everything else, he managed to regain control and do what he did best.

*Think.* What did he know about Keene? He wasn't staying in town. He'd already shown a preference for the Coyote Mountains. It was where Esmée had first encountered him, and where he had disposed of Richie's body. It was also where the Angel Cave, the deadly limestone cavern, was located. Dr. Wilson had said Richie's body showed he was killed somewhere that left limestone traces on his body. Keene was a survival specialist who was unlikely to be put off by the dangers of the cave. And he'd moved the body from its first burial site because he didn't want it right outside the place where he was staying.

Was he prepared to gamble Esmée's safety on a hunch? Right now, his intuition was all he had. In the darkness of his despair, the only ray of light he had was this tiny hope that he was right about where

Keene had taken her. If he acted on it, at least he would be doing something.

He spared a few minutes to call Shane. "Get over to Sarah Mull's place. I think the guy who's been after Esmée has taken her, but I don't want to take any chances. It could be a double bluff. Keep Rhys safe until I get back."

This time when he called the dispatcher, his voice was firm. "I'm heading out to Angel Cave."


Lulu parked her car at the farthest point from the public restrooms. "Don't try anything. I promised I'd bring you to Keene. I can still do it, even if you have a bullet in your knee."

As Lulu exited the vehicle, Esmée moved fast. Her fingers were trembling so much she wasn't sure they would work properly, but she managed to undo her seat belt and lean down. She snagged her phone and jammed it into the back pocket of her jeans. When Lulu pulled open the passenger door, Esmée was shaking so badly with nerves, she could barely move.

"Get out." Lulu waved the gun at her.

"You don't have to do this." She figured she had nothing to lose by giving negotiating one last try.

"I'm not going to stand here talking about it." Lulu's voice was almost a shriek and she took a moment to get it back under control. "I need to get Venus back."

She grabbed Esmée by the wrist and hauled her

out of the car, slamming the door closed after her. Even if Esmée had wanted to draw attention to herself, there was no one else around. Any thoughts she may have had about making a run for it soon ended when Lulu linked an arm through hers and jammed the gun in her ribs.

"He wants you alive, but I'll hurt you if I have to. Don't make me choose between you and my baby."

Keene wanted her alive. It was an interesting piece of information. The person who had set fire to Jack's apartment and the driver of the SUV had certainly appeared to be trying to kill her. Could he have been trying to frighten her into leaving town? Now it seemed things had changed. Esmée had something Keene wanted. But what? She had no idea. Soon she would be face-to-face with the Neckbreaker and he would know that. He would soon discover she was no use to him. At which point, she was very much afraid the scare tactics would end and he would no longer want her alive.

They walked in silence down the steep track. So much had happened since the last time Esmée was here, it was hard to believe such a short time had passed. She still struggled to believe her first encounter with Keene was anything other than chance. If he had followed her and Rhys up to the ridge that day, why would he have waited until she found the knife to confront her? He'd had the advantage over them the whole time. Setting aside the fact that he was a giant, he had been armed. While they had been enjoying a picnic under the trees followed by a game of hide-and-seek, he could have attacked them at any time.

That was why Esmée believed he hadn't followed them on their hike. No. The truth was so obvious, she could have laughed out loud. If there hadn't been a gun in her ribs, she probably would have. *He was here all the time.* Keene had been hiding out in the cave when she and Rhys had walked right into his front yard. No doubt they had disturbed him with their laughter and he'd started spying on them. When they'd discovered the hidden knife, Keene had been forced into action.

They were on level ground now, and Lulu marched her along the bottom edge of the cliff toward the distinctive rock structure that looked like angel's wings. If Esmée could turn back time, she would have chosen a different place for their picnic. But then, she supposed, the series of events that had led to her getting to know Brayden wouldn't have happened. Would she change that? The thought brought a rush of tears to her eyes and she blinked hard to get rid of them. No matter how they had reached this point in time, she had fallen in love with Brayden. She would never turn the clock back on that.

*And I will see him again.* She had to hold on to that thought.

A faint sound reached them, making Lulu gasp. It was a baby's cry.

"If she's crying, she's alive." Esmée said it for her own sake as much as for Lulu's. The thought that Keene had snatched a baby to get at her was sickening.

Although Lulu had a gun trained on her, the woman was being blackmailed into it. Would she have dealt with things differently if Keene had taken Rhys and told her the only way to get him back was to kidnap someone? She didn't know. The only thing she knew for sure was that Lulu wasn't the bad guy.

"Yeah." Lulu gulped hard, as she moved faster. "She's alive."

When they reached the angel-wing rock, Lulu shifted their positions so that Esmée had to go ahead of her around the rock and into the entrance of the cave. The sudden gloom was hard on Esmée's eyes and she took a few moments to adjust. The baby's cries were louder here, echoing in the rocky depths.

"Keene? I brought her…just like you told me." Lulu's voice quavered desperately.

There was a sound—boots scuffing on rock—and Keene appeared. Esmée had told herself he couldn't be as big as she remembered, that her imagination had made him into a caricature. She was wrong. He was bigger. He towered over her and Lulu, making them look like children in comparison to his bulk.

*I missed the self-defense class about how to deal with a giant in a cave.*

Keene was holding Venus Love awkwardly in one arm. In his hand, he held the strange rattle Esmée had seen at Lulu's apartment. Although the baby was red-faced and screaming, she didn't appear to have suffered any harm.

"Please." Lulu choked back a sob. "I did what you asked. Let me take her."

"Give me the gun first." Keene's smile took in Esmée's face then Lulu's. He placed the baby's rattle on a waist-high rock. "I don't want the two of you getting any ideas about female bonding."

With a shaking hand, Lulu held out the weapon. Keene took it and gave her the baby in exchange. With a cry that went straight to Esmée's heart, Lulu seized Venus and clutched her tight to her chest.

"Get out of here." Keene used the gun to gesture toward the cave entrance. "And remember... I know where you live."

"I won't talk. I swear."

Lulu reached for the rattle, but Keene shook his head. "Leave that here."

It was an odd instruction, one that triggered a question in Esmée's mind. Since she had more important things to think about it went unanswered. Nevertheless, it lingered. Why would Keene want to keep the baby toy?

As Lulu dashed from the cave, Keene turned his attention to Esmée. "It's just you and me."

"What do you want from me?" She was pleased

with the way her voice sounded. Calm and controlled, it gave no hint of the churning of her insides.

He placed the gun next to the rattle and cracked his knuckles purposefully. "Information." Esmée's gaze dropped to his hands. He was reminding her of what he could do with them. The scare tactics were working. "And I suggest you give it to me."

When Brayden arrived at the Eagle's Nest rest stop there were only a few other vehicles in the parking lot. It was about what he'd have expected on a weekday morning in April. As he opened the rear door of his own car to allow Echo to jump down, one of the vehicles at the farthest end of the lot caught his eye. It was impossible to miss Lulu Love's bubblegum-pink Mustang.

That had to merit further investigation. Lulu didn't strike him as an outdoor girl, and even if she had suddenly changed her ways, would she come out here with a newborn baby? There was a chill wind blowing and the forecast was for rain later.

Brayden put in a quick call to Frank. "Her car is here at Eagle's Nest, but get someone to check out Lulu Love's apartment."

The dispatcher responded with his usual calm efficiency. "I'll have a unit stop by there right away."

Brayden made his way down the incline with Echo at his heels. He had nothing belonging to Esmée, so he couldn't send the dog ahead to seek her out. He decided against sending Echo on an air-scenting search. The problem with that type of trail was that his partner would alert to any human he found. Brayden didn't want distractions. He was certain Keene was hiding in the Angel Cave and, if he was right, that meant Esmée was with him.

As he reached the bottom of the slope, a figure came running toward him. Before Brayden could reach for his gun, he recognized Lulu. Clutching her baby and sobbing wildly, she was only a few feet away when she noticed him.

"Lulu. What the hell—" He reached out a hand, but she cowered away like a frightened animal.

"Get away from me!" She attempted to step around him, but Brayden blocked her path. Turning her head to look over her shoulder, she came to a trembling standstill. Her eyes were hidden behind huge shades, but tears had left tracks in her makeup and her cheeks were still wet. "Please. Just let me go."

"Not until you tell me what's going on." Impatience and instinct were at war inside him. He needed to find Esmée and he had to do it fast, but his gut was telling him Lulu's fear must be connected to Keene.

The fight went out of Lulu and her whole body slumped. Brayden caught hold of her by the elbow and led her to a large rock. He took a moment to check on the baby, but she looked fine. "You don't understand." Lulu hitched in a breath. "You don't know what he can do."

"Tell me." He kept his voice firm and calm, sensing if he offered her sympathy, her distress would increase. He would get her help later. Right now, he needed her lucid.

"He said he'll kill me and my baby—"

"He won't be able to do that if he's behind bars, Lulu. Now, where is he? Is he in the Angel Cave?" She nodded. "And Esmée is with him?" Another nod. "Is he armed?"

"Gun." Lulu swallowed hard. "He took my baby... made me bring Esmée to him."

Brayden was aware of time slipping away. Lulu still didn't know Keene had killed Richie. If he broke that news to her now, he couldn't give her the support she needed and go after Keene. Esmée's life was in danger. Even if she wasn't the woman he loved—even if they'd never met—saving her had to be his priority.

"This is what I need you to do." He squatted beside Lulu. Speaking slowly, he made sure she was looking his way in spite of the oversize shades. "Get back in your car. Drive to the Red Ridge PD building and go to the front desk. Tell the secretary there Brayden Colton sent you. Ask for a K-9 cop called Juliette Walsh. When you see her, I want you to tell her the whole story."

"I can't." Lulu cast another glance along the track toward the cave. "He said..."

"Lulu, this is the only way you are going to keep your baby safe." If she didn't respond this time, he would have to leave her. He couldn't waste any more of Esmée's precious time.

To his relief, Lulu got to her feet. "Okay." Her lip wobbled. "I'm so sorry."

He gave her a gentle shove in the right direction. Only time would tell if she listened to his advice, or got in her car and took off. No matter how the forthcoming confrontation ended—and Brayden was determined to make sure it ended the right way for Esmée—Lulu would be needed as a witness against Keene. He hoped she'd make it easy on herself and stick around.

Brayden gave Echo the command to stay at his heels, then broke into a run and covered the distance to the cave. He drew his gun and paused at one side of the entrance, taking a moment to breathe deeply before he prepared to step inside.

As he did, a woman's scream echoed off the rocky walls.

# Chapter 18

"I don't have any information for you. I don't know anything about you." Although it was the gun that stopped Esmée from running, she was more worried about Keene's hands. *Neckbreaker.* She couldn't get the word out of her head.

"That's what I thought you'd say." Keene gave an exaggerated sigh. "But we both know it's not true. And I don't have time to waste on chitchat. I have business associates in Red Ridge who need to get moving on a deal we've made, but your habit of making friends with police officers could screw things up for me. I've waited a long time for this. I need to know who you've spoken to and what you've said. Then I can tidy up here before I move on."

Esmée was trying to maintain control over her thoughts, even as they were skittering wildly in every direction. She hadn't seen Richie Lyman's body, but Brayden, a hardened police officer, had been badly shaken by what he'd witnessed. She had a feeling Keene's idea of "tidying up" was to dispose of anyone who got in his way. When he talked about her friendship with police officers, he must mean Jack and Brayden.

Jack had known about the safe-deposit robbery, but her friend was dead. Telling Keene what Jack knew couldn't hurt anyone, and it might buy her some time. "Are you talking about the robbery that took place ten years ago at the bank?"

"See? I knew you were a sensible woman. Not sensible enough to get out of town after I gave you a few warnings, but not so stupid that you're going to pretend you don't know what I'm talking about." He cupped his fingers invitingly around his ear. "Tell me more."

"Jack Parkowski suspected you and Richie Lyman were involved, but he had no proof."

"You're telling me stuff I already know. Let me make it easier for you so we can skip over the next bit. I got a call from Richie that our old friend Detective Parkowski had shown up here in his hometown. Richie wasn't happy to see him. He liked Red Ridge. Had a girlfriend, baby on the way, was working for some guys who run the place like a well-oiled machine. He asked me to pay a visit. Wanted me to come to Red Ridge and get rid of Parkowski once and for all. But there was something more in it for me as well. Richie's bosses were interested in some items I have. Let's just say they're pretty special and the market for them is rare." He took a step closer. "When I reached town, turns out this crazy Groom Killer everyone's talking about had already done the job for me with Parkowski. But then *you* started snooping around."

Esmée swallowed hard. "I wasn't investigating you. I'm making a documentary about the Groom Killer."

"I know that." He flapped an impatient hand at her. "I even know you and your kid didn't come snooping around here deliberately the day you found my knife." His eyes narrowed. "I should have finished you off then, or all the other times I had the chance. But I already had Richie's body on my hands. Like I said, my business associates don't want any trouble coming their way. They just want a nice pay-off when we dispose of these items."

He seemed happy to talk. *Keep him talking.* "Why did you kill Richie?"

A frown descended on Keene's brow. "He knew I had these items, even though he didn't know where they were hidden. Ten years ago, he helped me get away and we agreed he'd get a share of the proceeds when they were sold. I caught him snooping around in this cave one day." He cracked his knuckles again. "So I got rid of him. I wanted to cut him up small." Esmée shuddered at the way he said it so matter-of-factly. "You know, so I could spread the pieces over a wider area and there'd be less chance of him being found? Didn't work out." He shrugged. "With him gone, I get a bigger share of the payout. And Lulu? She thinks she walked away just now? I'll be visiting her again soon. I don't leave any loose ends."

Esmée guessed he was planning on killing her as well by the amount he was telling her. As far as Keene was concerned, there was no way she was leaving this cave alive. "I still don't know what you want from me."

"I need to know what your new guy has on me. He's the one my business associates are worried about. They won't risk this deal if there's a chance the cops will come sniffing around them and Richie's body already has them jumpy." He reached out a hand, gripping her upper arm so tight she thought his fingers would embed themselves in her flesh. "This is where you tell me all about the Colton search-and-rescue cop you've been cozying up to. How much does he know about me? Do I need to get rid of him as well as you?"

"No!" The word came out on a gasp. "We haven't talked about you."

His eyes narrowed and she knew he'd been toying with her. Telling Lulu he needed her alive, claiming he wanted information from Esmée... Keene enjoyed psychological torture as much as he enjoyed violence and killing. He had said it himself. He didn't leave loose ends. He had wanted to find out what she knew, but he didn't intend to keep her alive. Once he had killed Esmée, he would go after Brayden and anyone else who stood in his way. If his business associates didn't like it, he would move on without a backward glance. The Angelika diamonds were timeless. One day, Keene would sell them and get his billions.

Now that she knew she had nothing to lose, her spirit came back. He might be bigger and he might have killed, but this man was a bully the same way Gwyn had been. After that day in Wales, Esmée had sworn that if she was ever in a position where another person sought to browbeat her by using superior physical strength, she would fight back. She would never cower in fear again.

*I guess the time has come to put that to the test.*

In her self-defense classes, she had learned one simple rule. Her instructor had taught her the basics, but, ultimately, there were no rules. Whatever it took to get away was what she had to do. There were some key body areas she could strike. No matter how big her opponent may be, he was still vulnerable to a well-timed blow.

"You're lying," Keene growled as he pulled her closer.

Esmée hit him in the throat with the heel of her

hand. At the same time, she jerked her knee up hard between his legs. Although he grunted and released her arm, as she turned to run, he twisted his hand in her hair and dragged her back to him. He swung a fist like a sledgehammer in the direction of her face and she managed to dodge it at the last minute. Even so, he caught her on the shoulder and she screamed in pain, the sound echoing off the rocky walls.

One chance. That was all she had. He wouldn't miss next time. As he raised his arm again, Esmée braced herself against the wall of the cave and kicked out with both feet. She hit Keene hard in the stomach and, as he staggered back, she scrambled wildly for his gun. Her hand closed on something hard and she grasped it. As she pointed it at Keene, she realized to her horror that she'd picked up Venus Love's rattle instead of the gun.

She had one chance, and she'd blown it. She was confronting the Neckbreaker…with a baby toy.

Keene stayed on his knees, staring up at her with a wary expression. "Give me that."

That was it? No fist slamming into her face? No hands closing around her throat? No swiping her legs out from under her? Just his eyes fixed on the baby rattle and that quiet tone. She looked again at the ungainly plaything. What was it about this toy?

"You want this?" She held it up like it was one of Echo's balls. "You go get it."

She threw the rattle as hard and as far as she could,

then waited for him to get to his feet and dash after it before taking off in the opposite direction. Her feet skittered over the uneven rocky surface and she held one hand out in front of her in the darkness. With the other hand, she fumbled in the back pocket of her jeans for her cell.

Forcing herself to remain calm, she checked the screen and almost cried. She had no signal. All her clever plans had been for nothing. Her phone was useless. She couldn't even use it as a light source in case she gave her location away to Keene.

There wasn't a moment to catch her breath. She could already hear Keene approaching. As she tried to slide her cell back into her pocket, it slipped from her hand. Unable to see it in the gloom, she left it. She didn't have time to waste on something that wasn't going to help her.

With a growing sense of despair, she moved deeper into the tunnel.

At the sound of Esmée's scream, panic rose up inside Brayden. It was like a wolf tearing into his chest with sharp teeth and claws. It threatened to devour him, leaving him useless and incapable of action. All he knew for sure was, if he gave in to it, he would hear more of those screams. With no more hesitation, he went into the cave.

It was impossible to see anything, so he unclipped the small flashlight from his belt and held it in front of him. It gave him some light, but only a few feet in front of him. He thought he heard the sounds of a scuffle and voices up ahead, but he couldn't be sure. The acoustics in the cave made it difficult to hear and it was impossible to distinguish the direction of a sound.

His initial panic subsided slightly. The fact that he could hear some sort of interaction must mean Esmée was still alive. That was good news. It also meant she was with Keene, which was not as good. If he called out to her, he would alert Keene to his presence and lose the element of surprise. All he could do was keep moving deeper into the cave in search of them. Echo seemed to sense the danger and kept his nose pressed up against the back of Brayden's leg.

There was a reason why the town council had issued a warning about this cave. The layout was unlike the smaller caves lower down the trail. In the Angel Cave, there was a large cavern with several tunnels leading off. The rocky floor was treacherous, often becoming dangerously steep or even opening out without warning into sinkholes.

Brayden moved carefully. With his gun in one hand and his flashlight in the other, he couldn't steady himself against the rock wall. Once he reached the cavern, he shone the light around. It was a dramatic sight, with limestone structures and huge stalactites hanging from the roof. He could see several tunnels leading off from the main cave and he paused. Which way should he go now? An object on the ground caught his attention. Pausing to put on a pair of disposable gloves, he stooped to pick it up. It was Esmée's cell phone.

At least now he could do something more than wander blindly through the dangerous tunnels. It wasn't an ideal situation. The cell wasn't a good scent article. It wouldn't hold Esmée's smell the way a piece of clothing would. But she had been holding it recently and Echo knew her. The other problem was the cave environment wouldn't carry a scent to the dog's sensitive nostrils the same way the outdoor air would.

He was counting on his partner. Echo was an experienced dog. They'd been in difficult situations before. Maybe none with so many variables as this. A hostile environment, a killer…*and the woman I love just happens to be down here somewhere*. He had to stay focused. Putting his personal feelings aside and staying professional was hard, but it was the only way to save Esmée.

He held the cell phone out to Echo. The dog sniffed it all over. Soon, his tail began to wag eagerly.

"Go find Esmée." Brayden didn't want to speak too loud, but Echo needed to hear the familiar order.

Echo took off along the narrow tunnel. Generally, Echo switched between sniffing the air and scenting the ground, but he kept his nose down, indicating that tracking Esmée was easier that way in the cave.

Brayden followed close behind, shining the flashlight ahead of him. He was conscious that Keene was still likely to be somewhere in this cave. He didn't think the Neckbreaker had fled. Keene still had unfinished business. The killer could be behind Brayden, or he could be up ahead, sneaking up on Esmée.

The thought of her in danger was like a dark storm cloud inside his skull, gathering and growing heavier, the pressure increasing until it was unbearable. The coldness in his limbs had nothing to do with the dank walls of the cave and everything to do with the fear that gripped him. He was working on instinct, his body going through the familiar, professional routine, while his emotions were in turmoil. His heart struggled to maintain a steady beat, almost as if it was pumping tar around his body instead of blood. Because Esmée had to be okay. He couldn't have waited all this time to find her only to lose her this way.

They reached a branch in the tunnels and Echo paused. Lifting his head, he scented the air, then sniffed the ground. Circling the area, he appeared to hesitate, and Brayden clenched a fist against his thigh. If the dog had lost the scent, they had no other way of finding Esmée. He would have to exit the cave and call Mountain Rescue. In the meantime, she would be alone down here with Keene on the loose.

Suddenly, Echo took off into a passageway so low Brayden had to bend almost to his waist to follow him. It slowed his progress and he lost sight of the dog completely. Biting back a curse as he hit his head on and overhanging rock, he paused as he heard a sound up ahead.

"Echo?" He spoke softly in case it was Keene. Although how the hell that guy would fit down this tiny burrow…

The dog gave a soft *woof.* It was unmistakably his alert, but the clever hound was doing it quietly as though aware he shouldn't draw attention to them. With a pounding heart, Brayden made his way along the tunnel.

After she dropped her cell phone, Esmée tried to find her way through the tunnels that led off the main cave. But the warnings that she'd read about, the dangers of this underground system, stayed in her mind. She didn't want to escape Keene only to fall into a sinkhole, or break her leg and be unable to make her way out.

Trying to gain control over her terror, she forced herself to think. Keene had size on his side when it came to a confrontation, but maybe she could use that against him. If she could hide in a small space, he wouldn't be able to find her. Stuck in a cave in the dark, with no way of knowing where Keene was, or what he was doing…it wasn't a perfect plan. But it was better than his hands around her throat, or a bullet in her back.

With no light to guide her, she felt her way along the tunnel wall, sliding a foot in front of her to check she wasn't in danger of tumbling into a hole. When she found a narrow tunnel with a low ceiling, she ducked into it. Making her way along the passage, she discovered a cleft in the rock wall just wide enough for her to be able to squeeze into. She curled into the tight space, tucking her knees up to her chin.

Despite the cold rock walls surrounding her, sweat drenched her skin. Tension was a throbbing pain behind her eyes, and her heart thumped wildly against her rib cage. Her hands were curled into fists, nails digging into her palms. She tried to regulate her breathing, scared it was coming so fast and hard in and out of her lungs it would give her away and Keene would hear it.

*Brayden.* She wanted him so much it hurt. The fear of not seeing him and Rhys again was smothering her. Every time she thought about it, she began to tremble. Her whole body wanted to shut down in panic, but she fought it. Each time it happened, she forced herself to face her fears, to be stronger.

She had to see Brayden again to tell him how he made her feel. All this emotion inside her couldn't just die. It had to have a happy ending… It would if she could get out of this, because she knew he felt the same way. She hadn't known him for long, but loving him felt right. It was meant to be. They had both been burned in the past and they loved each other despite, or maybe because of, what they'd been through.

When she was with Brayden, Esmée was at peace. She was completely at home with him. From the first moment of meeting him, there had been no need to hold back or pretend. And she loved the way he was with Rhys. Her little boy was going to grow up with the best role model. She scrubbed a hand across her eyes, brushing away a tear. She wanted to spend the rest of her life thanking her stars she'd come to Red Ridge and found Brayden Colton.

*Just let me get out of here...*

A faint sound reached her ears and she froze, straining to listen. There it was again. Something, or someone, was coming toward her. She could hear panting. Pressing her knuckles to her mouth, she stifled a sob. She had been so sure Keene wouldn't be able to get down this tunnel.

Without warning, a wet nose thrust into her hand and a warm, furry body pushed up against her. *Echo?* She wondered if she might be hallucinating, then she heard Brayden's voice calling out to the dog. The sound was muffled, but it was unmistakably him. When Echo gave an answering bark, Esmée wrapped her arms around the dog's neck, letting her tears soak into his thick fur. Echo accepted the situation in his usual calm manner, turning his head to lick her cheek.

She could see a faint light approaching. "I'm here." Her voice was painfully wobbly, but she got the words out.

Clambering out of her hiding place, she managed to throw herself into Brayden's arms even though neither of them could stand up straight. She didn't know whether to laugh or cry, so she did both. Brayden held on to her as if he was never going to let her go. And that suited Esmée just fine.

"Keene?" She almost choked as she whispered the name.

"I don't know where he is." Brayden was hunched over in the enclosed space. "Let's get out of here. The K-9 team will search for him later."

She shivered. He was right. They had to get back above ground, but she'd have felt so much better if he'd told her Keene had been captured. The thought of the Neckbreaker on the loose in the cave as they made their way out sent her pulse rate spiking again.

"He has a gun." She kept her hand in Brayden's as he led the way into the wider tunnel. Echo was behind her.

"So do I." His voice was grim.

At least this time, she was making her way through the caves at Brayden's side and they could see where they were going. When they reached the large cavern, she started to breathe normally. Maybe, just maybe, it was going to be okay. Perhaps Keene had moved onto a new hiding place. When she glimpsed daylight through the cave exit, she tugged on Brayden's hand, urging him into a run.

She was focused on that patch of sunshine, those trees. She could almost smell the rich, forest smell...

The hand that gripped her upper arm came from nowhere, jerking her away from Brayden and pulling her against a body that appeared to have been hewn from the same rock as the rest of the cave. Something hard and cold was pressed into her ribs.

"Drop the gun, Officer Colton." Esmée couldn't see Keene, but the triumphant note in his voice made her flesh crawl.

Brayden slowly turned, keeping his eyes fixed on hers. She could read his expression. He was asking her to trust him. Did he have to ask? Her belief in him was unshaken. She hoped that, even with a gun in her ribs, she could convey that to him.

Brayden tossed down his gun. As Keene kicked it aside, Esmée heard the sound of a rattle and realized he was holding the baby toy in his other hand. *Still?*

"Time to say goodbye."

Everything seemed to slow down. She expected to hear the gun go off and feel the impact of the bullet. Instead, Keene pushed her aside and raised the gun, aiming it at Brayden. Her brain took a second to register that he was dealing with the greatest threat first.

In the same instant, Brayden lifted his arm and pointed at Keene. Echo, obedient to the silent signal, leaped across the distance between the two men, knocking Keene to the ground. Clamping his jaws onto Keene's leg, Echo held on tight.

Esmée, swinging around to see what was happening, could tell this was different from the time Echo had pinned down Corey Gage. That had been a harmless hold. This was a bite.

Keene still had hold of his gun, but he had dropped the rattle. Now everything was happening too fast. Brayden dived for his weapon at the same time that Keene tried to point his gun at Echo's head.

Desperate to save the brave dog she had come to love, Esmée lunged forward and snatched up the heavy rattle. Holding it in both hands, she lifted it high and brought it down on Keene's head. It made a crunching sound as it connected, confirming her suspicions about its unsuitability as a baby toy. As Keene grunted and collapsed, the rattle split open, spilling its contents on the ground.

Esmée could finally see why the rattle was so important to him. Even in the gloomy light of the cave the stones that tumbled from the broken toy were mesmerizing. Esmée had never seen a blue diamond, but she knew what these were instantly. The hiding place of the Angelika diamonds was no longer a secret.

"Release." Brayden gave the order to Echo at the same time as he cuffed Keene's hands behind his back. The dog immediately let go of Keene's leg.

"Is he...?" Esmée didn't dare touch the slumped

figure. Blood poured from the wound she had inflicted on his temple.

Kneeling, Brayden checked Keene's pulse. "He's alive and his pulse is strong. Let's get outside so I can make some calls."

Leaving Echo to watch over the injured man, he slid an arm around her waist. Esmée leaned against him gratefully as they walked the few yards into the afternoon sunlight. When they stepped from the cave into the woodland, the sound of voices reached them. Esmée looked up to see a group of four K-9 officers and their dogs descending the slope from the Eagle's Nest rest stop.

Brayden stepped forward to greet them, introducing Esmée to a female officer. "This is Juliette Walsh. Did Lulu tell you what was happening?"

"Yes. She wasn't making much sense, but she said you were in danger and Frank already had your location."

Brayden's arm tightened around Esmée. "There's a guy in the cave who needs medical attention. He took a blow to the head and Echo had him in a bite hold on his leg. He's the suspect in Richie Lyman's murder. He's also the person who's been targeting Esmée. Oh, and the Chicago police will want to speak to him about a bank robbery that took place ten years ago, particularly as he's surrounded by blue diamonds."

As Juliette organized the rest of the team, Brayden

guided Esmée to a large rock so she could sit down. After a few minutes, Juliette sent Echo out to join them. Leaning her cheek against Brayden's arm, Esmée watched the activity as the police officers checked the area.

"When I was in that cave, when I thought I wouldn't see you again, I swore I wouldn't let another minute pass without telling you…" She hitched in a tearful breath, unable to continue.

He placed a shaking finger on her lips. "I know. I did the same. But not here. Not with Keene still around." He smiled and she saw everything she needed to know in his eyes. All the love, strength and warmth she'd ever want, or need, was right there. "Let's do it properly. At home…our home."

"Can we go there now? I have to see Rhys. I need to hold him."

Brayden kissed the top of her head. "Me, too."

The next evening, Esmée was seated on the porch watching Rhys play on the grass. Echo dozed at her feet. When Brayden came out of the house, she edged along the bench to make room for him.

"For the first time since we moved in here with you, I don't feel the need to look over my shoulder."

He placed his arm around her. "I just got off the phone with the chief. Keene didn't suffer any ill effect from the blow to his head and Echo's bite didn't even break the skin."

"Oh." She stayed very still, staring out at the view of rolling countryside and tall trees. "What happens now?"

"He'll be charged with Richie's murder and with attempting to kill you." He ran his hand down the length of her hair. "There'll be a trial, of course, and you'll be a witness."

She nodded. "I can do that. He needs to be behind bars for the rest of his life. Will he implicate the Larsons?"

"Keene's not talking at all right now, but Finn isn't hopeful he'll provide the breakthrough we need when it comes to the Larsons. Even if Keene admitted they were the mystery 'business associates' he's been dealing with, it will be his word against theirs. The sale of the diamonds never went beyond the talking stage. The Chicago PD have been in touch and a couple of officers are coming to interview him about the robbery. They know he was involved, of course, because he had the diamonds. Their real investigation will center on the murder of the security guard." He smiled. "And they will have some news for you."

"For me?" Her brow furrowed. "What do you mean?"

"You, Esmée da Costa, are due a reward for the recovery of the Angelika diamonds."

She started to laugh. "Are you serious?"

"Very. Finn said it's not life-changing, but it's a nice sum."

She still appeared torn between amusement and disbelief when Sarah and Hester arrived. They were both concerned over what had happened, but relieved that everyone was okay. Brayden quickly transferred Rhys's car seat to Hester's vehicle and they were ready to go.

Hester took the little boy's hand. "Say goodbye to Mommy and…" She stopped, looking from Esmée to Brayden with a question in her eyes.

"Rhys calls me Bray." He was fine with that. They could take their time over anything else.

"Bye, Mommy. Bye, Bray. Bye, Ko."

"I think Rhys has unrealistic expectations about what feeding the ducks in the park, followed by a visit to the ice-cream parlor, may entail," Brayden said, as Hester and Sarah drove off with an overexcited Rhys.

"Hester may have even more unrealistic expectations about why you and I wanted some time alone. I think she could be picturing a white wedding in the near future."

He leaned against the door frame, looking down at her. "What are *you* picturing?"

"I, um…" She looked adorably confused. "I just want to be with you, Brayden. I love you. I don't need bells and ribbons."

His pulse raced with joy every time he looked at her. Hearing her say she loved him in return made his heart do a backward somersault. "Esmée, before I met you, I thought life was complicated. It was like a puzzle that everyone else understood and I didn't get. I tried falling in love once and it was too damn difficult. Now I know that was because it wasn't love. I was dazzled by something that was dressed up to look like it. Finding you was like finding a missing piece to the puzzle. Suddenly, everything made sense. There was nothing complicated about it, after all. I just needed you to make me complete. Loving you is the easiest, simplest thing in the world and I'm going to do it for the rest of my life."

Her mischievous smile peeped out. "I thought I was the talker?"

"Shh. I'm not finished." He caught hold of her around the waist. "Now that I've found you, I *do* want bells and ribbons. I want everything with you. I want to buy you the biggest engagement ring Red Ridge has ever seen. I want a wedding that will rock Bea's Bridal back on its heels. I want Quinn to be working until midnight every night for a month on the cake. I want Rhys to have the cutest page-boy outfit so Sarah and Hester don't know whether to laugh or cry. I want it all and then I want forever."

By the time he'd finished, she was crying and laughing at the same time. "But the Groom Killer…"

"I know. I'm crazy about you, Esmée. But I'm not *crazy*. We'll keep this between us until the killer—the killer who is *not* my sister Demi—is caught." His heart was pounding as though he'd run a marathon. "Say something."

"I want all those things, too, Brayden." She stood on the tips of her toes and looped her arms around his neck. "Before I came to Red Ridge, I'd convinced myself I could live without love, but that was because I didn't know what love was." She took a deep breath. "And because I was scared. The first time you took my hand, my fear vanished. I know you'll always be there for me and Rhys. You're my emotional security blanket as well as the person who sends electrical currents running through me every time I look at you."

"I do that?" He drew her closer. "Wow."

"*Every* time." Her voice was husky.

"There's just one thing." No matter how much he wanted to lose himself in this moment, he needed to ask a final question. "What about your job? You need to travel for your work, and I'm based here in Red Ridge."

"I've been thinking about that. Come with me." She took his hand and clicked her fingers to Echo, who had been snoozing on the porch.

Bemused, Brayden let her lead him around the side of the house. When his grandfather bought the property, it came with plenty of land. *Everything as far as the eye can see.* That had been Grandpa Colton's saying.

"Echo helped Rhys with his talking, and that got me thinking about dogs as therapy. I'd never really been around animals until then, but I can feel it myself. When I'm around Echo, I'm more relaxed." She tucked her hand into his arm. "I still want to make my documentary. Demi's story needs to be told, but after that I want a change of focus. I've been thinking about opening an animal-assistance center. Dogs are used to support people with all sorts of conditions, including depression, autism and Alzheimer's. They also help people recover from physical ailments and injuries. I would need to do some training, and we'd need to do some building work. I was going to look into whether my savings would cover it. But now that you've told me about the reward money—" She waved her arm to indicate the large square of land at the side of the house. "What do you think?"

"I think it would be perfect. We'll need to extend the house to make room for Rhys's new brothers and sisters when they come along, but there is enough land to do both." He gave Esmée a sidelong glance and saw the answering smile in her eyes. He ruffled Echo's head. "And this guy can teach the newbies how to behave. The only thing left to decide is how many kittens we let Rhys have?"

"Uh-uh." Esmée shook her head. "The only thing left to decide is what we do with the remaining time we have until Sarah and Hester bring Rhys home."

In response, he slid one hand under her knees and the other around her waist, lifting her off her feet. "I've already decided about that."

She linked her arms around his neck as he marched

toward the house. Her eyes sparkled as she gazed up at him. "You have? Will I like it?"

"I hope so. It will be intense and demanding and we'll both be exhausted when we're through." When they reached the porch, he set her on her feet. "But we need to search the house to find out where Rhys has hidden my watch."

\* \* \* \* \*

**IF YOU ENJOYED THIS BOOK
WE THINK YOU WILL ALSO LOVE**

HARLEQUIN
ROMANTIC
SUSPENSE

*Danger. Passion. Drama.*

These heart-racing page-turners will keep you guessing
to the very end. Experience the thrill of unexpected
plot twists and irresistible chemistry.

**4 NEW BOOKS AVAILABLE EVERY MONTH!**

She lunged forward, slamming him against the brick wall
at his back, her forearm against his throat. "Who are you?"
she snarled.

Stunned, he didn't resist her. Clearly, Rachel had some
serious self-defense training, which only furthered his
certainty that this was a woman who believed herself to be
in mortal danger.

"I told you," he rasped past her forearm. "I'm Marcus Tate."

"That's your name. Who are you?"

"I don't understand—"

"How did you follow me without me spotting you? How
do you know I look in shop windows to check my six? For
that matter, why are you here? Why did you think you could
take down some bad guy who might be following me?"

Ah. He didn't usually talk about his job, and certainly not
with civilians. But this situation was not usual in any way.
"I'm a soldier," he gasped.

All of a sudden, the pressure from her arm was so heavy he couldn't breathe, and he abruptly feared she might actually crush his larynx. Urgently needing to breathe, he reached up in reflex and pinched the pressure point in her hand between her thumb and fingers.

She yelped and jumped back from him, settling into a fighting stance with her hands in front of her and her weight lightly balanced on the balls of her feet.

"I mean you no harm, I swear," he said desperately. "You were just cutting off all my air."

"Who. Are. You," she bit out.

"Lieutenant Marcus Tate, US navy SEAL."

She hissed in sharply at that. Welp, she knew who the SEALs were. More to the point, she wasn't thrilled he was one. Which was weird as heck. Most people would be jumping up and down for joy that a SEAL had their back.

He continued doggedly. "I messed up my shoulder a couple of months ago. Had surgery on it a few weeks ago, and I'm here in Sunny Creek to rehab it. I'm staying with my old teammate, Brett Morgan, at Runaway Ranch. He'll vouch for me and everything I've just told you."

Speaking of which, his shoulder was screaming in protest at all the exertion he'd just put it through.

"If you don't mind," he said carefully, "I'd like to walk back to my truck and get some ice for my shoulder. It hurts like a sonofa—" He broke off. "It hurts a lot."

"You can walk in front of me. I'll follow behind you," she said grimly.

*Don't miss*
Her SEAL Bodyguard *by Cindy Dees,*
*available May 2022 wherever*
*Harlequin Romantic Suspense books and ebooks are sold.*

Harlequin.com

# *Love Harlequin romance?*

## DISCOVER.

Be the first to find out about promotions, news and exclusive content!

Facebook.com/HarlequinBooks

Twitter.com/HarlequinBooks

Instagram.com/HarlequinBooks

Pinterest.com/HarlequinBooks

YouTube.com/HarlequinBooks

ReaderService.com

## EXPLORE.

Sign up for the Harlequin e-newsletter and download a free book from any series at
**TryHarlequin.com**

## CONNECT.

Join our Harlequin community to share your thoughts and connect with other romance readers!
**Facebook.com/groups/HarlequinConnection**

**HARLEQUIN**

*Heartfelt or thrilling, passionate or uplifting—Harlequin is more than just happily-ever-after.*

With twelve different series to choose from and new books available every month, you are sure to find stories that will move you, uplift you, inspire and delight you.